MW01248938

SOMEONE WANTS *YOU* DEAD

Dick Bartlett

COPYRIGHT PAGE

ISBN: 1493539167
ISBN 13: 9781493539161
Library of Congress Control Number: 2014900141
CreateSpace Independent Publishing Platform
North Charleston, South Carolina

ACKNOWLEDGMENTS

This is my first book, so you can imagine the help I must have needed. These are the people who gave it to me. Many thanks to them all.

Lynette Benton, my creative writing instructor. She educated me in English for the second time, largely due to her knowledge, her manner, and her everlasting patience.

Dave Barclay, a tutor and new friend, who has guided me through the mysteries (at least to me) of the internet.

The men and women I've met in Lynette's classes at both the Waltham and Arlington Massachusetts Senior Centers, all of whom were pleasant and helpful. In particular, Connie Younkin, who did a great proofread for me.

Barbara Boudreau, a genealogist, computer instructor and member of both my writing classes. She got me started with computers, corrected many of my early blunders, and was responsible for my never having thrown it away.

A few good friends who took the time to read my first, lengthy manuscript and offer helpful comments. In alphabetical order—Donna Bartlett, Harriet Fraser, Bill and Polly Rosen and Kathy Zambello.

DEDICATIONS

To Mary, my best friend and longtime companion,
Who still puts up with me.
And
My three kids: Dawn, Richard and Julie
Also
My five grandkids: Katie, Dan, Ciara, Bryan and Julia.

CHAPTER ONE

Hannon covered the last half mile of his almost-daily "jog-walk" in a few seconds under six minutes and with a satisfied smile on his face. "Jogwalking" was the name he'd given to his morning exercise when he'd stopped jogging the entire three-mile route and had begun walking half and jogging half. This he did in alternating intervals. The change was in deference to his age. He was pushing seventy and had concluded that the pressure he relieved his legs of was well worth the extra time spent. What a perfect way to start a day where his Boston Red Sox were only one win away from becoming the wild card in the league's championship series. "Bad things don't happen on days like this," he said aloud. Like many older people who lived alone, he often talked to himself.

He was standing on a huge, smooth boulder that rose evenly from the sand to a height of nearly eight feet at its center, looking out over MacMaster Cove, taking his pulse. He glanced at his watch. "Damn," he said aloud. "First senior blunder of the day."

He had forgotten to click his stop watch off. It didn't really matter. His time was good, perhaps a personal best, and that gave him a feeling of accomplishment.

He had broken a good sweat, and his pulse rate was well over a hundred. Not bad for a man his age.

He stepped down onto a paved bike path and walked toward his one-room beach house. Beyond it was the small peninsula that made up the MacMaster estate. His father had been the gardener there for many years. His house and the pristine beach it sat on were once part of the estate but had been given to his father twenty years ago. He had never been told why.

He reached the house, climbed the steps onto the deck, and moved to open the huge sliding glass door. The black drapes inside were closed. They usually were. He slid open the screen door and the glass door, neither of which had been locked, pushed the drapes aside, and slipped through. Sunlight seeped into that side of the room. He turned to shut the screen door. The other side of the room was dark, and even if he'd looked, he would not have seen the man sitting in the black recliner next to his bed. He leaned forward onto the door frame, looked out over the cove and checked his pulse again.

The man in the chair was holding a length of rope. Silently he rose, moved quickly past the couch that fronted the drapes, and flipped the rope over Hannon's head and around his neck. Hannon was stunned into a nearly unconscious state. A chocking sensation pushed a desperate cough from his mouth and sent a sickly feeling of terror through his body. He was powerless. He heard his attacker's voice snarling. "Murderer, remember your victim while you die."

The voice shocked Hannon into awareness. He was being strangled. Instinctively, he reached up to try to loosen the rope. His right hand couldn't move. It was already there, covering his throat, inside the rope. That was how he took his pulse. He was still able to breathe. The assassin spoke again, but Hannon didn't understand. He decided to play dead. He made a choking sound, a gasp, and fell limp. The killer made one last tug on the rope, pulled him out of the corner, and hurled him across the room. He landed between the recliner and his bed, smashing his face into the leg of a night table. He lay there motionless, hoping the killer would think him dead.

His attacker was exhausted. He sat on the bed. Hannon lay face down on the floor, bleeding and thinking. Play dead and hope his attacker did not realize he had botched the job, or reach under the bed and find the claw hammer his ever cautious father had always kept there. Slowly the fingers of his right hand crept forward, silently seeking the wooden handle. He found it and gripped it. What now?

A knock on the door answered his question. It would be Linda, his friend and companion. He knew she had a key and would enter. The murderer would have to kill her too. He couldn't let that happen. The man on the bed stood. Hannon pushed himself up onto his knees. The key turned in the lock. The door opened. Light poured in. Her voice called out, "Hannon, I've got groceries."

The killer moved quickly toward her. Hannon rose and went after him, hammer in hand. Linda screamed, dropped her groceries, and turned to run, but she fell.

"Hey, you!" Hannon shouted. The killer turned to face him. He had a knife but was taken by surprise. Hannon swung the hammer wildly and drove it into the man's throat. Blood erupted from the wound, spurting over Hannon's arm and onto the floor. He tried to pull the hammer back to strike again, but it was stuck. He had gripped it backward, and the claw end had sliced into the killer's neck. Hannon could see his attacker was dead. He released his grip on the hammer, allowing the dead man to crumple to the floor. He looked at Linda, who was trembling, trying to get up. He went to help her but could only collapse beside her.

"What the hell's happening?" she managed to ask as he put his arm around her.

"Bastard tried to strangle me," he answered.

"Why."

"I don't know."

"Who is he?"

"He didn't introduce himself."

"Is he dead?"

"Oh yes, dead as hell."

"We need the police."

He nodded. "We certainly do."

CHAPTER TWO

"You never saw the guy sitting there?" Hooper's Landing Police Chief Paul Cunningham asked.

"No," Hannon answered. "It was too dark"

"Do you always keep the drapes closed?"

"Yes—usually."

"And you were checking your pulse?"

"Yes, I always do—to make sure it's getting back to normal."

Hannon was sitting in his recliner, being debriefed. The chief was on the couch, taking notes. Behind him, the drapes were open. Outside, Hannon could see Linda on the deck, seated at the picnic table, staring out at the cove. The chief nodded toward him. "She's upset," he said.

"I know."

"But you, Mr. Hannon, seem calm."

"I work hard at staying calm."

"But you could have been killed. You should have been."

"I wasn't. I'm still here."

"But you're still in danger."

"Why?" Hannon asked. "He wasn't after me. He took me for someone else. Besides, he's dead."

"That's the point, for Christ's sake," Cunningham shot back. "He's dead. He's in the morgue and you put him there. He may have friends who don't give a shit it was self-defense."

Hannon wished he hadn't asked the question. The chief kept right on going.

"We have to start with the idea that the guy was after you. It doesn't matter whether he was or not."

They'd been talking for only a few moments. Prior to that, Hannon had told a crime-scene investigator from the state police the details of the attack. The investigator had indicated that the evidence supported his story. Now he was telling the same story to the chief and answering the same questions. He sensed his debriefing was becoming an interrogation. He was tired and sore. His swollen cheek had been stitched and bandaged. Worst of all, he knew Chief Cunningham was right.

It was quiet in the house, far different from the bedlam out front where a large crowd had gathered. There were cars parked along the bike path and up onto the access road that led to Route 1A. Spectators stood behind yellow police tape that formed a semicircle around the house. There were two television vans and crews from Providence, and a helicopter circled overhead. Half a dozen police cars dotted the area.

"What's going on out there?" Hannon asked.

"This is big stuff," the chief answered. "Hasn't been a murder in the village for fifty years."

"This is an attempted murder gone wrong," Hannon said.

Cunningham smiled. "Yeah, I guess so."

A woman's voice from outside interrupted them. "Need you out here, Chief."

"OK, be right there."

Hannon was getting a respite. He needed it.

As the chief left, Hannon noticed what a large man he was, over six feet, a height he had never quite reached. The chief was barrel-chested but paunchy, suggesting weight training and beer drinking. Hannon had stopped both years ago. He was a "jogwalker", probably in better shape than the much younger man who was questioning him. He enjoyed comparing himself with other men. What hair the chief had was brown, but graying. His was gray, going white. Both had receding hairlines. Neither had facial hair. Linda's voice interrupted his thoughts. She was leaning in from the deck.

"How's it going?" she asked.

"OK. How are you doing?"

"They gave me something. It's working. What have you been talking about?"

"Mostly about me. I gave him a quick picture of my life to date."

"The same thumbnail sketch you gave me when we met?" she said.

"Pretty much. I told him what I remembered about the attack—and what I didn't."

"You mean the second thing the guy said?"

"Yeah, he said I should work on remembering that."

"This is all very scary," she said.

"I'm still not convinced he was after me."

"Everyone else thinks he was."

"How do you know that?"

"I hear them talking. One of the cops lives in my building. We're friends. She said someone must really have it in for you."

Cunningham's voice interrupted them. "Could you excuse us, Mrs. Rizzo?" he said as he moved past her.

"Yes, of course," she said.

After she left, Cunningham sat down. "This is a large room," he said.

"It's practically the whole house," Hannon explained. "Use to be a recreation hall and beach house for the kids who lived on the estate. They had organized fun time here."

"Were there lots of kids?"

"Of course. If they were born here, they stayed here—had their own kids who also stayed here and so on for generations."

"One big Scottish clan," Cunningham said, "living life on a huge estate this house was once part of."

Hannon smiled. He knew where this was going.

"And they gave this little section to your father," the chief continued. "Why was that?"

"Maybe they were running short of kids."

"Probably not."

"He was their gardener," Hannon said.

"Must have been a damn good one."

"He was the best. The gardens were a show place— open to the public on weekends. They won awards and were featured in magazines."

"Must have been more than that."

"Maybe, but he never told me."

"Pretty expensive living here?"

"I scrape by. There's no mortgage."

"Still, limited income, taxes."

"I manage—if I don't go out to dinner too often."

The chief shook his head. "Sounds kind of strange." He stood up, took his jacket off, and loosened his tie.

He was in full uniform and looked hot and uncomfortable. Hannon still wore shorts and a T-shirt but not the same blood stained ones as earlier. They had been taken as evidence.

"Mind if I use the bathroom?" the chief asked.

"Course not," Hannon said. "Front of the house." He pointed as he spoke. "Hook a left in the kitchen, through the closet."

The chief wasn't gone long. When he got back he looked like he'd splashed cold water on his face. "The man who attacked you called you a murderer," he began.

"I'm not," Hannon said quickly.

"You need to think about why someone might think you are."

Hannon hadn't done that. He nodded. The chief sat down.

"What about those last two words the guy said?" he asked.

"I missed them, Chief. They're gone."

"Keep trying. Only been a few hours. You're too calm. Maybe that's shock. You got anything to drink?"

"Sure." Hannon pushed himself out of the recliner. "I got water and nonalcoholic beer."

"I'll try one of those."

Hannon got a couple of O'Doul's from the refrigerator. As he opened them, he thought of something. He asked a question on his way back, before Cunningham could start up again.

"You really think the guy was a professional, don't you?"

"Yes."

"No question he was after me?"

"Not in my mind."

He gave the chief one of the beers and sat down. He didn't like the answer, but he knew that was the way things would be handled. He took a couple of sips of his beer while Cunningham gulped down what looked like half of his. "This stuff's not bad," he said.

"I don't know anyone who would want me murdered," Hannon said.

"You haven't even thought about it."

"I never hurt anyone," Hannon said softly,

"OK, I'll give you that, but someone out there thinks you have."

"What's that mean?"

"It means you have to think about things you've said or done that might have offended someone without your realizing it."

"Do I look like I can read minds?"

"None of us can, Mr. Hannon. That's why we make enemies without knowing."

Hannon leaned forward in his recliner. The chief was making sense.

The chief finished his beer while Hannon had a couple more sips.

"People keep things to themselves," Cunningham said, "and sometimes, they never forget."

Hannon was getting the idea. "So they just sit back and seethe," he said.

"Yes."

"And over time," Hannon continued, "they make a nuclear warhead out of a cherry bomb."

The chief nodded. "Something like that."

"And they have you killed?" Hannon said. "I don't have enemies like that."

10

"You don't know for sure."

"No, guess I don't. These people—they're not normal, right?"

"Hell, yes. They're paranoid and they feel victimized."

"That opens up a lot of possibilities."

"That's my point, sir."

Hannon finished his beer.

Cunningham looked pleased. "Let's try a few questions," he said.

"Fire away."

"Had much violence in your life?"

"No, not really. Mostly controlled."

"You mean rough stuff like football?"

"Yeah."

"Any martial arts?"

"I was on the group boxing team in the Army."

"So you know how to fight?"

"I know how to duck and protect myself. I was only a sparring partner."

"You protected yourself pretty well this morning."

"I got lucky."

"Still, the Army can be violent. They teach you how to kill."

"We were between wars when I was in. I learned to shoot at targets and stab dummies with a bayonet."

Cunningham smiled and held up his empty can. "Got one more of these?"

Hannon got two more cans.

The chief let him get seated before asking the next question. "Ever involved in a bad car accident where people died or got hurt?"

"Never."

"How 'bout stuff like barroom brawls?"

"No."

"You used to drink a lot."

"I couldn't afford to drink in bars. I was a package store guy."

"How about relationships? I'm assuming yours would have been with women."

"That's right. I've had a few."

"Any bad breakups?"

"Not so you'd notice."

"How about road rage?"

"Nah." Hannon shook his head. "I get horns blown at me. Nothing more."

"The killer's last two words, think it was a name?"

"Probably."

Cunningham stood up and took a deep breath. "I have to ask this," he said.

Hannon knew what the question would be. He was ready. Cunningham continued.

"Was it a name you recognized but don't want to share? Someone you offended or hurt or whatever, legal or illegal?"

"No! I heard a noise. It might as well been a dog barking."

"OK." The chief sounded disappointed.

"I'm not holding out on you, Chief. If I have an enemy like that, I don't have a clue who it is."

There was a burst of activity on the deck. A cop entered the room. She was carrying a black wet suit. "We found this under the deck, sir," she said, "along with an air tank."

The chief looked quickly at Hannon.

"Not mine," Hannon said.

"You mean the guy swam here?" the chief asked.

"Looks that way." The officer said. "He must have come ashore when it was dark and hid under the deck until Mr. Hannon went running. We found snack wrappers and bottled water. He must have come in at high tide. No footprints."

The chief turned to Hannon. "This guy's a real professional. No question he was after you. Someone wants you dead, Mr. Hannon — murdered. Search your mind. We'll talk tomorrow morning, my office at ten o'clock. Bring Mrs. Rizzo with you."

Hannon nodded.

CHAPTER THREE

The day's turmoil left Hannon confused, tired, and angry. His morning jogwalk had been the only bright spot. He felt cheated. He was seated on the edge of the concrete boat ramp that ran from the bike path into the water, staring out at the cove, reliving what had happened. He was still wearing jogging shorts but no shirt. Linda called out to him from the deck.

"The chief's on TV."

"I'll pass."

"Don't you want to hear what he's saying?"

"I guess so."

She came down from the deck and sat beside him, being careful not to get her feet wet. She looked much better then she had. The color had returned to her face. She pushed some hair back over her shoulder revealing her full, tanned face, a perfect centerpiece for her auburn hair. She smiled. He loved her smile. She was beautiful when she smiled.

"Are you OK now?" she asked.

"I'm fine."

"Are you sure?"

"Yeah, I'm sure."

She shook her head. "You should be frightened, at least worried."

14

"I try hard not to be either. What did the chief say?"

"A man's been killed. It's being investigated."

"Did he call it murder or attempted murder?"

"Suspicious death."

He frowned.

"You don't think he believes what happened?" she said.

"Yeah, he does. The state cop says the evidence backs the story up."

"What evidence?"

"The rope burns on my neck, the fact that he had a knife."

"So what's the problem?"

"They think it's an attempted revenge killing. The guy called me a murderer. They want to know who I killed."

"But you didn't kill anybody." She paused. "Did you?"

"Of course not. Are there still people out front?"

"A few," she answered. "Couple of reporters, a few curiosity freaks, cars driving by."

"That's morbid."

"What did the chief ask you to do?" she said.

"You heard him. He didn't ask, he ordered. I'm to come up with a list of people I might have harmed or offended without realizing it."

"Can you do that?"

"I don't think so. My mind's a blank. No names, no ideas."

"I can help. I've known you over five years."

"He wants to go back further than that."

"Like, how far?"

"As far as it takes."

15

Linda shook her head and stood up. "That's a tall order," she said.

"It is," he agreed. "And he wants another meeting tomorrow morning."

"OK." She put her hand on his shoulder. "Tell you what. I'll get us something to eat, and you start a fire. Want me to stay over?"

"Damn right I do," he said.

"I wish I had some wine."

"I think you left some in the fridge last time."

"I hope so. Don't stay out too long."

She started back to the house but stopped abruptly after only a few steps. "Where's your car?" she called out. "It's not in the driveway."

"Oh," he called back, "I left it at Sam's Garage yesterday. The brakes felt a little soft."

"What about the appointment with the chief?"

"What about it?"

"How do you plan on getting there?"

He hadn't thought about that. It took a moment to answer. "Isn't your bike here?" he asked.

"Yes."

We'll use that," he said. "You stand and peddle. I'll sit behind you."

"Very funny." She was smiling.

"Maybe I'll take my boat over," he said. "It's still out on the mooring."

"Are you coming in now?" she asked.

"It a minute."

Linda went into the house, grabbed one of his sweat shirts, and brought it out to him.

"Put this on," she ordered. "It's getting cold."

"You take such good care of me," he said.

16

"You saved my life today. He would have cut my throat if you hadn't come after him."

"I had to do that. I had no choice."

"Yes, you did have a choice. You didn't have to do that."

"Of course I did," he said emphatically. "Letting him harm you wasn't an option."

She realized he was right. She knelt down in the water and put her arms around him. When she spoke, her voice quivered. "I'm so sorry. I should have known."

"It's over and we're still here. What's for supper?"

"How about my own special blend of macaroni and cheese."

"Sounds great."

At that moment their focus for the evening was altered. They would relax and enjoy each other's company. Little if any progress would be made on searching the past and producing a list of potential enemies. That would have to wait until tomorrow He would build a fire in the massive stone fireplace across the room from his bed, and they would eat her mac and cheese. She would drink wine and he would have O'Doul's. They would both sit in the recliner and watch the fire, perhaps listen to music, and reminisce about the time they had spent together. He wouldn't even watch the Red Sox game.

***

They had met on the bike path five Septembers ago. The locals knew her as "the bicycle queen" because she rode every day on the path or on her way to work or for errands or appointments. She did not own a car, because she had never learned to drive. She dressed in regular clothes rather than the popular elastic bodysuit, and she never wore a helmet. She was also known to ride at speeds that many considered excessive.

He was still jogging the entire three miles of his run, and wore a calf-to-thigh brace in order to ease pain caused by a lack of cartilage in his left knee. He liked to think the problem was the result of an old football injury, but he'd recently learned it was actually a form of arthritis. If they met on the path going in opposite direction, there was always a nod of recognition but no more than that.

On one particular day when they were going in the same direction, he drifted out from the edge of the path while she was coming from behind him at her usual high rate of speed.

"Passing on the left," she called out.

He misunderstood and moved left directly into her path. She squeezed her hand brakes and turned her wheel, but it was too late, and they collided, sending her headlong over the handle bars and onto the pavement while knocking him sideways onto the gravel side path.

"Moron," she screamed.

He had no immediate reply.

"Idiot." The tone of her scream rose.

He was getting himself up but still had no reply.

"Are you deaf?" she demanded, still lying on the path.

"Not yet," he answered calmly. Those two simple words had become his usual reply to questions related to his physical or mental health. Whatever common malady consistent with old age he was being asked about, he didn't have it yet. Hopefully that would bring any discussion about elder health to an abrupt end. This time it didn't work.

"Did you forget your hearing aid?" she persisted.

"Actually, it's in the repair shop," he answered playfully. It wasn't a good idea.

"Oh, my God," she said in a perplexed tone. "You're a stupid old man."

Stupid was one of his least favorite words, but the collision had been his fault and he knew it.

She'd scraped her knee on the pavement and was bleeding. He took his red bandanna out of his pocket and knelt down beside her.

"Maybe we should start over," he said. "That's my place back there." He pointed toward the house. "Let me walk you there on your bike. I'll clean and bandage your knee."

"With that?" she said, gesturing at his bandanna.

"I have a first aid kit," he said quickly. "I do good work." He thought he saw her smile.

"OK," she said after a short pause. "I'm Linda Rizzo."

"My name's Hannon."

***

In the five years they'd spent together since then, those few moments and the verbal banter they'd engaged in created a scene so memorable that they would often break spontaneously into a back-and-forth, word-for-word recital of it. Now, sitting in front of the glowing fireplace, they were in the midst of that recitation when Linda suddenly burst out laughing.

"You didn't even have ointment in that damned first aid kit," she said.

"No," Hannon countered, "but I washed and cleaned the scratches and bandaged them."

"It took you twenty minutes."

"I didn't want you to get an infection."

"You just wanted to keep me there."

"Of course I did. I wanted to become friends."

"We certainly did that—friends, best friends, companions."

"Lovers," he added.

"Yes," she smiled, "that was nice."

"I never expected that," he said.

"Why not?"

"Age. I'm almost twenty years older. I don't know what you saw in me."

"A gentle, considerate man who's made me happier than I ever was before."

"Thank you for that," he said.

It was a few moments before they spoke again.

"I hope what happened today won't change anything," she said.

"We won't let it."

"We know so little about each other's past," she said.

"We agreed not to be invasive about the past."

"Was that a mistake?"

"No. You know all my headlines—a marriage that didn't work, two grown kids, a job I didn't like but didn't have the guts to get out of. The booze."

"They're going to search your past."

He turned to face her. "There's nothing there to find."

She turned and put her arms around him. "They'll take a close look at me too."

20

"Is there anything you should tell me?" he asked.

"No, nothing."

They turned to watch the tiny flames dance in the fireplace, satisfied that the day they hoped to forget had become a pleasant evening.

"I'm going to brush my teeth and go to bed," she said.

She got up and walked into the small kitchen, turned, and framed herself in the entrance. The glow from the burning embers illuminated her. She looked beautiful.

"You may want to think about doing the same thing," she added.

A moment later he heard the shower turn on. He closed his eyes, took a deep breath, and felt a surge of anticipated pleasure. When she returned a few minutes later, she was naked. She flipped him the towel she was carrying as she flashed by and slid into his queen-size bed. "I left the water running for you," she said.

Hannon hated to hurry. He felt it caused older people to make mistakes and become confused, but he could still move in double time when the situation called for it. He was in and out of the shower in minutes with his teeth partially brushed. He raced out of the bathroom, through the closet, and stopped in the kitchen. He had forgotten to turn the shower off. Linda laughed as he corrected his mistake. He was walking when he returned. He moved passed the glowing embers straight to the near side of the bed where she waited for him. It was as spontaneous as anything they had ever done, and he was as aroused as anyone his age could ever hope to be. She was just as excited.

CHAPTER FOUR

By the time Hannon woke in the morning, Linda was already up, sitting at the kitchen table, drinking coffee. Not surprisingly, she was dressed in the same brown shorts and blue shirt she'd arrived in the day before. Hannon pushed himself up into a sitting position and looked at his watch. It wasn't on his wrist. "What time is it?" he asked.

"Eleven o'clock." She answered.

"Why didn't you wake me? We're due at the police station."

"Not yet. We had a call from the police earlier that woke me up. I couldn't find your phone, so they left a message. I called back and spoke with Rose. The meeting's postponed till two o'clock. Get dressed."

"Close your eyes. I'm naked."

She smiled and opened her eyes wider. He got up and headed for the closet.

"And who is Rose??" he called out.

"She's the police officer I'm friendly with."

"What else did she tell you?"

"Sergeant Costello was with her. He's the state police crime-scene investigator who was here yesterday. He believed us, but he thinks you may be holding something back."

"Damn it," he said. "Why would I tell them what he said and hold back a name if I recognized it?"

He came back into the kitchen wearing shorts and a T-shirt. He poured himself some coffee.

"Christ," he continued. "If the guy hadn't said something, I'd be dead."

"What do you mean?" she asked.

"I was comatose. It was the voice that snapped me out of it and got me thinking about staying alive. Do we have anything to eat?"

"Cheerios and bananas."

They had breakfast on the deck watching the cove fill up with pleasure boats. It was Saturday, and the weather was warm and sunny, a perfect day to start the long Columbus Day weekend. The cove was a popular place for boats to anchor or raft together for a day of family sunbathing, swimming, and beer drinking. There was a large sandbar two hundred yards offshore where there was only three feet of water at low tide. A great place for kids to swim and dive for sand dollars and for adults to soak up the sun and listen to music coming from radios or small televisions. Hannon was always impressed by the sight of MacMaster Cove filling up with boats and activity that covered the water from the small peninsula that made up the estate to the rocky, tree-lined coast that curved around to Seagull Rock, which walled off the small village of Hooper's Landing.

"Such a pretty sight," Linda said.

"Yeah. Wish we could be out there."

"I wonder if the MacMaster family members are annoyed by all that's going on in their cove?" she asked.

"They don't own it," he said. "It's just named after them."

"Lot of things in the village are named after them."

"Why not?" Hannon said with a shrug. "They're rich and powerful. Their ancestors were the founders of the village"

"It's just one family living there now, isn't it?" she said.

"Yeah, old Charles is still alive, and one of his sons is there with his family."

"That's it?"

"Yep, and his two grandsons are off in college."

"Sounds lonely."

"Don't sell them short," he cautioned. "They still swing a big stick."

"I better get going," she said, getting up from her chair.

"Aren't you going with me? The chief wanted you too."

"I can't."

"How come?"

"I left my phone at the office Thursday. I've got to check messages and drum up some business."

"Things not so good in the travel business?"

"Awful. People aren't traveling. Besides, you know me and boats. You go too fast, and I don't swim."

They started walking back through the house. He decided to change the subject. Maybe a little kidding would lighten the mood.

"What is it with you?" he asked sarcastically. "You don't drive or swim. What do you do?"

She stopped in the middle of the kitchen and took his arm. "You," she said emphatically, "have a very short memory."

They went out into the yard where her bicycle was leaning against the house.

"Any idea who won the ball game last night?" he asked as she mounted the bike.

"Red Sox. They play again Tuesday. Probably against the Yankees."

"Come back tonight," he said. "I'll cook spaghetti and meatballs."

"Good idea. What will you tell the chief?"

"I'll think of something."

After she left, Hannon realized he should be in a hurry. He didn't want to keep the chief waiting. He thought about shaving and brushing his teeth, but all he did was the teeth. Facial stubble had become part of the contemporary male image, even if it was gray. He put on long pants and a black T-shirt and headed out the back door. His eight foot rowboat was under the deck. He pulled it out, ignoring the yellow police tape, and hauled it into the water. He was rowing at a good clip when he heard a motor churning behind him off his port side. It was the MacMaster's forty-foot schooner, its sails already down, cruising toward its mooring. Dr. Mark MacMaster was at the helm, hunched over it in a crouch that hardly allowed him to see over the cabin and made him look even shorter and heavier than he was. Fully dressed, with the tip of his cap pulled down to touch his thick, rimless sunglasses, he was completely involved in his landing, while his wife, Charlotte, barefoot and wearing a two-piece bathing suit, moved swiftly and smoothly about the boat, cleaning, and tying up the sails.

Hannon stopped rowing as they glided by only twenty yards to his port side. He hoped they wouldn't see him.

"Get up to the bow and hook the mooring, Charlotte," Mark called out in his best command voice.

Quickly she rose and, with only a few strides of her long, well-tanned legs, glided to the bow and turned to pick up the mooring hook stick. She spotted Hannon.

"Hey," she called out. "What's happening with you?"

"Haven't you heard?" he yelled back.

The schooner slipped past its mooring without her catching it.

"God dammit," Mark yelled. "Pay attention."

"Hannon," she called again, ignoring her husband. "What's going on?"

He noticed she'd cut her hair and was showing streaks of gray, but was still as attractive as ever.

"Did someone really try to kill you?" she persisted.

"Looks that way," he called back. "I'm surprised you haven't heard."

"Just bits and pieces." she said.

Mark was guiding the schooner around Hannon's rowboat for another run at the mooring. He looked annoyed.

"Are you all right?" Charlotte asked. There was genuine concern in her voice.

"I'm OK."

"Get ready, Charlotte," Mark yelled as they slipped past Hannon. "We want to be home before sunset."

"Good morning, Doctor," Hannon said.

Mark nodded. "Hannon."

"Is there anything we can do?" Charlotte asked.

"I'm all set," he said. He knew she meant anything *she* could do, not *we*.

"Drop over and see us later," she called out after catching the mooring and taking the lines onboard.

Hannon knew that meant see *her*.

"I've got to be at the police station," he yelled.

"Stop by when you get back." She wasn't going to take no for an answer.

"OK," he said. He wished he hadn't.

Hannon watched them climb off the schooner onto the small rubber craft that would carry them to shore. It was equipped with a small outboard motor. No pulling on oars for Dr. Mark.

Hannon started rowing toward his boat, a twenty-two foot Aquasport Odyssey with a 175 horsepower outboard motor. It was the third boat he had owned, all called *Vagabond*, in his thirty years as an avid boater. When he got there, he tied his bowline onto a cleat on the Aquasport and climbed aboard. He noticed the line wasn't as long as he remembered. He moved past the steering console to the hatch, which was not padlocked. He opened it and slid down into the small cabin where he'd left his boat bag. The boat keys were in the bag, and it occurred to him that if he had padlocked the hatch, as he always did, he would now be unable to start his motor. He'd made two mistakes last time out, and the fact that they had offset each other didn't matter. It had been a double senior moment.

He shook his head in disgust. "Idiot! Moron!" he uttered.

He dug the keys out of his bag, climbed back onto the deck, and lowered the motor into the water before slipping the engine kill switch in under the ignition. He put the key into the keyhole and turned it.

Nothing happened. The engine didn't turn over. He was about to turn the key again when he remembered the third thing he hadn't done on his last ride. He'd forgotten to turn the bilge pump off after clearing out the water the boat had taken on. It had been draining the battery for five days and the battery was dead. It had been a true, triple-header lapse of focus. He shook his head again.

"Ah, what the hell," he muttered. "Just fix the problem."

He smiled. He could do that. The boat carried two batteries. All he had to do was change the leads. He got his tool box from the cabin, moved to the stern, and flipped up the starboard seat that covered the battery well. He didn't like what he saw. There was a small, arrowhead shaped device next to the dead battery. It was filled with what looked like gray putty. There was a black thread of wire leading from the putty to the battery lead.

"Holy shit," he said. He knew a bomb when he saw one.

CHAPTER FIVE

Deputy Police Chief Orlando Cruz was sitting in the harbormaster's launch, docked at the town wharf, when Hannon's distress call come over his radio.

"Get off the boat," he ordered. "Keep the other boats away."

"There's nothing within a hundred yards," Hannon answered.

"Keep it like that," Cruz said. "I'm on my way."

Cruz threw off his tie lines, turned the motor on, and slammed the throttle down, causing the boat to shoot off into the harbor leaving a huge wake that would have cost any other boater a fifty dollar fine.

As he raced out of the harbor and turned left toward the cove, he called the police station and told Officer DiMartino to alert Costello and the chief.

"And call Carl Bucci from the state police," he added. "He knows bombs."

He reached the mouth of the cove in under five minutes and slowed down to head speed so as not to alarm boaters on the pleasure boats anchored there. He cruised slowly past them, acknowledging the friendly waves of some who knew him and carefully avoiding swimmers, until he spotted Hannon sitting in his rowboat, a safe distance away from his boat.

29

"Morning, Hannon," he said as he reached him, "how are you holding up?"

"I'm fine," Hannon answered. "Nervous, but fine."

"Why didn't you call 911?" Cruz asked.

"I forgot to bring my cell phone."

"You're too old to be out on a boat alone."

"I also forgot my walker."

"Ah, the plight of the elderly," Cruz chuckled, "You sounded a little out of sorts on the radio."

"Did I? It's not every day I almost get blown up. Do you think it's on a timer?"

"Nah, goes off when the motor starts, like a car bomb."

Hannon took a deep breath and lowered his head.

"What's the matter?" Cruz asked.

"I tried to start the motor, but the battery's dead."

"Holy shit, man. You should be dead."

"I should have been dead yesterday."

"You seem pretty calm. How the hell do you manage that?"

"Years and years of practice."

"Well, you're really pissing the chief off. He can't figure you out. He doesn't like that."

"I'll try and be more nervous next time I see him."

"That's a good idea."

Hannon and Cruz were good friends. At the core of their relationship was the friendship that had developed between Hannon's father and Cruz's grandfather when they had worked together on the MacMaster estate. According to Cruz, Hannon's father had persuaded Earl MacMaster to hire his grandfather as a chauffeur and car mechanic. He'd also been a great comfort to the older man when Cruz's father, a policeman, was killed in a shootout. Cruz had been impressed and grateful, and Hannon had welcomed the friendship, having been especially pleased that Cruz was a policeman. He had always felt a pleasant rapport with law enforcement people whenever his work brought him into contact with them.

"I'll stay out here and keep the other boats away," Cruz said. "You get back to shore and wait for the cavalry."

The cavalry didn't take long. Hannon was only halfway back when a state police car pulled up to the house and a rather short, somewhat overweight man with glasses stepped out and waked briskly toward the boat ramp. Hannon recognized him as the crime-scene investigator from the day before.

"Where's Cruz?" he asked.

"Keeping the other boats away," Hannon answered.

"We'll wait for the bomb guy," Costello said. "Then we'll go back out."

"What do you mean, *we?*" Hannon asked. He couldn't resist.

"I mean him and me. You stay here." Costello was all business

"Will this bomb guy be in full battle gear?" Hannon asked.

Costello smiled. "He won't exactly blend in."

He was right. The bomb guy arrived minutes later in a red pickup truck, and he was anything but inconspicuous. He had a welder's mask sitting on the top of his head and was carrying a heavy iron box. He wore a gray coverall suit that looked heavy. He looked like an astronaut ready for blast-off.

He introduced himself to Hannon. "I'm Trooper Bucci. Tell me about the bomb."

Hannon description was apparently good enough. Bucci turned to Costello.

"Need your help, Sergeant."

"Ain't I the lucky one," Costello responded.

"We'll take this guy's rowboat," Bucci said. "Hope we clear this up before the media gets here."

"How would they find out?" Hannon asked.

Bucci gave him a questioning look and shook his head. "You got the harbor master's boat out there, I look like a fuckin' moon man, and everyone out there has a cell phone."

Hannon wished he hadn't asked the question. So much for his rapport with cops.

The whole operation took less than ten minutes. Hannon looked on while the two men rowed to his boat. Bucci climbed aboard with his box and, moments later, passed it back to Costello... They were halfway back when they heard the unmistakable sound of a helicopter approaching. Even over the sound of it, Hannon could hear Bucci's rather crass two-word reaction.

"You are a lucky man, Mr. Hannon," Costello said when they reached shore.

"Clever littler device," Bucci said. "C4 with a shaped charge pointed directly at the steering wheel—very professional."

Hannon was glad he was sitting down. "You mean it would have blown up in my face if the motor had turned over?"

"Not to belabor a point," Bucci answered, "but actually, it would have shot right up your ass, then vaporized."

"Vaporized?" Hannon said. "Wouldn't that make it look like an accident?"

"That's what it's supposed to do."

Hannon was puzzled. "That doesn't make sense. The guy yesterday wasn't trying to hide anything. Are there two different guys?"

"I doubt killing you would be a two-man job," Costello said. "No offense."

"Yesterday was so damn personal," Hannon said. "The prick was rubbing it in, telling me why I was dying. Sending a message. A bomb doesn't do that. You never know what hit you."

"Listen to this guy," Bucci said with a chuckle. "Just became a detective. He should be shaking in his boots."

"I'm scared as hell," Hannon said. "But I don't want to give myself a heart attack."

"Handle it anyway you want," Costello said. "Fine with us. Right now, we should get out of here before the media show up."

"Good idea." Bucci said. "Give me a hand with the box."

Costello and Bucci picked up the box and started off toward the cars.

"I'll need a ride to the station," Hannon called out to them.

"Ride with me," Costello said.

"I need to get my cell phone and make a call," Hannon said as he started toward the house.

"Call from the car," Costello yelled back. "We're in a hurry."

Hannon sprinted into the house and found his phone on top of a cardboard chest of drawers in the walk-through closet. When he reached the police cruiser, Costello had started the engine and Bucci was gone. He was only halfway into the passenger seat when

Costello hit the accelerator, and the cruiser sped away toward the access road to route 1A. They turned right onto the paved surface and were halfway to 1A when Hannon spotted a convoy of cars and TV trucks and interested spectators headed in the opposite direction.

"Here they come," he said.

"They can eat our dust," Costello said. "Let them talk to Cunningham at the station."

They didn't speak the rest of the way. Costello was driving, and Hannon was trying to call Sam's Garage to see if his car was ready. He wasn't getting any answer. Route 1A was a blur. Costello muscled the cruiser up to almost eighty miles an hour with the lights flashing and the siren blaring. They were running parallel to the bike path, with buildings in between, one of which was Linda's apartment building, backed up to the bike path only a half mile from Hannon's place. He didn't even see it. He was deep in thought. Costello finally slowed down to make a left onto Main Street. Sam's garage lay ahead.

"Can we stop at Sam Engels' garage," Hannon asked.

"No," Costello said abruptly. "I don't want the media catching up."

"For Christ's sake," Hannon chuckled. "They haven't even got turned around yet."

Costello laughed, but kept on driving.

Hannon didn't mind. They'd just turned a thirty-minute boat trip into a ten-minute charge, and he had come to a conclusion he was comfortable with.

"I think," he said, as they pulled into the police station parking lot, "it was only one guy."

"What?" Costello asked.

"One killer," Hannon said. "Same guy that set the bomb tried to strangle me. We thought maybe it was two different guys."

"You thought that," Costello said. "I was thinking backup plan."

"More likely it was panic plan," Hannon said.

"What's that mean?"

"It was one guy, probably someone who specialized in explosives, and somebody—maybe his client–changed his mind for him."

CHAPTER SIX

The Hooper's Landing Police Station was located in the center of the village's small business area, halfway between Route 1A and the harbor. It occupied the rear section of the first floor and the entire basement of the Town Hall. The front part of the first floor housed the municipal offices and the entire second floor was the library. The chief's office, a holding cell and four desks with computers were on the first floor. The cells used for long term incarcerations, an interrogation room, a weight room and a seldom used firing range were in the basement. Hannon and Costello entered directly into the first floor area from the parking lot.

"Pretty nice setup for a small village," Costello said, "having its own station and chief."

"You can thank the MacMaster family for that," Hannon said. "They have very little crime. Cunningham told me this was the first murder in fifty years."

"That wasn't murder," Costello said. "It was attempted murder."

Hannon smiled. Maybe he and Costello would get along.

The duty officer, Tom Fisk, came out of the restroom. "Chief's running late. He's hung up at State Police Headquarters."

"We'll wait in the office," Costello said.

"Chief don't like anyone sitting in his chair," Fisk cautioned.

Costello nodded, went into the office, sat in the chief's chair, and put his feet on the desk. "I don't blame him," he called back to Fisk. "It's comfortable."

Fisk didn't answer. Hannon sat in front of the desk and waited to be questioned, but Costello seemed more interested in resting.

"How many cops are here?" Hannon asked.

"About eight, counting the chief."

"Are they up to handling this situation?"

"We'll see. It's their jurisdiction, but it's a major crime, not like handing out speeding tickets or arresting drunks."

"Will the State Police help?"

"Of course. We'll be around, but it's Cunningham's case."

"Will anyone be interested in my take on what just happened?"

Costello smiled. He knew Hannon had a theory. "I'll listen to any input you have. You think we only have one killer and he changed his mind."

"I said he had it changed for him. Isn't it true these killer-for-hire deals often involve intermediaries?"

"Yeah, I guess so."

"People in the middle who could screw things up?"

"You're pushing the idea they hit the wrong guy."

"No," Hannon said emphatically. "I'm saying the person who wants me dead and the actual hit man never met. The guy doing the killing didn't get all the right information."

"Like what? He knew who you were and where your boat and your house were. He knew your habits."

"But he didn't know how personal it was," Hannon interrupted. "He didn't know he was supposed to tell me why."

Costello looked surprised. He took his feet off the desk and leaned forward on it.

Hannon continued. "The hit man's on my boat. He's set the bomb so he calls someone to tell them it's a go."

A look of enlightenment came over Costello's face. "OK," he said. "And this someone tells him it's a revenge killing. He has to tell you why you're dying."

"Right," Hannon said. "Now it's panic time for him."

"So it's on to a hastily conceived Plan B," Costello said. "He swims ashore, hides under the deck and jumps you when you get back from your run."

"That's how I see it," Hannon said. "I think he decided to strangle me while he was under the deck. It looks like he cut some rope off the bowline of my rowboat"

"Why not use the knife? He didn't know squat about strangulation."

"No, he didn't. Maybe he thought it would be easier to take me from behind."

"Makes sense, but we didn't find any cell phone on him or the boat."

"Must have tossed it overboard."

Costello had to think about that.

"The boat sits right over a sand bar," Hannon continued. "A diver might find it. Then we'd know it could have happened that way."

Costello got up from the chair and walked around the desk. He leaned back on it, folded his arms, and gave Hannon a long look.

"Have you ever had experience in this line of work?" he asked.

Hannon was surprised by the question. "I've done some snorkeling but never any scuba stuff."

"That's not what I mean," Costello said. "We have our own divers, for Christ's sake. I mean have you ever been involved in investigative analysis?"

"What's that?"

"It's like what I do for a living."

"You mean detective work? No, not really."

"You have a knack for thinking things through, putting two and two together."

"I had time to think while you were driving. I don't like things that don't make sense. If I'm puzzled, I like to know why."

"That's good. You also like to appear calm and in control, don't you?"

"Yeah, I do," Hannon said emphatically. "I've been working on that all my life."

"But you must be worried about what's going on now."

"I try hard not to worry about bad things after they didn't happen. I have some disturbing concerns about the future. That's where my attention is. Whoever they are, they haven't got me yet. I like to think you can help me with that."

"That's what we do, Mr. Hannon."

CHAPTER SEVEN

Chief Cunningham didn't get back until five o'clock. Costello passed the time working on reports, while Hannon attempted to find out the status of his car. He finally got a message on the garage answering machine, one that told callers the shop had closed at three o'clock and wouldn't open again until Tuesday after the long weekend. Sam's home number was unlisted, so Hannon would be without a car. Sam was probably halfway to Maine for a fishing tournament by now. When they first heard the stampede of media people rushing to surround the chief's car, Hannon went to the window and watched the chief push his way through the crowd.

"Out of my chair." He bellowed at Costello as he entered the office. "Took me eighteen years to get that seat."

"Find out anything at headquarter?" Costello asked as he vacated the chair.

"I found out a good deal about Mr. Hannon here," the chief answered, "but not a damn thing about the dead guy. He's a real spook."

"Nothing on any file or list, no rap sheet?" Costello asked.

"Not in this country. He has to be an illegal. They're checking foreign links now."

40

Cunningham sat down in his chair. He also leaned back and put his feet on the desk. Costello and Hannon sat down.

"Did you get the news about the bomb?" Costello asked.

"Hell, yes. What was that all about?"

Costello gave him the details. When he'd finished, the chief shook his head.

"What's going on here," he asked. "They can't kill you twice? Is there more than one killer?"

"We have a theory," Costello said. Hannon smiled.

Costello told the story, but he didn't get any further than the reason the bomb hadn't detonated.

The chief was thunderstruck. "This is unbelievable! This guy is alive because he left the bilge pump running and killed the battery?"

"That's right," Hannon said meekly. "I've been lucky."

"Lucky?" the chief shouted. "You're bloody blessed."

"Looks that way," Hannon nodded.

Costello got through the entire scenario after that.

Cunningham, had a few questions. "Why didn't the hit man disarm the bomb before he came ashore?"

"Who knows?" Hannon answered, "Panic, maybe he forgets."

"Or maybe he leaves it armed as a backup in case Plan B doesn't work," Costello added.

"My guys didn't find any cell phone onboard," Cunningham said.

"Must have tossed it." Costello said. "We should send a diver down."

"For Christ's sake," Cunningham chuckled. "There's only three or four feet of water at low tide. We could go wading and find it. I'll have Cruz look."

"Good idea," Costello said. "A diver might attract attention and that means media."

"Why didn't he do the job when he first came ashore?" Cunningham asked.

Hannon answered this question. "Doors and windows were locked."

"Professionals don't have a problem with locks." Cunningham said.

"But the guy's been watching me," Hannon said. "You said that yourself. He knows my habits and routines outside the house, but he doesn't know what's inside. It's the middle of the night. I could be awake. I could be armed. He doesn't know the layout."

A smile came over Cunningham's face. "Unless someone close to you filled him in."

"That's not happening," Hannon insisted. "He knows I jog in the morning. Easier to come in while I'm out."

"That makes sense," Costello said.

"That way he could surprise me from behind and give the message while he's strangling me."

"With your own rope," Cunningham said.

"I think so."

"Nice touch."

"What do you think, Chief?" Costello asked.

"Better than nothing, I guess. We still have to find out who sent him and if they're going to send someone else. They'll think twice about it now that we're involved."

Officer Tom Fisk knocked on the door, opened it meekly, and entered.

"Damned reporters are driving me crazy, Chief. They got questions I can't answer."

"Give them evasive answers, my boy," Cunningham said in a loud voice Hannon recognized as a mediocre attempt to impersonate the great W. C. Fields. "Tell them to go fuck themselves."

Costello burst out laughing. Tom blushed. Chief Cunningham seemed pleased. Hannon was glad to see Cunningham had a sense of humor.

"I can't tell them that," Fisk said.

"I'll be out in five minutes," Cunningham said.

"What did you find out about Hannon today?" Costello asked after Fisk left.

"Ah, yes," the chief began. "It seems Mr. Hannon once worked for a large, now defunct, department store in Boston and had more than a passing interest in security work. He was a special policeman, carried one of those little badges, had a license to carry a firearm, assisted in several arrests, and logged in a large number of appearances in criminal court testifying against a whole hoard of assorted felons."

"Well," Costello said. "What do we have here?"

"Mostly involvement with fraudulent credit card use," the chief said. "Bad checks, internal theft. Stuff like that."

The two men looked at Hannon. He didn't say anything. He remained seated.

"I'd forgotten about that," he said after a pause. "I don't know why. It was the only time I ever enjoyed working for the company."

"You better tell us about it," Cunningham said. "And make it quick." He glanced at his watch.

"I don't remember all that much. It was thirty years ago. Mostly I questioned customers who were using a credit card that had been reported lost or stolen and determine if we had a crime in progress."

"You had to make that decision?" Costello said.

"Yeah, security people were standing by, but I had to tell them when to get involved."

"By getting involved, you mean make an arrest?"

"Yeah."

"And you might assist in the arrest?"

"Sometimes."

Cunningham took over. "And you went to court and testified and, maybe, made yourself an enemy."

"Yes, I guess I did."

Cunningham rose from his chair and leaned forward on the desk. "You sent people to jail," he bellowed.

"Some went to jail, a lot got off with a six-month suspended sentence."

"What's that matter? They still might become enemies. Remember what we spoke about yesterday?"

Hannon had to think about that a moment. "People who seethe, turn firecrackers into nuclear bombs," he finally said.

"Close enough," Cunningham said."

Hannon knew the chief was right. "I'm sorry," he said. "You're right."

Cunningham smiled. "Now we need details about your life as a crime fighter."

"It's all pretty fuzzy."

"Let me jog your memory. Do you remember a Boston detective named George McCarty?"

"Sure. He worked the big stores, prosecuted most of our cases. We were friends. He's dead now."

Once again, Cunningham smiled. "He sounded alive when I spoke to him this afternoon."

"George is alive?" Hannon was astonished.

"Alive, well, living on Cape Cod and semiretired. Boston police put me in touch with him. He remembers you. Says you helped him out of a jam once."

"Did I?"

"According to him you did, and he wants to help. He's going to Boston Tuesday and look through some of his old files."

"I'd like to talk to him."

"I'll give you the number. Meanwhile, do some thinking yourself. See what you come up with. Are we clear now?"

"We are."

"Then we'll meet again Tuesday, eleven o'clock, right here. Things should be quiet till then. The bad guys need to regroup. Make sure Mrs. Rizzo is with you. I wanted her here today. Meanwhile, you stay out of sight. I'll have Cruz contact you." He checked his watch again.

"Are we done?" Costello asked.

"You guys are. I've got to get rid of those reporters. Any questions?"

Hannon had lots of questions, but this didn't seem like a good time. Cunningham was in a hurry. It was Saturday night. Hannon figured he was headed for a big time at the Knights of Columbus.

CHAPTER EIGHT

Hannon was surprised when Costello offered him a ride home. Another chance to work on his rapport with cops. As they were leaving, Officer Fisk handed Costello a note. The parking lot exit was blocked by one of the TV trucks so Costello read the note while they waited for Chief Cunningham to finish his live interview on the six o'clock news.

"You're right," Costello said. "He used rope from your rowboat to strangle you with. I had the lab people check."

Hannon nodded. He was pleased.

The chief's comments took almost ten minutes, even though he had very little to say. Hannon didn't pay much attention. He was thinking about his own questions. Would a guard be posted near his house? He didn't think so. Should he even be staying there? Why did Cunningham want Linda to be with him on Tuesday? Would the chief consider reissuing his permit to carry a firearm, which had long since expired, and would he be able to use the firing range at the station for practice? He hadn't fired a weapon in years.

"Let's move out," Costello said when the exit was clear. "I need to set up a watch on your place for the rest of the weekend."

Hannon was glad to hear that. And it turned out Costello was in a talkative mood. By the time they reached Route 1A, he had some of his questions answered. Hannon's safety, overall, would be the responsibility of Deputy Chief Cruz. Hannon liked that. Maybe Cruz, who was also the harbormaster, would commandeer someone's yacht as a safe house. Not likely. Costello didn't think much of Hannon's arming himself and he didn't think the chief would either. Also, use of the firing range didn't seem like a good idea.

"The place isn't soundproof," he said. "They get a lot of complainants about the noise. It doesn't get much use."

"So none of them shoot very well?"

"No need around here for sharpshooters. Until now, maybe."

They were cruising along at half the speed they'd been going on the way in, and Hannon was much more relaxed.

"As far as Mrs. Rizzo is concerned, no getting around it," Costello said. "She has to be checked out along with anyone else who's close to you."

"That's a waste of time."

"No it's not. Statistics tell us a large percentage of murderers are close to the people they kill."

"Familiarity breeds contempt," Hannon said. "That was my mother's favorite old saying. She could explain anything by just quoting an old saying."

He would have ambled on about that subject had Costello not interrupted him.

"Mrs. Rizzo is a significant other. She has to be checked out. It's standard procedure, crime solving 101."

"And all my friends as well?"

"Yes," Costello answered firmly.

"So everyone is a suspect until they prove themselves innocent."

"That's the way in works until we get to court. You should know that"

They were coming to the access ramp that led to the beach house.

"Take a right here," Hannon said.

"I was at your place yesterday. Remember?"

"Christ, yes. I'm trying to think of too much at once. I guess I'm in some denial about what's going on. I've had that problem before."

Costello seemed surprised. "Denial about what?"

"Alcohol and angina."

"So how did you master those denials?"

"Sobriety and stents."

"But before the solutions you had to realize the problems."

"Yeah."

"So, can I make the point that you shouldn't be in denial about your current problem?"

"You may, everyone else has. Do you think they'll try again?"

"Hard to say," Costello said, measuring his words. "Depends on the resolve of the person who's paying the fee. With all the media attention and police presence, it wouldn't be a surprise to see them cut and run."

"What if the hit man has a friend or family member seeking revenge?"

"That's not likely. Professional killers are loners. Murder is just a job they do for money. They don't have close friends or families who give a damn if they screw up and get themselves killed. If anyone else shows up it will be because the client hasn't given up."

They slowed down on the access road to see if there was anyone left at the house. It looked clear.

"You might want to think about taking a little vacation," Costello said. "Visit friends or family. You have kids, don't you?"

"I have two grown kids and three grandkids, and I'm not going anywhere near them. I don't want anyone caught in the crossfire."

"Don't you have a sister out West somewhere?"

"Yeah, Arizona. I'd like to see her again. It's been twenty years. Maybe when this is over. I'd like her to meet Linda."

"That's Mrs. Rizzo, huh?"

"Yeah, she's divorced."

"What was her name before?"

"I don't know. Never asked."

"Maybe you should, before Tuesday."

Hannon nodded. He got the message.

"I'm not too keen about going into hiding," he said.

"It's not a bad idea. Why make it easy for them? Talk to Cruz about it. He's had experience with major crimes and the SWAT team, and his father was a damn good detective."

They were on the dirt road that ran parallel with the bike path, approaching the house.

"Someone's waiting for you on the deck," Costello said.

"That would be Linda." Hannon really couldn't see that far without the glasses he seldom wore.

Costello drove past the house and started to make a U-turn just before they reached the two ten-foot high stone pillars that marked the boundary of the MacMaster estate. He stopped the car.

"Where the hell's the gate?" he asked. "There should be a gate there."

"There was," Hannon said. "A huge, black, wrought iron gate. There was also almost two hundred yards of iron fence that stretched out on both sides of the pillars to the water. It walled off the whole peninsula like a moat around a castle."

"What happened to it?"

"Turned over to the war effort in '42," Hannon said. "Tore it all down to make tanks and guns. The whole village showed up to watch it come down. They cheered. Some people cried. It was a big deal."

"Very patriotic."

"That's the way things were back then. The only thing that mattered was winning the war. I was just a kid, but I remember it. All the young guys went off to war. All four of the MacMaster boys went. One of them didn't come back."

"And the fence didn't make it back either," Costello said.

"No. When my father got the gardener's job, old Earl, who was king of the clan at the time, had him plant that whole row of trees you see walling the compound off. They wanted their privacy back."

Costello finished his U-turn and headed back to the house to let Hannon out.

"Was it really a clan?" Costello asked.

"You bet it was. Always three generations of family there. They homeschooled the kids till they got to high school, then they paved the path to the village so the kids could ride their bikes to the school bus. They had livestock and vegetable gardens."

"Christ," Costello said. "It's a wonder they didn't all end up farmers."

"Real estate was more profitable. Plus they had their fair share of doctors, lawyers, and politicians."

They had reached the house. "Thanks for the ride," Hannon said as he got out. "See you again."

"Count on it," Costello said.

After he drove away Hannon went to the deck, expecting to see Linda. It wasn't her. It was Charlotte MacMaster.

CHAPTER NINE

Hannon had forgotten Charlotte's invitation but tried not to show it. She was sitting at the table facing the cove, sipping a drink she'd brought with her.

"How'd it go?" she asked.

"Not bad."

"How's Police Chief Paul Cunningham?" she asked sarcastically.

"He's getting help from the state guys, hanging in there."

"Any clues or leads?"

"No."

"Do they know who the man was who attacked you?"

"Not yet."

He sat down on the other side of the table facing her. He didn't like all the questioning.

"What was all that business on the cove this morning?" she asked.

"Watch the eleven o'clock news, and you'll know as much as I do."

She frowned. "Under investigation, is that it?"

"Yeah." He smiled. "What brings you down off the mountain?"

"I knew you wouldn't come up the mountain, so I came down."

"Maybe I should just ask why you're here."

"Perhaps I just wanted to see you."

"Why?"

She smiled and finished whatever it was she was drinking. "There's something I should tell you."

"I'm listening,"

"It's about this house."

Hannon was surprised. They had never talked about the house before. Charlotte got up and came around the table to lean on the railing. She seemed nervous. He was also feeling anxiety. Linda might arrive at any moment.

"Did your father ever tell you how he got this house?" she asked.

"No. We didn't talk much."

"Did you have a falling out?"

"No, we got along. It never came up. I didn't get here often."

"Why not?"

"The sofa bed was a backbreaker. We kept in touch by phone."

"Didn't you ever wonder?"

"No, I didn't. It happened in the mid-eighties. I wasn't around. My older brother, Billy, died. He had cancer. A couple months later, my mother and father separated. She went to Arizona to live with a friend. My sister went with her. My father was all alone in the big house on Edgar Avenue. I guess he was lonely. Anyway, I got a call to help him move. He'd sold the house and was coming here. I didn't know he owned the place. I didn't find that out till he died."

"Six years ago," she said.

"Yeah. How'd you know?"

"We met the day you moved in. Remember?"

Hannon remembered.

She smiled. "It was one of the best days I ever had." Whatever tension she had felt seemed to be gone. "It was fun, wasn't it?"

"Yes," he admitted. "But it's over."

"I know. You were looking for something less complicated?"

"Something like that."

She turned to face him. "And you found it," she said softly.

"That's right." His response was emphatic. "What about the house?"

"Oh, that," she said. "Do you really believe Charles just gave it to him?"

"I've wondered about that. So have a lot of other people."

"I know," she said. "But what do you think?"

"I think my dad was more than just a wonderful gardener who made the estate famous. He and Charles were damn good friends. I think Charles felt sorry for him after my mother left him alone in that big house."

"Yes. But why give it to him. He could have just lived here."

"I don't know, Charlotte. Why is this so important?"

"You know my brother-in-law, Harry, of course," she said.

"I remember him. Short, red hair?"

"And gay."

"I was going to say he was the youngest of Charles's three sons."

"He's also chosen an alternative life style. He lives in Providence with his partner, Ricardo. They have their eyes on this house."

"It's not for sale," he said.

"They're in no hurry."

"The way I see it, it won't be for sale while I'm alive."

Charlotte turned away. She didn't say anything. She let him figured it out for himself.

"Oh, come on, Charlotte. You think they might want to do me in?"

"It's crazy, I know, but someone wants you dead, and Harry's a person who gets what he wants."

"We're talking murder here, Charlotte."

"I know, but Harry can be violent, and so can this partner of his."

"I don't know about the partner." Hannon stood as he spoke. "But the Harry I knew wouldn't break an egg. And even if I was out of the way, he'd have no claim on the place."

"I think he's working on Charles for that, looking for some kind of loophole in the sale."

"That's twenty years ago." He began to pace.

"Harry thinks that Charles may have been coerced," she said.

"Coerced? He thinks my father was a blackmailer?"

"That word hasn't been used yet, but he thinks Charles was somehow cheated."

"Men like Charles don't get cheated by men like my father." He stopped pacing, and sat down again.

"I know that," she said, "but I think it's important you know what's going on. I'm only trying to help."

"I know. I'll have to tell Cunningham. I'll try and leave you out of it."

"Don't worry about that. Harry knows how I feel. I have to be back." She started to leave, but remember something. "I forgot to mention. I saw a note on your front door when I came by."

He nodded and smiled.

"Good to see you again," she said as she was leaving

Hannon knew the note would be from Linda and what it would tell him. She had a second job waiting tables at the Sail Loft restaurant and had been called in to work the evening shift. She would be back around midnight. Linda never missed a chance to work there. She was a good waitress and was first in line for the next full-time opening. Unfortunately, there was little turn-over. The restaurant was always busy, and the tips were lavish. It was the best seafood restaurant in the county, some would say the state, and had recently been given an added boost when a food critic for Channel Six said the owner and head cook, Dan Gallagher, ought to give frying lessons to his contemporaries and competitors. Linda's note verified what he already knew. He was glad she had the work but disappointed he would be alone. He had hoped they might make progress on his situation, something they had failed to do the previous evening. Perhaps it was just as well she was working.

He was building a fire in the huge, stone fireplace, which took up half the wall across from his bed and recliner, when he suddenly realized how hungry he was. He hadn't eaten since breakfast but was in no mood to cook. He couldn't go out. He had no transportation. His car was in the shop, and his boat was a crime scene covered with yellow police tape. He settled for a can of chicken soup with plenty of crackers.

By the time he finished eating, the fire was blazing and he was thirsty. He opened a bottle of nonalcoholic beer, sat down in his recliner, and leaned back. He didn't turn the television on or grab anything to read or play music. This was time to think about his predicament, to search his mind and flush out enemies who would harm him. But that didn't happen. His thoughts took him back to the mid-seventies and an old friend he had helped out of a jam.

CHAPTER TEN

The Mid-Seventies

He first met Detective George McCarty on the fourth floor of the new Boston courthouse located one street up from what use to be Scolley Square but was now Government Center and City Hall Plaza. He didn't remember exactly what year it was, but he knew Gerald Ford was president. When he was young, he had spent many happy evenings in the square, usually at the Old Howard Burlesque Theater watching comics like Mike Sacks, strippers like Rose La Rose, and the left-handed fiddler who led the pit orchestra. As he stood looking out the window, waiting for his case to be called, those old memories slipped back into his mind. He scanned the Government Center trying to pick out the exact spot where the Old Howard was. It was long gone. So were the bars and the pawn shops, the tattoo parlors and the arcades and the all -night movie theaters. The area that Hannon had once called a "neon paradise" was now a semicircle of red brick buildings, a red brick plaza, and a City Hall constructed of red brick. At the moment, it was all getting rained on.

"Are you Hannon?" a man said, interrupting his reverie.

"I am."

"I'm Detective McCarty. Let's go. We're up first."

McCarty was no taller than Hannon but had more bulk and looked to be about the same age. He was dark complected and had black hair. He hadn't shaved for a couple of days.

"You don't look Irish," Hannon commented.

"My mother's Italian." McCarty said.

"You're the guy who prosecutes our cases now?" Hannon asked as they hurried toward the courtroom.

"Yes," said McCarty. "And Judge Ketch doesn't like to be kept waiting."

"I know."

"Been here before?"

"A few times."

"Well, I've been doing this for six years, and I hate to lose."

But they did lose. The defendant, a scrawny young man named Chain Links, had shoulder-length blond hair and was a biker who had just arrived in town without any money. He'd found another man's credit card in the men's room of a local bar and was buying a black leather jacket with it when Hannon arrested him.

"I was just getting something I could sell for food money," he'd pleaded. "I was going to pay the guy back when I got a job."

No one in the courtroom, including Judge Ketch, believed him. No one except the short, pale young man sitting beside Hannon. It was his credit card, and he no longer wanted to press charges. George McCarty argued that Chain's criminal record should be taken into consideration.

"He hasn't been here long enough to get one," Judge Ketch said. "Let's not dig too deep here."

The case was dismissed. Detective McCarty was not happy.

"What the hell happened?" he asked Hannon.

"I think the guy whose card it was made eye contact with the defendant. Love at first sight."

McCarty didn't look like he liked the answer.

They were in court together many times during the months that followed, but it was all business. There was no friendly banter or discussions about sports or politics or family. Hannon did get to a point where he called the detective by his first name, but he never knew whether George knew his first name. . That was OK. Not many people did. The cases they worked were routine, and they usually won. It was on a cold winter day shortly after Jimmy Carter became president when their friendship really began.

Hannon was getting on the up escalator from the third floor when a woman from store security called out to him.

"There's a big fight in men's suits," she yelled. "Some guy's stealing a bunch of Hickey Freeman suits. George is trying to arrest him. I'm going for the cops."

Hannon turned and ran back down the escalator and around the corner into the suit department. He saw a crowd at the other end of the floor watching George and a massive black man struggling. He ran toward the action, not knowing exactly what he would do. George was trying to handcuff the man, but suddenly the huge thief uncorked a wild, roundhouse punch that smashed into George's face and knocked him to the floor. Hannon reached his right hand into his jacket pocket and closed his fist around the roll of pennies he carried there. The thief hadn't seen him yet. He was busy picking up his loot. Hickey Freeman suits were the Armani suits of that era. George got up and stumbled toward the man and slammed his shoulder into his back, trying to knock him down. It didn't work. The thief turned and hit George with a left hook. George's head snapped back, but his body fell forward. He took the man in a clinch and held on like a weary boxer. Hannon moved into the fray without being noticed. He tightened his right fist around the roll of pennies and cocked the fist behind his right ear. His eyes focused on the side of the black man's jaw. Target zero—the quintessential sucker punch. The thief turned to look at him but it was too late. Hannon swung his shoulder around with all the speed and power he could muster and drove his fist into the thief's jaw. There was a loud crunching sound. Hannon felt a sharp pain in his right hand. The thief stumbled backward and then dropped to his knees. He put his hands on the floor so that he fell no further. Hannon turned and slid the penny roll into his pocket. The crowd of onlookers cheered.

George McCarty stood in relived awe. "What kept you?" he asked.

Hannon had no answer.

"You cold cocked him," George said.

"Damn right," Hannon said. "What else could I do?"

Ralph Hall, the store's head of security, arrived and began shouting orders. "Move the crowd out of here, Hannon. Get the cuffs on him, George, and get him into the stockroom."

"Don't we need to line up some witnesses?" Hannon asked.

"No," Hall shouted. "We got witnesses—me and you and George."

Hannon didn't press the matter. His hand was throbbing. He hoped it wasn't broken. George and Hall pulled the black man up and dragged him toward the stockroom.

"It's over, folks," Hannon said. "The police will be right here."

As the crowd dispersed, Hannon moved quickly to the stockroom. As soon as he was through the door, he heard a loud scream coming from the far end of the room. He rushed toward it. When he got there he didn't like what he saw. Ralph Hall stood over the prisoner with a blackjack in his hand. Before Hannon could stop him, he smashed it into his jaw. As he drew back to strike again, Hannon grabbed his arm. "What the hell are you doing?" he shouted.

"You keep the fuck out of this," Hall snarled as he pulled his arm out of Hannon's grip and struck another blow into the fallen man's kidney.

The man shrieked in pain.

Hannon turned to George who was down on one knee. "We've got to stop this," he said.

"I know," George said. "But I can't get up."

Hannon looked back to Hall who was leaning down whispering in the black man's ear.

"You slimy prick," Hall said. "I'll break your spleen in half."

"I can't let you do that," Hannon said.

Hall stood up to face him. Hannon assumed a defensive position. He turned slightly sideways with his right foot ahead of the left, his hands belt high in front of his body, and his eyes fixed on Hall's hands.

SOMEONE WANTS *YOU* DEAD

"I'm not finished with him yet," Hall said.

"Yes, you are," Hannon said. He knew he was in too deep to back down. Hall was bigger and appeared to be fit. He had been army military police for many years, and Hannon knew he could handle himself. Hall's craggy face was red and beaded with sweat. Hannon could even see sweat under the short cropped hair on his scalp. He seemed to be trembling with anger.

"I'll have my blackjack back now," McCarty said as he stood. "You'll kill him. We don't need that."

"Goddamned moron don't deserve to live," Hall said fiercely.

Hannon shook his head in disgust. Two uniformed policeman entered the stockroom, and the confrontation ended.

"Get this guy out of here," McCarty said. "Read him whatever it is you have to and get him booked. Larceny and assault on a police officer."

The big man didn't go easily. "I'll break you in half someday," he shouted. "That's a promise."

"That's a threat," Hall yelled. "You guys are witnesses. If I ever see this guy again, I can shoot him on sight."

He pulled a .32 caliber revolver out of his shoulder holster and stuck it against the man's throat. "And that's exactly what I'll do."

That's enough, sir," one of the police officers said. "Holster your weapon. We're leaving."

And they did.

Hall had only one word for Hannon and George as he left. "Assholes!"

The two stood and look at each other.

"He's one ignorant bastard," George said. "I never realized he was that far gone."

"He's a sadistic bigot," Hannon said. "And he doesn't have a clue. Ignorance is bliss, as my mother used to say."

"How's the hand?" George asked.

"I think it's OK."

"I'm sorry I couldn't help out sooner. I was a little short of breath."

"Better get that checked out."

But George never did.

Hannon never found out how it all turned out. He and Hall hardly ever spoke again. He was sure the black man had gone to jail. Hall left the company a year later. A couple years later, Hannon heard he had died under strange circumstances. He and George became good friends. They worked together and drank too much together after work. They talked at length about crime and sports and problems they were having at home and how they both hated their jobs. Hannon's only working pleasure was his limited involvement in police work, but George was fed up with it and looked forward to early retirement. Both men were addicted to exercise and worked out regularly at the police athletic club. Hannon got George interested in jogging, and George got Hannon into weights. Occasionally they would go a couple of rounds in the boxing ring. The last time they did, George had to stop because of a chest pain. Their friendship, except for a few phone calls, ended about the time Ronald Reagan moved into the White House, and Hannon was transferred to another location. A few years later, Hannon heard George McCarty had died of a heart attack.

CHAPTER ELEVEN

It was ten o'clock when Hannon woke up. He had fallen asleep without meaning to. He couldn't have spent three hours reliving his time with George McCarty. What had made him think George had died? He didn't remember. It didn't matter. Cunningham had spoken with him. He was alive and was going to help. He felt good about that. He got up from the recliner and began to pace the floor. This was his usual procedure for heavy thinking. After three trips to the front door and back, he realized he wasn't thinking; he was counting steps.

"For Christ's sake," he said aloud. "I don't need to measure the room."

He sat down on the couch and looked at the room. He hardly ever saw it from this prospective. It looked larger and rather sparsely furnished. Everything he saw, except the kitchen table that fronted the wall closing off the closet and the bathroom, was backed up to either the right or left wall and facing out. His recliner, a night table, the bed, his father's ancient bureau, and a bookcase ran down the left side, while his television, the fireplace, a couple of storage units, and the kitchen filled the right side. One of the storage units was a huge stereo console with a radio and record player that had elaborate woodwork on the front covering the speakers. He had gutted the inside for storage space. The other unit was his old army footlocker. He thought about putting some music on the small record player on top of the console but quickly decided it was a bad idea. He couldn't do two things, listen and think, at the same time. He started to pace again, but his mind was blank. He got a beer, drank half the can in two or three gulps, and settled into the recliner.

A few minutes later he came to his first conclusion. The last two words the killer had spoken had to be a name. Why hadn't he seen that right away? Chief Cunningham had. OK, so what, move on to the big question. Who the hell wanted him dead and why? He didn't have a clue. He moved on to a new topic. "I need some kind of weapon," he said aloud. "They'll never let me get a gun."

He remembered his father's old starter pistol. It was still in the top drawer of the bureau. It fired only blanks because the firing pin had been filed down, but just carrying it around might provide him with some sense of security. Perhaps the pin could be replaced so it would fire live rounds. That would surely be illegal, but he would check it out. He spent some time lamenting the fact that he had a permit to carry a firearm for thirty years but had never bought one.

He moved to the kitchen table, sat down, and noticed the stone paper weight that was there. It was a smooth beach rock that had been given to him at his twenty-fifth high school reunion. Helen Cogsworth, who had been the class secretary, had given them out to the twenty-two members of the class who lived in Hooper's Landing and had been bussed to the regional high school, eleven miles away, for four years. She had gathered the small rocks from the massive rock pile at South Beach, where most of them had learned to swim. They were all about the same size, and she painted them red with a black *'53* on the front. Red and black being the school colors and 1953 the year of their graduation. He had never thought of it as a weapon, but as he picked it up, he was reminded of the roll of pennies he used to carry around.

"Just have to hit with this instead of knuckles," he said aloud.

He finished his beer and got another one before heading back to the recliner. He was feeling tired again. He began thinking about other ways he might protect himself and wondering whether he was getting a little paranoid. He sat down on the couch. Before long, he fell asleep again.

He was abruptly jarred from a deep sleep when the kitchen light flashed on. Instinctively, he jumped up from the couch. He still had the red rock in his hand. He drew his arm back as if to throw it.

Linda was standing in the door frame. She lifted her hands up in front of herself. "Hannon," she cried out. "It's me."

He dropped the rock.

"A little jumpy, aren't we?" she said.

"I was asleep. Didn't hear you unlocking the door."

"It was open."

Hannon shook his head. The budding king of caution had left his front door open all evening.

"I'm sorry," he said. "Cunningham's got me on high alert, and I'm getting nothing. Christ, it could be anyone—people I don't even remember."

"Concentrate on the ones you do know."

"Good point."

"Have you eaten?"

"Soup and crackers."

"I brought you some fried shrimp from the Loft. I'll heat them up."

"You're too good to me."

"Actually, it was Danny's idea. He and his father are hoping you're still going to run in their road race Monday."

"Son of a bitch! I forgot about it."

"Not surprising, considering all that's going on. Do you think you will?"

"I don't know." He said "It would piss Cunningham off. He doesn't want me exposing myself."

"Well, make sure you have clothes on." she chuckled.

The Columbus Day road race had become Hooper's Landing's biggest event of the year, and this was the tenth anniversary. It was a five-mile run that had been started by Danny Gallagher and his father, Max, co-owners of the Sail Loft, to benefit leukemia, which had claimed the life of Danny's daughter, Carol, over twelve years ago. Hannon had been visiting his father when the first race was run and came in second in the over-sixty division. There had been less than two hundred runners that year, and only seven were in the older group. When he moved into the beach house five years later, there were over sixteen hundred participants, almost two hundred in his age group. He finished twenty-ninth. He had competed every year since, with diminishing results, and had acquired several sponsors from his high school classmates, who made pledges to leukemia research in Carol's name. The amount of money they contributed was based on Hannon's finishing position and had always been substantial.

"You are going to run, aren't you?" Linda asked. "They're expecting over two thousand entries."

"I'm not sure," he answered. "I don't want to put anyone in danger."

"The crowd is protection," she said. "Plus there's lots of police."

"Good point. I love that race, and I certainly don't want to be scared off."

"Give it some thought."

"I don't like them losing the money my sponsors donate."

"They'll probably give it anyway."

"I guess. Still, I'll feel better if I earn it."

"Sleep on it."

"The hell with it. I'll run. I'm not going into hiding."

"Good for you," she said.

CHAPTER TWELVE

When Hannon woke up the next day, Linda had gone out. He hoped it was to buy food. He'd had another good night's sleep and wondered why the stress of his situation hadn't kept him awake. He felt calm and relaxed. He didn't get any further with his thought. Linda was back.

"Are you still in bed?" she asked.

"Looks that way," he said. "Where've you been?"

"Cumberland Farms. I'm going to make brunch."

"You mean breakfast?"

"I mean brunch. It's almost noon. I'm making hash and eggs plus my special hash-brown potatoes with peppers and onions sautéed in olive oil."

"Life is good," he mused.

Linda outdid herself. They ate on the deck watching the boats fill up the cove. There were many more than the day before.

"Maybe there hoping they'll be another attempt on my life," he said.

He started to tell her about the bomb, but she'd already heard.

"It was the topic of conversation at the restaurant," she said. "There was a different version at every table."

"Cunningham danced around it with the reporters," he said.

"There are tons of theories."

He chuckled. "Everybody's a detective."

He was telling her his theory about the sequence of the two attacks when they heard his cell phone jingle.

"Where's that coming from?" she asked.

"Sounds like somewhere in closet. I'll get it."

"You should get your land line back," she called after him. "You're not ready for twenty-first century technology."

"I'm hearing this from someone who doesn't drive a car."

"Don't be nasty, Hannon."

By the time he found the phone, there was only a voice mail from his son, Sean. The news of his dilemma had reached the Portland, Maine, area, and Sean's message expressed concern.

"You call him right back," Linda said. "He must be worried."

"Can't have that. I don't want him involved."

"At least call him back. Give him my best."

She washed the dishes and cleaned the kitchen while he and his son talked. She liked what little she knew about Sean. He had his own landscaping business in Maine, having followed his grandfather's lead instead of his father's. She often wished that Hannon had done the same.

"How is it with him?" she asked when they were done.

"Good. He's concerned, wants to come down. I told him things were under control."

"Did he believe you?"

"I don't know. I'll keep him posted. He's going to call his sister and let her know what's going on. He thinks I should cool it at his camp in Millinocket until this blows over."

"Good idea," Linda said.

"I don't want him involved. If they found me up there, he'd be in danger. But I'm glad he called. We had a nice chat."

"We should see more of him and your daughter."

"Yeah, maybe when this business is over. You'd like it in Maine."

"Yes, I would," she said. "Finish your story about the attack and the bomb."

He did. He also told her about George McCarty.

"And he's going to help you dig up the past?" she said.

"Yes. I may have made some enemies back in Boston. You're going to know a lot about me when this is over."

"And you about me," she said. "But that's OK. We should have done it years ago. Can you tell me one thing I've always wondered?"

"Sure."

"In all those years, why did you hate your job?"

"I made a poor career choice," he said. "The retail business sucks unless you're a merchant, buying and selling. Sales supporting jobs are second class with no future and no money."

"Why didn't you get out?"

"No guts, plain and simple, scared to death of not having a paycheck."

"Maybe you should have been a policeman. It sounds like you enjoyed working with George"

"Maybe, but right now, I'm going to go for a run, get ready for the race."

"Are you going to run the entire five miles?"

"'I'm going to try. No damn "jogwalking" for me."

"Will you be using your knee brace?"

"If you can find it."

He did a few stretching exercises while she found the brace in his footlocker. He pulled it onto his left leg, strapped it tight, and pumped air into it with his little rubber squeeze ball. He got up and walked around.

"How does it feel?" she asked.

"Uncomfortable. It's going to take some getting used to."

"Are you sure it will hold air after all this time?"

"I don't see why not. Moths wouldn't eat it, would they?"

"No," she said with a chuckle. "They wouldn't. Why don't I pace you on my bike?"

"OK, but I want a slow, easy pace."

"Of course."

The problem was that Linda didn't know what slow and easy meant. In the first half mile she had to stop and wait for him twice. That was OK. He wasn't out to break any records, and, as he jogged along, he became much more focused on his surroundings than he ever had been before. It was like seeing his route in a new light. He wasn't looking to the right—he knew Route 1A well enough. But he had never paid attention to the woods on his left and realized how dense the forest was and how easy it would be to hide in them and ambush someone. And it was large. It stretched out over the south side of the cove all the way to the jagged cliff of Seagull's Rock, plenty of space for a killer to hide in and watch. He wondered if the police had searched there. He was almost two miles into his run when the woods gave way to the village cemetery, open ground all the way to town. He started to run faster. He felt comfortable and was pleased that his knee brace wasn't losing air.

Linda was waiting for him, sitting on her bike at the beginning of Front Street where the town wharf and the Sail Loft were located. It was his turn around point.

"What kept you?" she asked playfully.

"Lack of wheels," he said. "Plus I was admiring the fall colors."

"Well, you're too slow for me. I'm going to turn it up a notch."

"Go for it."

"I saw Danny and his father on their way to the cemetery to visit Carol's grave. They're glad you're running. Max says you should stay with him tonight."

"Maybe I will," he said. "Be good to keep a low profile. Maybe I can stay upstairs till the race starts and jump in."

"Why don't we have dinner there tonight?" Linda said. "Max says we can eat in the function room."

"Looks like you and Max have a plan."

"You'll be out of sight, and I love their fried haddock."

"So I'll see you later."

"It's a date," she said as rode off back toward the beach house.

CHAPTER THIRTEEN

Hannon started back at a leisurely pace. He was good to go for the race, no need to burn himself out. He hadn't gone three hundred yards when Linda came flying back past him at a rate of speed that suggested she was out to set some new kind of new world record.

When he reached his house, he heard the sound of an outboard motor close to shore. It was the harbor master's boat pulling up to his own. Cruz was on board, wearing his wet suit, getting ready to search for the killer's cell phone. .Hannon decided he could help. He pulled his rowboat out from under the deck and rowed out.

"Need help, Big O?" he called out as he pulled up to the boats.

"Not from the elderly," Cruz answered.

"How'd you know it was me?" Hannon said, as he climbed aboard his boat.

"Your rasping, aging voice."

"The rest of me is youthful."

"Feeling your oats today, are you?" Cruz said. "Stay here and keep the other boats away. We can talk when I get out."

Cruz pulled his weighted belt and air tank on and slipped into the water. Hannon sat down behind his steering wheel. He noticed the hatch was still open. He hadn't closed it when he evacuated the boat after finding the bomb, but why hadn't the police closed it after their search. Had they actually searched or just put yellow tape up to keep people off until they got around to it? Perhaps Cruz was going to search after he came up. Hannon decided to save him the trouble. Impulsively, he slid through the hatch and down into the cabin. As he began to look around, he had second thoughts. "What the hell am I doing?" he asked himself aloud.

But it was too late. He had already seen the cell phone in the middle of the port side bunk. He shouldn't have come onboard. He should have let Cruz find it.

"What the hell," he said. "What's done is done."

He went back to the deck and looked out over the water, searching for Cruz's floating surface marker. It was about ten yards off the bow moving slowly, clockwise around the boat. Cruz would be below it. He took off his shirt and running shoes and dove into the water five yards in front of the marker. The water was much colder than he'd expected. Quickly, he swam to the bottom and turned to get Cruz's attention. When the two made eye contact, he gave a thumbs-up and they went to the surface. Cruz snapped the weighted belt off and swam to the swimming platform on Hannon's boat, pulling the belt along with him.

"You didn't put your ladder down, old man," he called out.

Hannon didn't answer.

"Common mistake among the elderly," Cruz continued as pulled himself quickly onto the boat. "Do you need the ladder down?"

"You know damn well I do," Hannon said.

"What's the problem?" Cruz asked when they were both on board.

Hannon told him.

"Bastards left it for me to do the search," Cruz said.

"I shouldn't have come aboard with all the yellow tape," Hannon said. "Boat looks like a float in the Rose Parade."

"It's your boat. Pull it off while I get my kit."

When Cruz returned with a metal case, the tape was down. He took out two pairs of plastic, white gloves and tossed a pair to Hannon. "If you want to play detective, you have to put these on," he said.

"Gee thanks, Dad," Hannon said with a chuckle.

Cruz put the phone into an evidence bag, and they searched the boat. It didn't take long, and they found nothing more.

"I didn't think we would," Cruz said. "He took everything else with him."

"So what happens now?" Hannon asked.

"We send the phone to the state police lab and see what they come up with."

"Think they'll come with anything?"

"If they get lucky, fingerprints that will match those of the guy you killed."

"So we'll know there was just one guy."

"Yeah, but we still won't know who he is."

"And you don't think they'll find anything else?"

Cruz shook his head. "Nah. The phones these people use are prepaid. They buy them at some drugstore, program them with false information, and destroy them after they use them."

"But they might have voice mail or contact lists," Hannon said.

"Not likely."

"I was thinking about something while we searched the boat."

"I didn't know you could do two things at the same time."

"I'd like to be part of the investigation."

"Sure. Tell us who wants you murdered."

"As soon as I find out, you'll be the first to know."

As Hannon rowed back to shore, he realized he hadn't told Cruz of his plans to run in tomorrow's race. He felt a bit guilty about that. When he got to shore, Linda appeared on the deck.

"Get a move on," she shouted. "Max is picking us up in half an hour. You need to shower and shave."

"Shaving is out," he called back. "Facial stubble is all the rage."

"Bullshit. You're not thirty anymore."

He quickly showered and shaved and was ready before Max arrived.

Maximilian Gallagher was one of the best players in the history of Regional High School football. He was huge, fast, and tough, and had he not suffered a career-ending knee injury in his senior year in college, he would certainly have gone on to play in the National Football League. He and Hannon had played together when Hannon was a senior and Max a freshman, but they hadn't become close friends. Max was younger, quiet, and didn't live in Hooper's Landing. He went on to have a successful career in the sporting goods business but retired after his wife and granddaughter died within six months of each other. Despondent, he moved to Hooper's landing to join his only son, Danny, in the restaurant business. When Hannon moved into his father's beach house and became one of the Sail Loft's best customers, the two became good friends.

When Max arrived in his Lincoln Continental, they were waiting on the deck. Linda had insisted they dress up for the event and was wearing what looked to be a new dress. Hannon had been surprised. She hardly ever wore a dress. He had been even more surprised when she'd insisted he wear a jacket with his black, mock turtleneck T-shirt.

"How do I look?" He had asked as he admired himself in the bathroom mirror.

"Resplendent. How 'bout me?"

"Awesome."

"Exactly what does resplendent mean?" he asked as they walked toward Max's car. "That's good, isn't it?"

"It's very good—almost inspiring."

Max went into his best family chauffeur act. He took Hannon's overnight bag, put it in the trunk, and ushered them into the back seat. "You guys ride here," he said. "No fooling around."

"Just keep your eyes on the road." Hannon said.

The ride to the Sail Loft was smooth and quiet. Halfway there, Hannon noticed Max was wearing a suit and tie and figured it must be a working night. He would be seating people and table- hopping to ensure their pleasure. He was good at that, and he had his favorites. Although he would never accept a tip from anyone trying to buy their way to the head of the line, he would always have a table for friends like Hannon when they came through the door. Hannon didn't like to be taken ahead of others who'd been waiting, but he'd never found a friendly way to decline. Now he was thinking what these people waiting in line might have been feeling. Were they as annoyed as he would have been? Would any one of them go home and seethe, work themselves into a fit of anger, eventually snap and seek revenge?"

"Stop this!" he said softly.

"What?" Linda asked.

"Nothing."

When they reached the Sail Loft. Max pulled into his private parking space and jumped out to open the car door.

"Where were you on the ride over?" Linda asked Hannon as they were getting out.

"Paying a visit to paranoia," Hannon said. "My mind is a dangerous neighborhood. I should never go there alone."

"Where did that one come from?" she asked.

"Alcoholics Anonymous."

Max led the way to the rear entrance and into the kitchen, where his son performed culinary magic with his deep fryers. There were several of them, all going full force. The sound of the bubbling oil and the aroma that rose up from the fry baskets were like an aphrodisiac for Hannon. He felt complete pleasure. His stomach announced its hunger.

"Nothing like the smell of deep fat frying," he said to Max. "You should bring all your customers through the back door."

"Don't have to," Max said.

"What's Danny's secret, Max?"

"Don't know."

"Where is he tonight?"

"He'll be upstairs."

Hannon noticed a substantial amount of shrimp cocktail on the dumbwaiter that carried food up to the second floor. He smiled.

"Party tonight, Max?"

"Sort of," Max muttered.

Hannon's deductive powers kicked in as they started up the back stairs. Everyone dressed to kill, fryers going full force, tons of shrimp cocktail on its way to the function room. He started working his way into surprise mode.

CHAPTER FOURTEEN

There were over thirty people in the function room. They rose as he entered, shouted the obligatory greeting, and applauded. Hannon recognized enough of them to know that it was a gathering of his sponsors for tomorrow's race—people from his high school graduating class and their spouses and friends. Linda and Max had rounded them up for the prerace meeting they usually held on race day, a half hour before the starting gun, on the town dock. It was their way of limiting his prerace exposure.

"Keeping me out of sight," he whispered to Linda while expressing surprise to the crowd.

"We all need a party now and then," she said.

Helen Cogsworth was the first to reach him. She was a small woman with white hair and thick glasses. She walked briskly with the use of a cane and had a hearing aid in her left ear.

"Hannon," she said, embracing him. "Handsome as ever."

"You're looking well, Helen," he said.

"Don't shit me. I look old, but I can still set up a hell of a party."

"All Max and I did was call her," Linda said. "She's a one-man band."

"She always was," Hannon said.

"Come say hello to your sponsors, Hannon," Helen said. "Get business out of the way so we can party. We're all counting on you, as usual. Lots of money for Danny and Max's charity. You remember my husband, Tom?"

Tom appeared from out of nowhere, ready for a big handshake. He was over six feet tall and could have passed for Helen's son. Hannon adjusted his vision level to span the height difference between the two.

"I don't see how you guys ever got together," he said with a chuckle.

They answered simultaneously.

"Love," she said.

"Shotgun marriage," he joked.

Hannon and Tom joined hands in the powerhouse handshake that happened every time they met. Tom Cogsworth was proud of his grip and pleased when anyone could gave it right back to him.

"Good man," he said. "I hope things are going as well as possible."

"They are," Hannon said. "Thanks for asking."

Helen took Hannon by the arm and guided him through the gathering of sponsors and friends. He shook many hands, none of them as strong as Tom's, greeted everyone with a friendly comment, and answered questions and concerns about his situation. Actually, it was Helen who led the way in easing their concerns. She never stopped talking. By the time everyone sat down to dinner, the points had been made that the police had the situation in hand, no further attacks were expected, and Hannon felt comfortable about running in tomorrow's race.

"I think that went well," Helen said as they walked to a table where Linda, Max, and Tom were waiting.

"You do good work, Helen," Hannon said.

"You know we'll all make our donations even if you decide not to participate," she said.

"I know, but I want to run. I don't want to be scared off.

"You never change. We all knew you'd say something like that."

The fried seafood dinner prepared and served by Danny Gallagher was outstanding. Hannon had both shrimp and haddock. He passed on the scallops but made up for that with extra French fries, which were delicious.

"It's hard to find good French fries today," he said to Linda. "Not ones like my mother made."

"That's because they can't fry them in lard anymore."

"She used to shake the grease off in a brown paper bag."

"Can't do that today, Hannon. Not healthy enough."

"I guess. She cooked for taste."

"Maybe that's why you have two stents in your coronary arteries."

"Good point."

A short time later, Hannon found himself alone at the table sipping a St. Pauli Girl nonalcoholic beer. Max and Linda, along with several other couples, were on the dance floor taking advantage of the music Max had arranged to have piped in. Helen and Tom were table-hopping. Hannon always enjoyed watching his friends dancing and drinking and conversing at parties, but tonight was different. He couldn't help wondering if there was someone in the crowd he might have unknowingly offended or embarrassed in the past. Someone who was angry at him, but said nothing. Someone who seethed.

"Dammit," he muttered. "Stop doing this."

"Talking to yourself, Hannon?" Helen Cogworth's voice startled him out of his paranoid thought.

"Sometimes it helps me keep things in order," he said.

"Come and join the rest of us," she said. "We're rehashing our favorite reunion topic."

Hannon knew exactly what she meant. He had hoped they'd get through the evening without it coming up, but that never happened. Every time Regional High School's class of 1953 members who lived in Hooper's Landing got together, the happenings of their graduation night became the topic of conversation. It was a tradition. It was the night of Hooper's Landing's first and only murder, and it had never been solved.

"I wish we could let that go," Hannon said.

"But we can't," she said. "It's part of our history. It had a profound effect on our lives."

"Not mine."

"Come on, Charlie Benson has a new theory."

"Charlie has a new theory every month."

"The cops questioned us all. We were suspects."

Hannon leaned back in his chair and chuckled. "No we weren't. They just wanted to know if anyone saw or heard anything."

"That's a laugh," Helen said as she sat down beside him. "We were all either drunk or asleep or trying to get laid. I was getting pregnant."

"Yes, I know," Hannon said with a smile. "We all know. You tell us every reunion."

"Oh, my God, do I? I do, don't I?"

"Yeah, it's part of the program, just like the moment of silence we have for Miss Hopkins."

"Come join us," she said. "I don't want you sitting by yourself worrying."

He took her by the hand and looked directly into her eyes. "I'm not doing that," he said firmly.

"But you must be. You could be dead."

"But I'm not," he said. "See." He spread his arms out, palms up. "I'm breathing. Alive, healthy, and not incarcerated. What else do I need?"

She seemed relieved. Linda and Max returned to the table.

"Get yourself into character, big boy," Linda said to Hannon. "Max ordered up a tango."

Linda loved to dance, especially the tango. Hannon did not but was never able to decline when she asked, and when it was a tango, she didn't ask, she insisted.

"Better get your dancing in before the big debate gets going," Max said.

"What debate?" Linda asked.

"You don't know?" Helen said. She sounded surprised.

Linda shook her head.

"Usually our meetings and reunions always end up in a discussion—sometimes heated—about the night of our high school graduation," Hannon said.

"Enlighten me while we dance," Linda said.

"You know I can't do two things at the same time."

"You don't have to. I'll lead."

The music was just starting as she took his hand and pulled him onto the floor. Quickly, he put himself in tango mode. To him, it was all attitudes; stand erect and stiff, do not smile, think Latin or Al Pacino in *Scent of a Woman*. She would do the rest.

"Remember to move your body first and let your feet follow," she reminded him as he tried to recall his basic step. He had no idea what she meant.

"So what's the big discussion about?" she said as she took her first twirl under his arm, stretched to arm's length and dipped backward gracefully before twisting back into his strong embrace.

That was his favorite move, and it surprised him that during it he was able to tell her that his high school music teacher, Margaret Hopkins, had been stabbed to death in her own home just three hundred yards from where he and his classmates were celebrating their graduation. Linda's moves came to an abrupt stop. "That was long ago," she said. "My God. You still talk about it?"

"It's a tradition, Linda. A periodic meeting of the Murder Club."

"You even have a name for it""

"Not officially. That's just what I call it."

"Do they think the murderer may still be among us, perhaps in this very room?"

"Of course not," he said quickly. He wasn't really convinced that was true. They started to dance again. "Everyone really liked her," he continued. "Haven't I told you this before?"

"Not really."

"It was pretty gruesome. They won't let it go. I think some of them feel guilt."

"About what?"

"We were all partying at South Beach, just down the road from her house. I guess there's a feeling that if we hadn't been drinking or paired off in cars, we might have helped. At least provide information to the police."

"You were questioned?"

"Yeah, but nobody saw anything or heard anything. We were too busy."

"You don't need to elaborate." She took another dip and bounced back into his chest.

"I guess the group feels we owe her something," Hannon said as they sidestepped across the floor. "The killer needs to be exposed. Charlie Benson and Ray Freeman keep it going, along with Tom and Helen and a few others. Charlie was sitting up by the road around midnight and thought he heard a car start up, but he was too drunk to look."

They were moving forward now, side by side, in perfect step with the music. As it ended, they turned to face each other and froze in a stately, upright pose with her right leg hooked around his left just below the knee.

"And they can't let it go?" Linda said on the way back to the table.

"Not a chance."

"Sad, very sad."

The party lasted another hour. The fifty-year-old murder of Margaret Hopkins was not solved, but there was the moment of silence in her memory. Hannon and Linda stayed on the dance floor and away from the murder discussion. The hugs and handshakes and good-byes were short, and, moments later, only Max, Linda, and Hannon remained.

"Wonderful evening," Hannon said. "Thank you both."

"Helen got it all together so you wouldn't have to meet them out in the open tomorrow," Max said.

"Best to keep a low profile, Linda added.

"I've also given you a new race number," Max said.

"I hope you didn't give my regular number to anyone else," Hannon joked.

Max chuckled. "I was going to give it to Victor."

He was kidding. Victor had been Hannon's nemesis in all the Columbus Day races. Victor had beaten him by only a few seconds in the first race, nine years ago, and Hannon had vowed to beat him, but that hadn't happened.

"We're closing," Max said. "Danny's giving Linda a ride home, and I'll get you fixed up here."

"Aren't you staying?" Hannon asked Linda. He had hoped she would.

"Sorry," she said meekly. "I'm setting up a water station at my building early tomorrow."

After she left, Max took Hannon to a corner bedroom, off the function room. He often used it as his home away from home. It was a large room with two rear windows looking out over the harbor and two side windows looking down Front Street toward South Beach. It was well furnished, but all Hannon noticed was the comfortable looking bed and the room-darkening shades on the windows. He liked that.

"Do you have a gun in your overnight bag?" Max asked.

Hannon shook his head. "I don't own one. I had a license to carry for years but it lapsed."

"Too bad. You should get it back."

"Pain in the ass these days, Max. Red tape, training classes, firing range instruction."

"Who the hell's going to train you," Max said. "Nobody on the force knows squat about shooting."

"Anyway, I don't push it. I never thought I'd need a gun. I never bought one, but it was a comfort knowing I could."

"You don't have that comfort now, at least not legally."

"I don't like being illegal."

"That's how the crooks and killers do it."

"Still, not my style."

Max went over to a bureau and pulled out an old, but pristine, Colt .45 from the top drawer.

"Try this on for size," he said. "It's clean and has a full clip."

"I'd go to jail if I got caught carrying that around."

"You don't have to lug it around. Just keep it close. I'm sure you know how to use it."

"I do."

"I'll put it in the drawer. You do whatever you want. See you tomorrow. I'll have Danny wake you up."

"Not too early. I'll sleep late and jump into the pack after the start."

After Max left, Hannon got his shorts and T-shirt out of his bag and changed into them. Max had already pinned his racing number onto the front of the shirt. He smile and went to bed, but it took him a while to fall asleep. He was thinking about the .45.

CHAPTER FIFTEEN

He woke up the next morning to the sound of some-one banging on the door.

"Time to get up," Danny called out.

"Yeah" he said. "Come on in."

Danny was almost as tall as his father but nowhere near as heavy. There was certainly no doubt whose son he was. "Race starts in a half hour," he said as he entered. "How'd you sleep?"

"OK."

"I'll get you some coffee."

"That would be much appreciated."

Hannon normally required more than a half hour to get himself ready for running, especially a five mile road race, but he was glad for the extra sleep, and the coffee got him going. He had two cups while he pulled on his knee brace, did a few stretches, laced up his running shoes, and pulled his cap close down over his sunglasses. He was down the back stairs and moving through the kitchen when he heard the starting gun. The fact that he wasn't out in the street didn't bother him. He knew the elite runners, who were up front at the starting line and running for prize money, would be on their way. The recreational runners were still moving slowly toward the starting line, caught in a huge mass of humanity. He went out the back door and up the alley between the Sail Loft and the Citizens Bank toward Front Street. He had never seen the race from a spectator's viewpoint and was anxious to see what it looked like. The exit from the alleyway was blocked, so he went to his right and climbed onto the deck of the Sail Loft to get a good look. He was startled by what he saw.

It was an exciting, magnificent scene of grandeur that stormed into his vision, panoramic and full of color and motion. It sent a shiver of tingling energy through his whole body. That feeling had happened to him on his first and only viewing of the Grand Canyon and when he first drove through the electric wonderland of Fremont Street in Las Vegas. But now it was the crowd of runners, jammed together as one along the entire length of Front Street, giving the impression there was not enough room for even one more person to join them. The same was true of the spectators, filling both sides of the street to maximum capacity, cheering, and shouting encouragement to the participants.

"Wow," he said aloud. "Glad I didn't miss this."

He felt a surge of energy and comfort and happiness. This was a major moment. There was nothing but the race and the panorama. He moved down from the deck and slipped into the hoard of runners. There was room for one more. He was crossing the starting line. He set his watch into chronograph mode and pushed the start button. He was off and running.

The hoard of runners headed north toward the bike path and Hannon's house. The first quarter mile would be a slow spreading out of the tightly packed mass until each runner had enough space to establish his or her normal pace. As the cemetery on his right became the wooded area, he fell into his normal stride and began to pass other runners. He felt comfortable and loose but realized he would soon reach the forward group of runners, the younger, faster men and women whom he had no chance of catching. Then he would begin to look for Victor. That didn't happen until he reached the access road to route 1A, a hundred yards before his house. He slowed his pace to save strength in his legs. Suddenly he felt the presence of two runners in back of him but not wanting to pass. They could be drafting off him to keep themselves out of the wind, but there was no wind. Who the hell were they, and what were they doing? Fear crept into his mind. He began to regret his decision to run.

"Wonderful day for it, Mr. Hannon," the runner to his left said as he pulled abreast of him.

"For what?" Hannon asked.

"For running," the voice answered.

It was a male voice. He didn't recognize it, and his peripheral vision was no help. He turned his head and saw a redheaded man, perhaps middle age, shorter than himself, and wearing sunglasses. He took a wild guess.

"Harry MacMaster? After all these years?"

"I'm surprised you remember me."

"Are you also surprised I'm still alive?"

"What a question. I did hear of your nasty brushes with the inevitable."

"And were you disappointed with the outcome?"

"No, sir, not at all. I wish you no harm. I'm afraid my sister-in-law gave you a wrong impression."

"She said you wanted the beach house back."

"Perhaps I do."

Harry sounded a little out of breath. The climb up the access road was taking a toll. He slowed down. Hannon slowed down with him. He could still feel the presence of Harry's companion behind him.

"I spent many happy hours there as a child," Harry said. "I was disappointed when my father gave it to your father. I never understood why he did that."

"Nobody did," Hannon said quickly.

"I think you know Charlotte has a vivid imagination and is quick to form opinions."

"Yes, I do."

They had reached the highway and turned onto it. There was a police car there to ensure that the runners kept to the left side, which had been closed off to traffic. Officer DiMartino was stationed there. Hannon felt his comfort zone returning. This was the spot he usually tried to pick up his pace. He turned his attention back to Harry. "Do you do a lot of running?" he asked.

"I think you've already noticed I don't," Harry said in a voice that told Hannon he wasn't going much further.

"But you came out today to see me?" Hannon said.

"And to keep my partner, Ricardo, company. He's younger and a serious runner. I've already held him up a great deal."

"So he's just hanging around for an introduction."

"It's a pleasure to meet you, sir," Ricardo said as he moved quickly ahead of Hannon. He was not out of breath, and he looked very much the serious racer. He was tall and slender, with long, black hair, and he seemed to take one stride for every two Hannon took. He also looked much younger than Harry.

"You should be way ahead of us," Hannon said to him. "Up with the elite runners."

"I'm not in a competitive mood today," Ricardo said.

Hannon turned his attention back to Harry. "Does he share your feelings about my house?"

"I'm afraid he's fallen in love with it, but he wishes you no harm."

Hannon turned back to Ricardo for conformation, but he was long gone. He was far down the road in an all-out sprint. He turned back to Harry, but he wasn't there either. He'd had it. The incident had unnerved Hannon and taken his mind off the race. He remembered what Charlotte had said about Harry always getting what he wanted and Ricardo's strange and perhaps violent nature. He tried to step up his pace, but the uneasy feeling wouldn't go away. He passed Linda's water station without noticing whether or not she was there. He slowed down to a walk and concentrated on clearing his mind. "Get your ass in gear," he whispered to himself. "This ain't no damned "jog-walk."

He picked up his pace and put more bounce into his stride. As he made the left turn off Route 1A onto Main Street, he spotted his nemesis, Victor, about fifty yards ahead. Like Hannon, Victor wore black. He also wore a red sweatband around his forehead to keep beads of sweat from running down into his eyes from his totally bald head. It was his trademark. No one could miss him. But Hannon also couldn't miss the tall runner who was with him, step for step, engaging him it conversation. It was Ricardo.

"What's that all about?" he asked himself aloud.

Several possible answers crept into his mind. Was Victor gay? Were they friends? Did Harry know they knew each other? Did they actually know each other, or was this just a casual exchange between runners. He gave up on the casual exchange when the two shook hands and Jose sped away. They knew each other, and it seemed important to Hannon to find out how. Perhaps it was just a coincidence.

As he reached Town Hall and turned right onto Edgar Avenue, he began to plan his strategy. He would shadow his nemesis the rest of the way and try to race past him in the last hundred yards. The element of surprise was in his favor. As far as he knew, Victor had no knowledge of his competitive feeling.

Edgar Avenue was one of the three avenues named for one of the four founding brothers of the village. Along with Bruce Avenue and Harold Avenue, it ran north to south, parallel to Route 1A, from Town Hall to the southern edge of Hooper's landing. The village itself was named for the oldest brother, Hooper. It took the runners to South Street, where they would turn left to South Beach. Another left onto Beach Street would take them to the finish line at the Sail Loft. Hannon knew it would not be easy to stay close to Victor, who was running at a good pace. His legs were holding up, and he was breathing well, but it was hot, and sweat was pouring off him. By the time he reached South Street, he was beginning to have doubts.

As he made the turn, an old memory took over his thoughts. It always did. The small white cottage where his music teacher, Margaret Hopkins, had been brutally murdered came into view. It had come to be called "the murder house," and across the street was the two-story colonial where Charlie Benson had lived.

Hannon bumped into a woman jogging in front of him.

"Sorry," he said timidly. "Lost my focus for a moment."

"Lots of people do at this place," she said.

Hannon looked for Victor but didn't see him. He had lost him in the crowd ahead. He picked up his pace to make up the ground he'd lost, but he was breathing heavily, and his feet were sending tingles up into the backs of his legs. He hoped he wasn't cramping. He had to be close to Victor at the finish line. Even if he couldn't beat him, he had to speak with him. As he reached the beach and turned the corner to head for town, he noticed a cluster of recreational joggers moving at a slow pace. He smiled. That would be the Rosie Randell cluster.

Rosie was a gym teacher and woman's basketball coach at Regional High School. She was a power walker and a damn good one. She was tall and well proportioned, a blond knockout of a woman with shapely legs, thought of by many men as voluptuous. She moved like a machine—long strides, arms bent at the elbows, pumping back and forth just above the hips, and the hip area itself darted from side to side like a metronome set to high speed. It was the hip action that caused male runners to slow their pace and show a reluctance to pass her. Victor was currently among them. Hannon caught up quickly and settled in only twenty yards behind him and waited. When Victor finally sprinted past the crowd and resumed his normal pace, Hannon took off after him. He had no trouble keeping up, and suddenly his adrenalin kicked in. He felt a surge of energy and a feeling of euphoria as all thoughts turned to the race.

He was gaining on his archrival as Front Street and the huge crowd that filled it came into sight. The cheering and shouts of encouragement electrified him as he raced past his nemesis with only a few yards to go. He heard a loud, hollow blast that sounded like a shotgun. He ducked. So did some of the other runners. He almost fell. He slowed down, confused and nervous.

Someone took him by the arm as if to hold him up. It was Victor.

"Not to worry, Hannon," he said. "It's just a firecracker."

"Damn thing gave me a jolt," Hannon said.

"I'm not surprised. I've heard about your problem."

Hannon was surprised. "You know who I am?"

"Of course. I've been looking for you all morning."

CHAPTER SIXTEEN

Hannon and Victor realized that they hadn't reached the finish line and were blocking other runners. They crossed it simultaneously and moved quickly onto the crowded sidewalk. Hannon accepted that as a tie but still had a question for Victor. They would to have to wait. His sponsors descended upon him in an avalanche of congratulations, pats on the back, and handshakes. He was in Tom Cogsworth's crushing grip when he heard Victor, still close by, whisper in his ear, "Can we meet later?"

"Yes," Hannon said. "Somewhere inside. Do you know Max Gallagher?"

"Yes, of course."

"He'll show you where I am."

Victor nodded and left.

Hannon moved away from his sponsors. He had no intention of standing out in the open. The firecracker had shaken him up. He needed to take cover. Another blast rang out but didn't sound as loud.

"What the hell's going on?" he asked no one in particular.

"Just kids, Hannon," a woman's voice answered, "Fireworks. You remember, don't you?"

He turned to see Molly Hammond, a childhood neighbor and his sister Erin's best friend.

"Damn thing scared the crap out of me, Molly."

"I'm not surprised. You should be in hiding."

He smiled and nodded and changed the subject. "Have you heard from my sister lately?"

"It's been a while now."

"Yeah, me too. I'm having trouble keeping up."

"We all are, Hannon." She smiled. "Nice to see you."

When he got back to Max's room, he went to the bureau and took the .45 out. It had a full clip, just as Max had said, and a round in the chamber. Just aim and shoot. But was it really necessary? Were things so bad that he should carry a concealed weapon without having a license? Risk jail time? He'd have to think about that. He put in back in the drawer and covered it over. There was a soft knock on the door.

"Anybody home?" It was Max's voice.

"I'm here, Max. Come on in."

"You got a visitor," Max said as he came in.

"A guy named Victor?"

"Yeah. Want me to frisk him?"

"I don't think so," Hannon said with a chuckle.

"Want me to hang around?" Max was smiling.

"Not necessary, thanks."

"I got beer in the fridge. Even put a couple of fakes in there for you."

"Much appreciated."

Max left. Victor came in. Hannon found the small refrigerator tucked away in a corner and got two cans of beer. He held up a Miller Lite for Victor to see and gave him a questioning look. Victor nodded affirmatively.

Hannon gave him the beer, sat down on the bed, and motioned him to sit in an easy chair. They both opened their beers and drank heartily. Neither seemed to want to speak first.

Victor broke the ice. "Is that nonalcoholic beer you're drinking?"

"Yes, it is."

"I take it you don't drink."

"Not anymore."

"That's quite commendable. I imagine you're curious about why I'm here."

"Yes," Hannon said. "But first, I'm curious about how you even know me."

"You're quite well known, especially after your weekend adventures, and we do have a mutual friend, Mrs. MacMaster."

Hannon was surprised. "Charlotte? How do you know her?"

Victor took a long drink of his beer, finishing it off. He held the empty can up to Hannon with that same questioning look Hannon had given him. He was thirsty. Hannon got him another one.

"This is my favorite," Victor said. "Max must have picked it out."

"You know Max?"

"Of course I do. Everyone knows Max. I've seen you here before."

"But you didn't say hello," Hannon quipped. "How you know Charlotte?"

"My law firm has represented the MacMaster family for many years."

"And your firm is?"

"Abrams, Levine, and Lewis. I'm Levine. We're based in Providence and have a branch in Westerly to handle our work with the MacMaster family."

Victor took another long gulp of beer. Hannon finished his O'Doul's. In a small way, he envied Victor. Miller Lite had been his favorite for many years.

"I assume you're here to represent Harry," Hannon said, "I saw you speaking with Ricardo this morning."

"Oh no," Victor said. "Harry and Ricardo prefer to have their own legal counsel. I represent Mr. Charles MacMaster."

"Wow. The old boy himself. Still alive and kicking, is he?"

"Very much so. His kick isn't all it used to be, but he still has control."

"How's his health?"

"He's ninety-four. What more can I say?"

"So Mark hasn't taken over yet?"

"Mark's a patient man. He knows he's next in line for the throne, so to speak, and he's ready."

"He spends a lot of time on that schooner."

"That's his only source of relaxation," Victor said. "But like his father and grandfather and all the Mac Masters who came before, he's ready to continue the family's prominence."

"You mean dynasty."

Victor smiled. "They do tend to think of it that way. After all, their ancestors were the founders. They built it and made it what it is today."

"And they control it."

"Of course they do," Victor said. "And their social and political influence reach far beyond this small village."

"Would that be countywide or statewide?"

"Perhaps even more."

"None of them has ever held public office."

"They prefer to remain in the background. May I trouble you for another beer?"

"Yes, of course. I'll join you."

Hannon got up and got the beers. They heard a loud cheer rise up from the crowd outside. The awards were being presented. He opened both cans, handed the real one to Victor, and took a swig from his fake.

"So you're saying they're kingmakers, not kings," Hannon said.

"Quite right."

"And yet my father always thought of them as regal."

"I'm sure they think of themselves as royalty. It's their nature."

"So why are you here?"

"I've been sent to fetch you, Hannon. My client, Charles MacMaster, wishes to speak with you as soon as possible."

Hannon was surprised but answered quickly. "I'd like that. When's the best time?"

"Actually, right now. We could catch him before his afternoon nap."

"Sounds good to me."

CHAPTER SEVENTEEN

After they finished their beers, Victor went to get his car. Hannon didn't change his clothes. He told Max where he was going.

"Might be a good idea to take the .45 along," Max said

Hannon gestured toward his running clothes. "Where would you suggest I conceal it?"

"Just a thought," Max said.

Ten minutes later Hannon and Victor were moving past Linda's building on 1A in Victor's silver BMW. There had been hardly any conversation. Hannon noticed her water station was taken down but she was nowhere in sight. He wondered where she might be.

"How did it feel to finally beat your nemesis?" Victor asked as they turned off 1A onto the access road.

"We crossed the finish line together," Hannon said. "I'll settle for that. We'll do it again next year."

"I'll look forward to it."

As they approached Hannon's house, he spotted Linda's bike in the front yard.

"Can I bring my girlfriend along?" he asked. "She's never been on the estate before."

"Of course," Victor said. "I'll give her the guided tour. Charles wants to speak with you alone."

Hannon found Linda on the deck. She'd always wanted to see what the compound, as she called it, was like, so she was happy to go along. She also seemed pleased to meet Victor.

"Who won?" she asked after they were introduced.

"Dead heat," Victor said.

They drove quickly through the towering stone pillars that no longer held iron gates and along the quarter-mile, tree-lined driveway that led to the main house.

"How long since you've been here?" Victor asked Hannon.

"I haven't seen it in daylight for over twenty years. I was here one night about six years ago."

Hannon wished he hadn't said that. Although he'd told Linda about his brief affair with Charlotte, he'd never gone into particulars. And that one night had been a particular. He and Charlotte had been swimming together, naked, and had made love on the schooner. Just before dawn, she swam back to the estate's private dock and returned to her husband's bed, and he swam to his beach house. He wondered if Linda had picked up any notion of what had happened.

"You'll find the place has changed," Victor said, interrupting his thought.

Hannon expected change, but the only one he noticed was that his father's magnificent gardens were gone. What had been a phenomenally colorful floral extravaganza was now an open field of weeds. Even the huge latticework that was home to the multicolored rose wall was gone. But the three-story main building and the string of garages still looked formidable and sturdy. They had been constructed by the four founding brothers with lumber cut from the forest that covered the peninsula. There were two other buildings that came into view just beyond the main house.

"My God," Linda said. "How many people lived here?"

"The four founding brothers all had families," Victor said. "Lots of kids. Seemed like more each generation."

They drove onto the circular driveway that led to the main house.

"So where are they now?" she asked. "What happened here?"

Hannon didn't answer. He was still looking back at what use to be the gardens as they reached the main house.

"Two world wars," Victor said. "Plus birth control and women's rights."

"Ah," she said. "Independence and revolt."

"The Second World War really started the population decline." Victor said. "One brother was killed, one wounded so he couldn't have kids, and a third died in a plane crash after the war ended."

"That's awful." Linda seemed deeply moved.

"The larger the family, the larger the chance for tragedy," Hannon said.

"It left only Charles to continue the family name," Victor added.

"Was the family name really that important?" she asked.

"Yes, to them it was vital. Charles was under great pressure from his father, Earl."

They arrived at the front door. Victor had a key, so they let themselves in.

A large entrance hall led to a circular staircase that climbed up through the second floor and on to the third, atrium style. There was a balcony on both levels that led to the various rooms. There was nothing in the entrance hall except doors and a small elevator next to the staircase.

"Charles lives a rather reclusive life in the large room on the top floor," Victor said. "Hence the elevator."

"I'm surprised they don't have the walls decorated with ancestral portraits," Hannon said. "Leaders of the clan in full Scottish dress, kilts and all, perhaps carrying bagpipes."

"More likely to be carrying weapons," Victor said. "They've always considered themselves warriors. You better go up now."

"Can't keep the old boy waiting," Hannon quipped.

"It's best not to," Victor cautioned.

"Is it safe to use the elevator?"

"It must be. It hardly ever gets any use."

Hannon entered the elevator and pushed the up button. The door closed slowly, and there was a quick jolt as it started to lift. It was small, perhaps large enough to accommodate two people, one of whom might be in a wheelchair, and it was slow. It didn't stop at the second floor, and when it got to the third Hannon saw that there was only a small space at the top of the staircase and two doors. The one on his left was a double door with what must have been the family coat of arms on it, along with a sign that asked visitors to knock twice before entering. He did exactly that and found himself in a large, sparely furnished room that he'd never been in before. His father had told him about it. It had been used as a ballroom and theater. Family meetings and entertainment provided by family members for the entire family and their invited guests took place there. At the far end of the room, along the back wall, Hannon noticed a large stage, perhaps three or four feet high, with ramps leading up to both sides. It was completely enclosed by tall, black screens. That, he assumed, would be Charles's bedroom. He was right. Before he had a chance to call out or knock again, an ancient man in a power wheelchair came rolling down the ramp to his left, swerved toward him at the bottom, and began motoring in his direction.

CHAPTER EIGHTEEN

Hannon hardly recognized the frail old man riding toward him. He looked every bit his age, much smaller than Hannon remembered, wrinkled, and tired.

"You look fit and well, Hannon," he said as he brought the wheelchair to an abrupt halt on a small carpeted spot with a desk and chair. His voice was still strong and clear.

"Thank you, sir," Hannon answered politely. "It's good to see you."

"I had hoped to see more of you when you became our neighbor. Your father and I were very close."

"Yes, I know. I'm sorry that didn't happen." Hannon saw no need to discuss the reason it didn't happen. They both knew it was Hannon's involvement with Charlotte.

"May I offer you a drink or some food?" Charles asked.

"No, thanks."

"Well, have a seat then. We have a couple of matters to discuss."

Charles maneuvered his wheelchair into position behind the desk while Hannon settled into the antique rocker opposite him. Hannon noticed a small oxygen tank clipped to the wheelchair. It wasn't being used.

"Charlotte's told you what she thinks Harry might be up to," Charles said.

"Yes."

"I believe she's overstating the matter."

"So did I, until he and his friend confronted me during the race today."

"They confronted you?"

"They shadowed me a couple hundred yards and then came abreast to exchange sarcastic pleasantries."

"Did they threaten you?"

"Not really. Harry said they mean no harm. Maybe they were just having some fun."

"Yes, that's quite possible. Harry has to have his little jokes, but he's completely harmless."

"Charlotte also said he was thinking of challenging your decision to give the property to my father in the first place."

"Rubbish," the old man thundered in a voice that reminded Hannon of the imposing and powerful man he once was. "On what grounds?"

"On the grounds that you may have been coerced into the transaction or that there may have been some error made."

"Pure bullshit, Hannon. The transaction was handled by Victor's father, Aaron Levine, a lawyer who didn't make errors. And it was authorized by me, Charles MacMaster, a man not easily coerced."

Hannon was impressed. The old boy still had some fire in him, but he was getting angry and upset.

"Can I get you a glass of water?" Hannon asked.

"You can get me a shot of whiskey," Charles said. "And then you and I will take a walk around the room."

Hannon didn't see a walker or crutches or even a cane, so he concluded that Charles could walk. He also didn't see any whiskey.

'There's a bottle in the bottom drawer of the desk," Charles said.

Hannon got the bottle and poured a generous amount into a glass. Charles quickly gulped it down before pushing himself up from the wheelchair and beginning their stroll. His pace was ultraslow and unsteady, but he was on the move with Hannon at his side, ready to catch him before he fell. They moved to the front corner of the room, and Charles stopped to look out the first of several large, rectangular windows. There were four each on both side walls. Hannon counted the eight windows with their long, blue drapes held open to let the light in. If they were going to make a stop at all of them, it would be a long trip.

"Did you know your father was my best friend?" Charles asked.

"Actually, no, I didn't."

"Your father was a wonderful man, and as a gardener and landscaper he was a magician. He made us famous."

They moved on to the second window. Charles pointed out at what was left of the gardens below.

"Now look at it. It's a disgrace."

"Does anyone tend it?" Hannon asked.

"No, Mark hired some damn foreigner and calls him a gardener, but he doesn't know a rose from ragweed. I think he's more a bodyguard."

"A bodyguard?" Hannon said. "Don't you have electronic security hooked up to the local cops? They'd be here in minutes if they drove on the bike path."

"They'd lose their way on the bike path," Charles said with a chuckle. "Our alarms go straight to the state police."

"Does Mark have enemies?"

"Everyone has enemies. You should know that by now."

Hannon nodded. It didn't seem like Charles wanted to talk about Mark.

They moved past the second window to the third and looked down at the hedge maze his father had constructed many years ago. It was completely overgrown and he had a hard time seeing where the pathways had been. Linda and Victor were standing at what Hannon remembered was the entrance. The old man's eyes seemed to fix on it. He didn't speak.

"You were about to tell me why you asked me here today," Hannon said.

"Yes, of course," Charles said. Hannon hoped he hadn't forgotten.

They skipped window four and began walking past the stage to the other side of the room. They made it to window five before Charles spoke.

"I wanted to make it clear that your father owned the beach house because I gave it to him for his years of service to the family and because he was the only real friend I ever had. It was getting little, if any, use. We didn't need it and I felt he did. He was devastated after your mother left him. He needed a change. He never asked for it or pressured me. It was his and now it's yours. Is that clear?"

"Yes, perfectly clear."

They were approaching the next-to-last window, and the old man was running out of steam. "I'll be needing my chair for the rest of our walk," he said.

Hannon moved quickly to get the wheelchair.

"What else did you wish to tell me?" he asked as he moved Charles back to the carpeted area.

"I want to tell you why your mother left your father." Charles said.

"I'd be interested in hearing that."

"I'll need another whiskey first."

Hannon got the old man another shot, and after Charles tossed it down quickly, he began speaking clearly and calmly. Ten minutes later, Hannon knew the whole story.

It had all happened in 1983 shortly after the death of Hannon's older brother, Billy, who had recently retired after thirty years in the army and was living on Long Island. The tragedy had been amplified for the family due to their inability to contact Hannon, who was working in Upstate New York, in time to attend the funeral. Also, his death was a shocking surprise to the family, who were not aware he had been battling cancer for over two years. Two weeks later, when Hannon's father was cleaning out Billy's army footlockers, he discovered a letter to Billy from a woman calling herself Babe and telling him she was being pressured to give their unborn child up for adoption. The letter was thirty years old. Hannon's father became obsessed with finding his grandchild and her mother and taking them into the family, but his mother wanted no part of it. She needed no further trauma in her life, and being a good Catholic, she feared the humiliation that came with a child born out of wedlock. But his father had persisted until Charles finally told him that his own wife, Mary MacMaster, who had given birth to three sons but could no longer carry a child, longed for a daughter and had been in contact with a woman willing to give up her unborn child if it was a girl. And, in fact, an infant girl had been taken into the MacMaster family and passed off as their own. However, the young child soon became erratic and mischievous and more than Mary could handle. Eventually she was placed in an orphanage in Providence. In order to quell thoughts of insanity in the family, word went out that she had died and been buried in the family cemetery on the estate. The births and deaths of the MacMaster family members were never questioned. Knowing that she might still be alive, Hannon's father hired a woman named Florence Bird to help him with the search.

"That was it for your mother," Charles said, finishing his story. "She couldn't take any more. She packed a bag and took the train to Arizona to visit an old friend."

"And she never came back," Hannon said softly.

"Never," the old man said emphatically. "She wrote to your sister asking for clothes to be sent, and finally Erin went out there herself."

"I never heard any of that. Why didn't Erin come back?"

"Who knows?" the old man said. "She came home for her belongings and left. Your father fell apart. He couldn't work, didn't eat, and drank too much."

"So you moved him over here?"

"It took a long time. He wouldn't leave the old place, but he wasn't happy there, too many memories. He snapped out of it after he got settled here."

"You saved him."

"I helped him. That's what friends are for. He saved himself."

Their meeting was ended by a loud scream that came from the gardens. Hannon bolted toward the door. The old man began maneuvering his wheelchair toward the third window.

CHAPTER NINETEEN

Hannon passed up the elevator and started bounding down the staircase. That was a mistake. Running down stairs wasn't as easy as it used to be. He felt uneasy, as if his feet weren't going to land properly, and was forced to grip the banister and slow himself down. He was all right on a flat surface and was able to sprint out the front door, around the house, and into the gardens. He saw Linda sitting on the bench near the entrance to the hedge maze. She looked distressed. Victor was sitting beside her and a short, stocky, bald man was standing beside them. Hannon concluded he was the bodyguard.

"What's happening?" he asked as he approached them.

"Little lady went into the maze," the stocky man said. "Kind of spooky in there."

"I'm all right," Linda said. "It just closed in on me."

"It's all overgrown," Hannon said. "It hasn't been taken care of."

He was looking for a reaction from the bodyguard. There was none. He noticed the man was taller than he first appeared.

"I'm Hannon," he said. "I was visiting with Mr. MacMaster."

They shook hands. The man had a large, strong hand and a stiff grip, but he was no gardener. His hand didn't feel rough enough.

"Old Charles," the bodyguard said. "How's he doing today?"

"You haven't seen him?" Hannon asked.

"No, not today."

Or any other day, Hannon thought.

"Have you finished your business?" Victor said.

Hannon nodded. "I think so." He knew Charles didn't want to talk about Mark's enemies. Maybe Victor would.

"Do you want me to run up and check?" The security guard asked.

"Yes, would you?"

The guard was out of sight before Linda gathered herself and they started walking to Victor's car. He was back before they reached it. No elevator for him.

"It's all set," he said. "He's in bed already."

Linda rode with Hannon and Victor back to the beach house to pick up her bike. She insisted she was all right after her episode.

"I don't know what came over me," she told them. "I'm a little embarrassed."

"Anything like that ever happen before?" Victor asked.

"No, never."

Hannon decided to wait until later before talking with her about it. He waited until she got out before asking Victor a question.

"Why does Mark need a bodyguard?"

"You spotted him, huh?"

"It wasn't difficult. He's very fit, someone you wouldn't want to mess with."

"Perhaps he's there to protect Charles."

"He hardly knows Charles is there."

"Quite so."

"So what's going on? You represent them. Why does Mark need a bodyguard? He must have enemies, and please don't tell me we all do. Charles already tried that."

"The old boy likes to keep the family secrets in the vault."

They had reached route 1A and were picking up speed. Hannon waited for Victor to continue.

"It's no secret Mark has enemies. I'm surprised you don't know that."

"We tend to ignore each other."

"If you knew him better, you'd realize he's a dedicated man with strong convictions. Men like Mark make enemies."

"Hope I'm not one of them."

"As you said, you tend to ignore each other."

Hannon smiled.

Victor continued.

"In recent years he's scaled down his medical practice and concentrated on administrative matters. He's chairman of the board at Mercy Hospital, and he runs a tight ship."

"Lots of people run tight ships without needing a bodyguard."

"He's deeply involved in medical malpractice affairs, and he's blown the whistle on several of his peers, bringing them up on charges, causing them to lose their licenses. He can't tolerate medical shortcomings."

"He has no trouble tolerating his wife's shortcomings."

"That's different," Victor said. "Nobody dies."

Hannon nodded in agreement. They turned off 1A and started down Main Street. Hannon was deep in thought. Victor noticed but didn't say anything until they reached the Sail Loft.

"What's on your mind now?" he asked.

"I'm thinking about Mark and me. We both have enemies and we both have boats moored alongside each other and we live in the only two houses on the shoreline."

"What's your point?" Victor said.

"How are we so sure it was me the guy was after?"

"You think Mark may have been the target?"

"It's a thought. It should be considered. The guy I killed wasn't very sharp. He's supposed to tell me why I'm dying, so he plants a bomb on my boat. How dumb is that? He's got a knife, yet he tries to strangle me. He could have been after Mark."

"All that means is that Mark is wise to have a bodyguard."

Hannon didn't have to think about that long. Victor was right.

"Yeah," he said. "It doesn't change my situation. I just want to believe it does."

"Will you tell the police what you're thinking?"

"No, I'm sure they already know about Mark's trouble."

"Keep your guard up, Hannon. You have to think of yourself as the target."

Hannon nodded and got out of the car. It had been an informative day for him. He'd learned a good deal about his neighbors' and his own family's tribulation. He thought about his sister in Arizona and wondered why he had lost contact with her when his mother had died. Why had she chosen to stay there? He felt a surge of guilt for not having stayed in touch. He would have to contact her. Molly Hammond could help him. He was tired and needed a quiet place to rest and sort out what he had learned. That would be Max's room. Moments later he was there, stretched out on the bed ready to contemplate and conclude. He fell asleep.

It was after seven when Linda woke him up. She was sitting on the bed wearing a white cloth bathrobe. The kind travelers often end up with after they've stayed at a four-star hotel.

"Where did that come from?" he asked, still half asleep.

"Max use to stay at a lot of fancy hotels," she said. "There's one for you too. You'll look good in it. We're here for the night."

She got up and moved across the room toward the side windows. He heard her strike a match. She lit two candles on a small table that had been placed there. It was set for dinner for two.

"Wow," he said. "Room service."

"It's been a long day. We need a time out."

And they took one. They dined quietly on medium rare steak, Portobello mushrooms, and Danny's famous French fries, speaking only of good times and happy thoughts. There was no mention of the hedge maze or tomorrow's meeting with the police chief. They removed themselves from the reality of the world outside. At ten o'clock, Hannon wheeled the table out into the banquet room. They had a nightcap, went to bed, and fell asleep in each other's arms.

CHAPTER TWENTY

When he woke up the next morning, Linda was not there. She was an early riser. Her clothes were draped over the easy chair and her robe was missing. She couldn't have gone far. He noticed the table was back by the window, and there were cups and a large pot of coffee on it. It was also set up with all the items that made up his favorite healthy breakfast—orange juice, bagels, cream cheese, Cheerios, and milk. What more could he ask for. He was pouring himself coffee when Linda came in. She was wearing her robe and had a large towel around her head.

"And a good morning to you," she said. "I thought you might sleep all day."

"Max has really outdone himself here," he said, choosing to ignore the comment about sleeping all day. "Did you have anything to eat?"

"No, I wanted to take a shower first."

"There's a shower up here?"

"Yes, it's in the men's room. There's a towel in there for you."

"Not until we eat."

"We're due at the police station by eleven."

"We have to eat, I have to shower."

"We'll be late."

"Who cares?"

She laughed. They had breakfast, and he showered. They were late but so was the chief.

"He'll be right along," Officer Tom Fisk told them. "Have a seat in the office."

"I'm not sitting in his chair," Hannon said.

"Take a chair from here in with you," Fisk said. "Nobody else is in till later."

Hannon wheeled a chair into the office and put it next to the one already there. Linda sat down. He started pacing the floor.

"Sit down and relax," She said. She knew what the pacing meant.

"I learned a lot yesterday. I've got to decide if any of it relates to my problem."

"Run it by me. Maybe I can help."

He told her everything: Charlotte's warning, the incident with Harry, and his conversations with Charles and Victor.

She wasn't surprised Mark MacMaster had enemies.

"It's been all over the television," she said. "He's relentless. You didn't tell me Charlotte came over."

"Yeah, I forgot. It didn't seem important. It still doesn't."

"At least you found out how your father got the house."

"Yeah, I was glad to clear that up."

Chief Cunningham entered the room. He didn't look happy. He walked briskly to the desk, fell back into his chair, put his feet on the desk, and got down to business.

"What the hell were you doing running in that fucking race yesterday? Excuse my language, Mrs. Rizzo."

"No, Chief, I don't think I will," she said firmly.

The chief ignored her remark and got right after Hannon. He was a damn fool with no regard for his own well-being or the safety of others. That was just the beginning of his rant. Why hadn't he kept him, or at least Cruz, up to date on his every move? Why did Charlotte MacMaster visit him? What was he talking to Harry about during the race, and what the hell ever possessed him to go to the estate and talk with Charles. That was even dumber than the race. Hannon waited calmly until Cunningham was finished before he spoke.

"You've had me under surveillance?" he said

"Surveillance!" the chief's voice rose and his face got red. "Cruz was trying to keep up with you for your own goddamned protection. I told him to take you into protective custody, but he didn't want to do that. He was looking out for you. That's his job now."

"I appreciate that."

"You damn well should. He likes you, for Christ's sake. He doesn't want to see you dead, and he doesn't think your property has anything to do with all this."

"I don't either, now that I've spoken with Charles."

"Well, I'm certainly glad to hear that."

"I guess I have to find things out for myself."

The chief looked like he might be about to go off on another rant. Linda cut him off. "I'm confused," she said. "I don't really know why I'm here. I told you all I know on Friday, and I'm late for work."

It worked. Chief Cunningham took a deep breath and turned to her.

"You don't have a driver's license," he said. "Was it revoked, or did you give it up?"

"Neither. I never had one, never learn to drive."

"That's unusual, Mrs. Rizzo. The thing is, under the circumstances, we need to know a little more about you. If you want to speed things up, Officer Fisk can give you a short form to fill out. If we need anything else, I'll be in touch."

Linda didn't say any more. She got up, nodded to Hannon, and left.

There was a pause before Cunningham spoke again.

"What do you know about her?" he asked quietly.

"I met her five years ago. I don't know much about her before that. I have strong feelings for her."

"We need to know about the time before you met."

"I can't help you there. We never talked about the past."

The chief got up and looked out the window. "Maybe you're afraid to know," he said.

"I don't think so."

"Let me tell you something. She fills forms out quickly. She's done already. I know this because I see her leaving." He pointed out the window.

"You did say it was a short form." Hannon said.

"Let me tell you something else."

Hannon had a feeling he didn't want to hear anymore. He sat down.

"Why didn't she come in with you Saturday? I was expecting her. She knew that."

Hannon shook his head. He had to think back.

"She told me she had to go to work," he said.

"What was so damned important? Did she have appointments?"

Hannon was trying to remember what Linda had said. It had surprised him that she wasn't going with him. Finally he remembered.

"She'd left her cell phone at the office Thursday. She had to see if she had messages."

The chief smiled before he spoke. "Officer DiMartino called your cell phone Saturday morning to tell you our meeting was put off until the afternoon. There was no answer so she left a message to call back."

"Yes. I was asleep and she couldn't find my phone. She heard the message and called back."

"Yes, she did," the chief said in a somewhat triumphant voice. "And she used her own cell phone."

Hannon swiveled his chair around to look at Cunningham, who was still looking out the window.

"How do you know that," he asked.

He knew he shouldn't have asked the question. He already knew the answer.

Chief Cunningham turned and headed back to his desk.

"Incoming call numbers show on our screen," he said. "Officer DiMartino recognized the number was different from yours. We checked. It was hers. She lied to you."

Hannon saw where this was going. "So you're saying she didn't want to go onto the boat."

"You were coming by boat, weren't you?" Cunningham said. "Your car was in the shop."

"Yes. I was going to use the boat."

"Isn't it possible she may have known something you didn't?"

"Like that the boat was rigged with a bomb? No, chief, that's not possible."

"Come on, Mr. Hannon. Don't let your feelings get in the way. What other reason could she have for not going?"

Hannon slumped down in his chair and folded his arms.

"She wasn't all that fond of being on the water. She'd go out because she knew I wanted her to, but sometimes she'd get nervous, especially outside the cove. She couldn't swim. She didn't have her life jacket."

The chief walked around the desk and leaned back on it, facing Hannon.

"You'd have jackets on board," he said.

"Yes," Hannon said. "Maybe she didn't want to row out without one."

The chief kept staring at him. Hannon looked up at him and smiled.

"I guess I'm just grasping at straws."

"You do agree we have to check this out."

Hannon nodded.

"I'll get the form she filled out," Cunningham said.

After he left the office, Hannon stood up and went over to the window to look out. He felt unsettled.

"This can't be," he muttered. "No way is she involved."

CHAPTER TWENTY-ONE

Their meeting lasted another twenty minutes. The information Linda had provided on the form was sparse, and the chief was not happy. He already knew what Hannon had planned to tell him, including the fact that Mark MacMaster had a bodyguard. As far as he was concerned, that was state police business. It didn't sound like he was happy about being left out. He didn't want to hear anything about a killer, no matter how dumb he might be, going after the wrong boat and the wrong man. Hannon didn't argue. They disagreed about who should speak first to Linda about her lie. Hannon wanted to talk to her first, but the chief wouldn't go for that either,

"This is a police investigation," he said firmly. "Keep your mouth shut till I've talked with her. I need to see her first reaction."

Hannon reluctantly said he would, but he wasn't sure how. As he was leaving, Officer Fisk gave him a note.

"Guy trying to reach you left a phone number. Wants you to call him."

"Did he give a name?"

"McCarty, I think."

The chief was standing in the office doorway.

"If he's got anything for you, let me know right away."

"Of course."

"He should be calling me directly."

"I'll be sure to tell him that."

He didn't get any response, so he left. When he got outside he heard muffled gunfire coming from the basement firing range. The locals were getting some practice. He hoped they didn't get any complaints. He headed up Main Street toward Sam's Garage, hoping his car was ready. No such luck. The only one there was Sam's wife, Phyllis, who told him Sam wasn't back, because of car trouble, and that his car wasn't finished yet. Hannon shrugged and left.

As he started back toward the Sail Loft, his mind began to focus on things he and the chief hadn't talked about. The cell phone he and Cruz had found on his boat wasn't mentioned. He decided that was a lost cause. Cunningham had said nothing about how the investigation was going, so he assumed there was no progress. It occurred to him that the chief wasn't really looking for new information. He'd made his mind up about something, but what?

He was back at Town Hall when it hit him.

"Damn it," he said aloud. "He's going to concentrate on Linda's possible involvement."

A woman passing by gave him a funny look. Quickly he pulled his collar toward his mouth and spoke into it as if there was a microphone there. "Get ready to move in," he said.

The woman turned away quickly and stepped up her pace. She didn't want to get involved in any secret agent stuff. He was just having a bit of fun with someone who'd caught him talking to himself. His mind was closing in on Linda. They had spent their time together in the present and never looked back. It had worked, but that phase of their relationship was over. Now there would be challenges to overcome. He hoped they were up to the task.

He had reached the Sail Loft and sat on a bench across the street. The chief was wrong. Linda could not be involved. What reason would she have? How could she possibly be part of a plot to harm him? Her mood and attitude would change, and he would notice. A feeling of relief came over him, but it didn't last. Suddenly the what-ifs moved into his mind. He thought he'd overcome them years ago. What if someone was holding a gun to her head or threatening to kill a family member? What if this, what if that, what if the planet blows up?

"Stop this," He whispered to himself. He was doing too much thinking about a situation that cried out for action, questions, answers, and logical conclusions. What a waste of time it was sitting around thinking paranoid thoughts. It was time to put the relaxation and pleasantries of retirement on hold and get busy solving a mystery. Time to find out who wanted him dead and take them down. He knew he could do it, but he didn't want to start with Linda. Let Cunningham open that door while he searched for the real enemy. What was he doing on a bench when he should be contacting his old friend George McCarty?

There was no phone in Max's room, so he went directly to the kitchen and asked Danny if he could use the restaurant phone. Danny got him a bowl of fish chowder and set him up in the office. Suddenly Hannon wasn't as anxious to make the call. He put two packages of oyster crackers into the chowder and peppered it heavily before devouring it. When he called the number Officer Fisk had given him, a woman answered. He didn't recognize her voice.

"Trying to get George McCarty," he said. "My name's Hannon."

"Is he expecting your call?"

"I'm returning his."

There was a silence. Presumably she'd gone to get George. She didn't sound like the woman George had been married to when he and Hannon worked together.

"Hannon, how the hell are you?" George's voice hadn't changed.

"Alive and well, George. I hope you're the same. I expect you know why I'm calling."

"Of course I do. I asked you to." Same old George, Hannon thought.

"Have you come up with anything?"

"A few odds and ends. I've got one of my men chasing them down today."

"You have guys working for you?"

"Sure. I'm a private investigator now. Too old and lazy for leg work."

Hannon was surprised George was still working.

"I'll send a report to the police chief down there," George said. "There is something else, but we can talk about it tomorrow when I see you."

"We're going to meet tomorrow?" Hannon asked. "Where?"

"Warwick, Rhode Island, about noon, at the mall just off I-95, in front of Macy's. Can you make it?"

Hannon didn't know whether he could or not.

"It's important," George added. "And I don't want your police chief involved."

"I'll be there. I may have to hitch a ride on the senior citizen shopping bus. No wheels at present."

"Come any way you can."

They only talked a minute or so after that. Hannon knew he'd get all the answers he needed tomorrow. George did things his own way in his own time. He enjoyed playing on other people's anticipations. Hannon didn't have a problem with that. His problem, at the moment, was transportation. Max solved it for him.

"Sure," he answered when Hannon asked for a ride to Warwick. "I'll look in on a couple of guys I know at Sports Authority, maybe get a free lunch."

Max also drove him to the beach house to get his phone, Molly's number, and a change of clothes for tomorrow's trip. He would sleep in Max's room tonight. On the way back, he tried to call Molly. He got her voice mail and left a message. When they reached the restaurant, he noticed Orlando Cruz walking up the gangway from the town wharf.

"I'd better check in with the big O," Hannon said. "He's in charge of my protection."

"Why don't you invite him to have dinner with us," Max said.

He started toward the wharf, but he didn't have to. Cruz had spotted him and was on his way over.

"For an old man, you're pretty hard to keep up with," Cruz said as he approached.

"I think you're up to the job, despite your youth," Hannon said.

"You should have told me about the race."

"You wouldn't have let me run."

Cruz smiled and nodded. "We need some ground rules," he added.

The three of them had dinner together in a small room off the main dining room. Cruz's wife was playing beano, so he was able to accept their invitation, and the ground rules were established over a fried lobster dinner. They were pretty basic. Hannon should stay out of sight, vary his schedule from day to day, and keep Cruz informed of his whereabouts at all times. Hannon told him about the trip to Warwick but didn't tell him the reason. Cruz had no objection. He thought Hannon's staying with Max was a good idea except that it shouldn't be a regular thing. Nothing should be regular.

"If there's anybody watching, keep 'em guessing."

"How's the investigation going?" Max asked.

"It's going nowhere," Cruz said. "We still don't know who the dead guy is or how he got here. We've checked planes and trains and car and boat rentals. Nobody saw anything. We checked for abandoned cars within a three-mile radius, nothing. We're getting help from cops in every village. It's like the guy was invisible."

"He's a good guy to have around," Max said after Cruz had left. "Shouldn't you have told him why we're going to Warwick?"

"I'll tell him as soon as I know. My friend George is a funny guy and sometimes he doesn't want people to know where he gets his information."

"Well, get some sleep. We'll leave around eleven tomorrow. You look tired."

"I am tired."

"Think we should take the forty-five along."

"Nah. If I know George, he'll be packing."

CHAPTER TWENTY-TWO

Hannon had a couple of things on his mind when he and Max started off the next morning. Molly Hammond hadn't called him back, but he was sure she would. He expected she'd have information about Erin, but all he really wanted was a phone number. His main concern was Linda. He hadn't heard from her either. He wasn't sure when Cunningham would interrogate her, but he knew she'd contact him once he had. Actually it was just as well she hadn't. He didn't want to speak with her until she'd been questioned. A conversation with her would be uncomfortable, since he'd been ordered not to tell her what was going on. He didn't like the way that made him feel.

"What's on your mind?" Max asked as they got onto I-95 and headed north.

"Nothing I can really explain."

"That's OK with me. I don't like much talking when I'm driving."

They were halfway to Warwick before Hannon decided he should at least call Linda and let her know where he was. He got lucky. He got her voice mail and left a message. He felt better. He hoped he hadn't sounded too abrupt.

The Warwick Mall was just off I-95. They pulled off the highway, made a couple of left turns, and stopped in front of Macy's at exactly noon. George was standing near the front entrance. Hannon knew George was younger than he was, but he didn't look it. He had lost weight and his hair was completely white. He didn't look as tall as Hannon remembered.

"George," he called out. "Hope we didn't keep you waiting."

George had a big smile on his face and plenty of energy when they shook hands. "Long time, buddy," he said. "You look good. Who's your driver?"

"Just a friend. My car's in the shop."

"He can't come with us."

"He's having lunch with friends. Want to meet him?"

"Not right now. We should hurry."

George went to get his car while Hannon told Max what the plan was. As Max was pulling away, George pulled up. He also drove a Lincoln Continental, almost the same color. They took a couple of left turns out of the mall, passed under the highway, and headed east toward the ocean.

"You still got your license to carry a firearm?" George said.

"No. I let it lapse a few years back."

"Too bad. Think you can get it back?"

"Hard to say. Our police chief doesn't think old guys should be totin' guns."

George shook his head and smiled. "Maybe I'll work on that. You shouldn't be traveling around unarmed."

"I think Max has one. I know damn well you do. I feel safe."

George drove fast, and he didn't slow down much for turns. He paid little attention to stop signs. There was still a lot of cop in him. All Hannon knew was that they were headed east. No matter the number of turns, the sun always came back to his right shoulder. It was another warm, sunny day, the sixth in a row with hardly a cloud: Indian summer.

Hannon's window was open. He could smell salt air. His curiosity got the better of him.

"Where are we headed?"

"I thought you'd never ask." George answered. "We're meeting an old friend."

"I didn't think we had any old friends."

"We have one."

Hannon didn't ask any more questions. He knew George loved surprising people. He enjoyed seeing their reactions. Hannon didn't mind. It wouldn't be long before he found out.

They turned left onto a long street with buildings on both sides that looked like old warehouses. Some looked empty and ready to be torn down, and even the ones that looked open didn't have much activity. Between the buildings, he could see the ocean. They passed a large Quonset hut that must have been built during the Second World War, and suddenly Hannon realized he'd been here before. He'd driven here in his first Mustang to pick up fireworks for his neighborhood's Fourth of July party. He had stuffed them into the small trunk, tied the top down because it wouldn't close, and driven home hoping his cargo wouldn't be spotted by some overzealous police officer. Fireworks were illegal in Massachusetts.

George slowed down and turned into the parking lot of a two-story, concrete building. There was a sign, but they were moving too fast for Hannon to read it. It was a large lot, but there was only one car, a Cadillac El Dorado, parked in front of a loading dock.

"Not much going on today," Hannon said.

"They're closed Wednesdays," George said.

They pulled into a striped parking space about twenty yards short of the loading dock and George got out. As Hannon opened his door he noticed someone standing on the dock. He leaned forward on the door and squinted. It was a huge black man. He recognized him immediately. It was the man they had come to call the "Hickey Freeman guy," the same man Hannon had sucker punched years ago in the men's suit department

"Christ's sake, George," Hannon said. "What the hell's going on?"

The man jumped off the dock and began walking briskly toward them. He was smiling. So was George.

"I didn't think you'd recognize him, Hannon. It's been thirty years."

The man quickened his step. He was closing fast.

"I coldcocked him, George. He threatened to kill us. Why wouldn't I recognize him?"

The huge man reached them. He grabbed Hannon's hand and starting shaking it.

"No, no," he said. "That's not right. I didn't mean you guys. It was that little shit with the blackjack. He would've killed me if you hadn't stepped in."

The man threw his massive arms around Hannon and hugged him. He was even taller than Max and must have weighed over three hundred pounds. Hannon felt as if he was being lifted off the ground.

"You saved my ass, man. You and Georgie. I been waiting years to thank you. My name's Patrick Hook, Come inside. I made some chili this morning. You like chili, don't you?"

"Yeah," Hannon managed to say. "I love chili."

CHAPTER TWENTY-THREE

The interior of the warehouse was nothing more than four walls and was practically empty. There were a few cartons stacked up on the far wall. The space they were in, near the door, consisted of two desks, only one of which looked like it was used, and a table with chairs. The table had been set for lunch. The fine aroma of chili told Hannon a room on the side was the kitchen. He didn't see stairs or an elevator but was sure the building had a second floor. Patrick came out of the room carrying three bowls of steaming chili on a tray. "I used to be a cook," he said.

"What business you in now?" Hannon asked.

He didn't get an answer right away. Patrick looked at George as he put the bowls on the table. George gave him and nod.

"Me and my partner, Nick, we're in the salvage business."

"What is it you salvage?"

Another look, another nod. "He's OK," George said.

"We grab up stuff on the cheap that someone else went broke trying to sell."

"They can't sell it, but you can?" Hannon asked.

"You can sell anything if the price is right," Patrick said. "Let's eat."

Hannon figured he was asking too many questions. He could wait. It helped that the chili was terrific. They were on their second bowl each when George started talking.

"I got to like Patrick during his trial so I helped him. Got him probation instead of six months in the slammer."

"Then he got me a job and made me finish school." Patrick said. "We've stayed in touch."

"He's made some good connections since he got into this business," George said. "He's gets a lot of information for me, if you know what I mean."

Hannon wasn't sure he did. They finished eating, and Patrick started to clear the table.

"You meet a lot of people in this business," Patrick said. "I don't kid myself that they're all on the up and up."

Hannon got the picture.

"Some of our customers want stuff but don't want anyone to know they have it or where they got it. Nick handles most of them, but I keep my ears open."

"What did you hear about me?" Hannon couldn't hold the question back.

"That's why we're here," Patrick said.

"Why don't you guys take a walk," George said. "I got some calls to make."

Patrick got two Miller beers for George and himself and bottled water for Hannon. They left the building through a back door and walked toward the shoreline.

"I'm grateful for what you did," Patrick said as they moved along. "I thought George had told you."

"I'm sure he thought he did, Patrick."

"I'm really sorry I scared you, sir."

"Don't call me sir, Patrick. My name's Hannon."

They reached the shoreline. It wasn't a beach, just a stretch of dark sand with plenty of rocks and pebbles and trash. There was no parking lot, but there were people walking, a couple of loose dogs running around, and a kid trying to fly a kite. Hannon sat down on the only bench in sight.

"What did you hear about me?" he asked.

"I heard about what happened. I recognized your name, so I called Georgie and asked if you were the same guy."

"I am," Hannon said.

"Yeah, so here's the story. I come to work Monday and Nick shows me a photo of the guy you killed. It was taken in the morgue. The local cops had been around asking if anyone had seen him. They come to us because they know we sell explosives, mostly legal. So Nick, he lies to the cops. Says he never saw him. But he did. The guy was here late last Thursday. Nick sold him some C4, plastic stuff, the stuff they found in your boat."

"Did he know the guy?" Hannon asked.

"Never saw him before, but he had a letter of introduction from a guy in upstate New York we do business with."

"Albany? I used to work there."

"Nah, further up. Watertown, near the Canadian border."

"Camp Drum. I've been there too. What about the guy who wrote the letter?"

Patrick paused and looked out to sea. They heard the low, slowly growing roar of an airplane coming out of the nearby airport. Hannon turned his head and saw a large plane headed toward them, climbing fast. Patrick was saying something, but he couldn't hear him. The plane shot right over them.

"Couldn't hear you," Hannon said as the sound faded.

"The guy's name is Alexander Kirilova. He's Russian," Patrick said. "I don't know if he has mob connections. He's got a couple of partners. They're brothers. I can't think of the name—couldn't pronounce it anyhow. They got a legitimate construction business, but most of their stuff is way off the legal charts. FBI's been looking at them for years. We sell them explosives."

"I'm guessing murder for hire wouldn't be much of a stretch for them," Hannon said.

"None at all."

Hannon got up and joined Patrick starring out at the sea. "This was Thursday?"

"Yeah, late Thursday afternoon."

Hannon shook his head. Something wasn't right. "The cops figured he was staking me out for days," he said.

"Well, he was here Thursday afternoon after I'd left."

"Did he have a car?"

"No. Nick figured someone dropped him off. He let him use one of our cars."

"And it hasn't come back?"

"No. We're kind of worried about that. We don't want it traced to us."

"They haven't found it yet."

"When they do, we're in deep shit."

"How come? You got a license to sell the stuff."

"Not in small quantities to strangers."

Hannon was getting the picture. Patrick was in a sketchy business. He wondered if George knew. Of course he did. Another thought slipped into his mind.

"Did he have anything with him he might leave in the car?"

"Nick said he had a backpack."

A whole new scenario flashed into Hannon's mind. "Did Nick notice if he was wearing boots?"

Patrick had to think about that. "Yeah," he said finely. "He said he was wearing hiking boots."

"Son of a bitch," Hannon said. "No wonder the cops can't find the car. He dumped it outside the police searching area and walked to my place."

"Is that important?" Patrick asked.

"It answers a question that's bugging everybody. It could me more important to you than me."

"How do you figure that?"

"We could find your car before they do."

"That would save us answering lots of questions. The C4 and our car, cops would figure that out in no time. Where would we look?"

"We got a guy with a backpack and hiking boots. My guess is we look for a hiking trail."

"Oh yeah." Patrick sounded skeptical. "There's hundreds of those around."

"That's right, Patrick, but I know one that's four miles long and ends in my backyard."

CHAPTER TWENTY-FOUR

Twenty minutes later, all three were in George's car headed south on I-95. Hannon was in the back seat with a map of Rhode Island and a pair of George's store-bought reading glasses. After he called Max to tell him about his change of plans, he began studying the map.

"Where the hell are we going?" George asked. They hadn't had time to fill him in.

"We need to get on Route 1A just past Hooper's landing and drive south a few miles till we come to a campsite on the ocean," Hannon said.

"And what makes you think Patrick's car will be there?"

"Call it a hunch."

"Please give me a little more than that."

Hannon gave it his best shot. When he finished, he wasn't sure George understood.

Patrick took over.

"I know that trail," he said. "It runs along the shoreline from where Mr. Hannon lives to a place called Cove Campsite."

"And this guy walked it at night?" George asked.

"That's what I think," Hannon said. "I've hiked the trail myself."

"Do you think he had a guide?" George asked. "One of the locals, maybe."

Hannon hadn't thought of that. His mind began to wander. He looked back at his map. "Take the next exit, George," he said. "Go east to 1A and start moving south."

George got back to the business of driving. Patrick slipped down in his seat as if he might go to sleep. Hannon's mind zeroed in on George's last question.

The killer must have had good directions. Was he briefed by someone who knew the area and also knew Hannon's habits? Was he actually guided through the darkness on his walk to kill Hannon by someone Hannon knew? How could he possibly know for sure Hannon would be jogging the next morning? He began to suspect the worst. The person who wanted him dead was closer than he thought, perhaps even someone he knew. That person could be Linda. She and Hannon had walked the trail twice.

George made a sharp turn onto Route 1A. Patrick was abruptly awakened. "Where the hell are we?" he asked.

"1A," George said. "I almost missed the damn turn. How much further, Hannon?"

Hannon didn't answer. He hadn't heard him. George asked him again.

"I'm not sure," Hannon managed to answer. "Couple of miles, maybe. Start looking for a sign." Patrick turned to look at Hannon. "You OK," he said. "You look like you seen a ghost."

"Something like that, I'm OK."

They spotted the Cove Campsite sign about ten minutes later and turned left onto a narrow dirt road in a heavily wooded area. A hundred yards farther they reached a two-door, wooden gate. It was closed and appeared to be padlocked. There was a sign on the gate that said, "Closed for the season."

"We're here," George said. "Now what?"

"Can either of you pick a lock?" Hannon asked.

They both could, but they didn't have to. The padlock was large and impressive, but someone had forgotten to clip it shut. Patrick pushed the gates open, and they drove another hundred yards into the campsite.

It was just as Hannon remembered it, a clearing in the woods on the ocean. There was no beach between the water and the land at high tide, although Hannon had seen people swimming over and around huge boulders covered with seaweed when he was last here. He suspected it was just mud and rocks at low tide. The shoreline was rocky and tree lined in both directions. The hiking trail ended on his left. There were six wooden buildings to his right. The largest one had two doors, one on each side, one for men and one for women. The five small buildings looked to be just one room each, probably for people who didn't bring their own tents. There was enough space for a dozen pop-up trailers. While Hannon was reliving his visits, George and Patrick found the car.

"You better take a look at this," George yelled to him.

"Is it Patrick's?" he called out as he started toward them.

"Bet your ass it is," Patrick answered. "You're a genius. I owe you another one."

It was an old Ford Escort parked behind the sleeping shacks. No further attempt had been made to conceal it. Patrick had brought the keys and had started it. George was looking through the trunk.

"Got anything?" Hannon asked.

"I'm afraid so," George said. "It's you he was after. No question."

He was holding a photograph of Hannon jogging on the bike path. He handed it to him. "There's some other stuff in an envelope."

Hannon looked at it. "It's me, all right, heading home in full stride."

"It looks current. You're still running, huh?"

"Yep."

"I stopped a few years ago."

"Excuse me, guys." Patrick said. "Might be a good idea to get the hell of here."

They agreed.

Patrick got out of the Escort and walked around to Hannon carrying a .32 caliber revolver.

"I want you to take this," he said. "I'll feel better if you have something to protect yourself with. It's loaded."

I don't want to lug it around without a license."

"Fuck the license, man. You're dealing with bad people. They'll be armed. They don't give a shit about a license, but they think people you like you do. They won't expect you to be carrying. That's an advantage for you."

"He's got a point," George said. "Keep it in the house while I work on a license for you."

Hannon smiled. They were right. He took the revolver. Patrick gave him a big hug and thanked him profusely. "I owe you, Hannon, big time," he said as he left.

"Do you think he ever caught up with Ralph Hall?" Hannon asked as they were getting into George's car.

"I don't know," George answered. "And I don't want to. Hall was a racist bully. End of story for me."

They didn't talk much on the drive back to Hooper's Landing. George had the radio on, and Hannon was busy reading the stuff in the folder George had found. It was his dossier and it was complete.

"Christ," he said as they sped past South Beach. "They know more about me than I do. They know how long my morning runs take."

"It looks like they know how long it takes you to piss," George said. "This whole thing could be closer to home than we think."

Hannon was thinking the same thing. He was beginning to understand Chief Cunningham's interest in Linda. He couldn't help himself.

"You got anything to eat at home?" George asked, "I'm hungry as hell."

"I don't, but I know a great place to stop."

"Just point me in the right direction."

CHAPTER TWENTY-FIVE

They stayed on Front Street all the way to the Sail Loft parking lot. As they were walking toward the entrance, George stopped suddenly. "I'm catching the scent of great fried food," he said.

"You don't know the half of it," Hannon said.

Max was seating customers. Hannon introduced them, and they got a window table on the harbor.

"How'd it go today?" Max asked after they were seated.

"It went well," Hannon said. "George has some good sources. Sorry we couldn't take you along."

"Not a problem. I had a good day. What do you guys want to eat?"

"Fried shrimp all around. That OK with you, George?"

"You know damn well it is."

"Are you staying here tonight?" Max asked Hannon.

"No, we'll stay at my place. We have some catching up to do."

Max nodded and headed off toward the kitchen. George took an envelope out of his pocket and handed it to Hannon. "I put together a list of people from the old days who might have it in for you."

"Do you think it's still relevant?"

"Yeah, it could be someone close, but we're not sure. I've got a guy checking on these people. I can also check on some of the locals."

"I wouldn't know who to start with down here."

"We can talk about that later. Right now I need a drink."

George's list was short and had a couple of names Hannon didn't recognize. They were probably people who got jail time.

"What's Rose Quinlan's name doing on here?" he asked.

"You worked together, remember, and you had an affair."

"I thought we parted friends."

"She didn't."

Hannon remembered the next name, Walter Buckley, a handbag buyer who had schemed with a manufacturer's representative to skim money off their invoices and line their own pockets. He and Rose had discovered it and turned their findings over to George, who quickly got the manufacturer's rep to turn states evidence. Company management decided to make an example of Buckley. He did hard time. Hannon remembered him being taken out of the courtroom after he was sentenced. Buckley had starred at him with tears and hatred in his eyes.

Max arrived with two heaping plates of shrimp and fries.

"What's that?" he asked.

"List of people who don't like me," Hannon answered.

"Don't look long enough to me."

Max smiled and left Hannon and George to devour their food. The list would have to wait. Hannon didn't look at it again until they were coming out into the parking lot raving about how good the meal had been.

"I need to stop at a liquor store," George said.

"Halfway up Main Street on your left. Who the hell is Bernie Lepke?"

"Guy you testified against and ended up alone with on the elevator."

"Oh, yeah, he took a swing at me. We came tumbling out of the elevator on the first floor and he got arrested again."

"Yeah, and the security guards worked him over. Plus he did time for assaulting you."

"You think he blamed me?"

"It's possible."

The only other name Hannon recognized was Vincent Nunziato, a fast talking sales manager from men's sportswear, who supplemented his salary by stealing from his salespeople's cash registers.

"There's a couple of names here I don't know," Hannon said when George came out of the liquor store.

"Don't worry about it. Tell me about this girlfriend of yours."

"Her name's Linda Rizzo."

"Is that her maiden name?"

"No, she was married once."

"What was her name before?"

"Don't know."

"You decided to leave the past in the past?"

Hannon nodded.

"I did the same thing, but the police aren't going to."

"I know."

"How long have you known her?"

"Going on five years."

Hannon told George about Linda and the lie she'd told and that Cunningham considered her a suspect. He told him about hiking with her to the campsite and her knowledge of his habits and jog walking schedule, and he told him about the doubts he had allowed into his mind.

"He told me not to talk to her until he'd questioned her. I don't know if I can do that."

"You have to. If you give her a head's up and he finds out, he's going to think you both have something to hide."

The pulled into Hannon's driveway and went in the back way through the sliding glass door.

"Wow," George said. "This is great, right on the water."

Hannon wasn't ready to talk about the water. "I need to know why she lied to me," he said.

"Come on, Hannon," George said with a chuckle. "People lie every day. You know that. It's a convenience. A little fib saves time. Maybe she don't like boats."

"You're right. I've forgotten some things about human nature."

"You'll get it all back. You always had a knack for thinking things out, like today when you found Patrick's car."

It pleased Hannon to hear that. He smiled. He went and got himself an O'Doul's and a couple of glasses. "You know I stopped drinking," he said on the way back.

"That's why I stopped and bought this," George said, pulling a pint of whiskey out of his pocket.

They settled in with their drinks. George got the recliner, Hannon the couch. He knew he'd end up there later anyway. Hannon told his old friend a little about what he'd been doing the last thirty years and everything that had happened in the past five days. George took notes.

"I don't think this house is your problem," George said when Hannon had finished.

"I don't either."

"I'll do a quick check on the gay guys and the girlfriend."

"I don't like involving her."

"For Christ's sake, she's already involved. Girlfriends always are. If she's got nothing to hide, she'll understand. Let it play out. And remember, she's not the only one who knows about the hiking trail."

Hannon was beginning to feel better. "You going to stay here tonight?" he asked.

"Of course. That bed of yours looks comfortable."

They talked almost two hours longer but not about Hannon's problem. This was catch-up time. Hannon was in the middle of a story when he noticed George was asleep. The whiskey had caught up with him. He opened the couch into a bed and tried to go to sleep. It took a long time. He knew it would. The bed was as unforgiving as it always had been when he visited his father. When he woke up in the morning, George was gone. He'd left a note saying he'd be in touch. Hannon switched to the bed and went back to sleep.

"Come on, old man, open the door." Cruz's voice woke him up. He was pounding on the door.

"Have you been standing at attention here guarding the house?" Hannon asked as he opened the door.

"We have more up-to-date means of protecting old folks."

"What brings you out so early?"

"Coffee. I'll have coffee, and its past two o'clock."

"Guess I overslept."

"No kidding."

Hannon started drawing water for coffee. Cruz headed for the kitchen table. "Have you seen your girl-friend?" he said as he sat down.

"No, I was away yesterday."

"Well, the chief can't find her. Looks like she's left town."

"What?"

"Took a taxi to the Amtrak Station in Kingston yesterday."

"Where did she go?"

"I was hoping you'd know."

Hannon shook his head. "I don't."

"The chief's pissed, so if you hear from her, let us know."

"Of course. You still want coffee."

"I'll have a cup with you."

Hannon sat down while the coffee brewed. Cruz had more news. "I told Sam to hold up on your car till I have the state police bomb guy check it."

"Think they'll be done tomorrow? I was going to take the boat over and have it pulled out. I'd like to be able to drive back here."

"I'm not sure."

"I can wait till Saturday."

"Better not. There's a storm due this weekend."

Hannon hadn't heard about that. After Cruz left, he tried to map out a plan to get the boat pulled. There wasn't much he could do today except wait to hear from Linda. He decided to settle in and call for takeout.

Two hours later there was a fire going it the fireplace, the original cast album of a recent revival of *Showboat* was playing, and he was dining on veal parmesan and spaghetti. He was done with problems and mysteries until tomorrow. Then he would pull the boat out of the water, pick up his car, and look for Linda.

Or so he thought.

CHAPTER TWENTY-SIX

Hannon woke up early the next morning full of youthful energy He'd had a relaxing evening and a good night's sleep, perhaps aided by the fact he'd locked his doors and kept the .32 close at hand. He got the bad news about the Red Sox on the radio while he was having his coffee. They had already lost the first two games of their championship series with the Yankees. Things looked bad— yet another year with no World Series trophy.

It was cool enough for long pants and a windbreaker, so he had jacket pockets for both his cell phone and the .32. It was low tide, so it didn't take long to row to his boat. He tied his rowboat to the stern, climbed aboard, and lowered the engine into the water. He slipped the kill switch into the back of the ignition and around his wrist, put the key into the front, and turned it. The engine started on the first try. He was about to cast off when his cell phone rang. It was George.

"Hannon, where the hell are you?" There was anxiety in his voice.

"I'm on my boat, pulling it—"

"Forget it," George interrupted frantically. "Get to shore and find some cover. We got a problem."

"What's going on?"

"Patrick called. Another guy showed up in the middle of the night. Nick was sleeping there. He sold the guy a sniper rifle. Patrick just found out."

"Was it the Russian, Kirilova?"

"It's a guy with a gun, Hannon, and he had a car. Get the hell out of there."

"Did you call the cops?"

"Yes, God dammit. Take cover."

George hung up. Hannon dropped to one knee and looked off toward Seagull Rock. He didn't see anything. He felt a shiver. His breathing became heavy.

"Calm down," he said softly. "You're better when you're calm."

Now on both knees, he began crawling toward the bow to cast off. He would make a run toward the safety of the harbor.

His cell phone rang. He hoped it was George. It wasn't. "Good morning, Mr. Hannon." He didn't recognize the voice.

He didn't respond immediately. Somehow he could picture himself in the cross hairs of a sniper rifle. His mind was racing. He took a deep breath and spoke. "Good morning, Mr. Kirilova."

There was a pause. He breathed a sigh of relief. He had bought some time. Now what?

"You know my name," the voice said.

"I do now," Hannon answered.

There was another pause. Hannon felt pleased with himself. He had hit a nerve.

"How do you know my name?" The voice sounded angry.

"It's a long story. I doubt you have time to hear it."

"Did Ivan tell you before you killed him?"

"I didn't kill him. He was careless. He tripped and fell on his knife."

"Liar," the voice yelled. "You killed him!"

Fear replaced anxiety in Hannon's mind. He had lost control of the conversation. Plan B. The boat motor was running. The throttle was in neutral.

"How did you kill him?" the voice demanded.

"What's that matter?" Hannon said. "What's important is why you're here. For vengeance or to finish the job?"

"Both," the voice snarled. "He was my friend, my sister's husband. I owe my life to him."

Hannon moved his hand onto the throttle. It was trembling.

"Then finish his job," he said firmly. "Tell me what I did. He never got around to that. I'm supposed to know."

"You're a murderer."

"Who the hell did I murder?"

He heard a name. He recognized it. He didn't have time to be shocked. He slammed the throttle down full force. The boat jumped up in the water and bolted forward. A bullet shattered the console's plastic window just missing his head. He lunged toward the port side, pulling the kill switch out from the ignition to stop the motor, and gripped the gunwale with both hands to pull himself over the side. Bullets crashed into the boat, smashing plastic over his face and body. Before he hit the water, he felt a sharp pain his left calf. He'd been hit. He went to the bottom in two strokes and looked around to assess the damage. There was blood flowing from his calf. He spotted more bullets entering the water and passing to his left. He had to get away from the boat. He flattened out on the bottom and gripped the soft sand with both hands to pull himself along. Then he switched to an overhead stroke, still digging his hands into the sand to move faster. He couldn't kick with his left leg so he used his right to push off. His wet clothing helped him stay on the bottom. He was moving quickly, but wasn't sure he was heading in the right direction. His intention was to reach the MacMaster schooner and pull himself up on the anchor chain. He had filled his lungs with air before he hit the water, but he didn't have much left. His clothes began to feel heavy, and the water was much colder than he'd expected. He stopped and spun around, looking for the anchor chain. Blood was still flowing from his leg. He felt weak and cold. He didn't see anything.

CHAPTER TWENTY-SEVEN

Officer Rose DiMartino was leaving for work when the call came to go directly to Hannon's house. She went down the back stairs two at a time and headed for her patrol car. She had almost reached it when she heard the first three gunshots in rapid succession. She stopped to determine the direction they came from. Two more shots rang out. They came from the east. Three more, and she knew they were not coming from Hannon's house. She started running through the parking area toward the bike path. She wouldn't need her car. The gunfire was coming from the woods. She had been a runner on her high school track team, and even the weight of her protective vest didn't slow her down. Her long strides carried her swiftly over the bike path and into the woods. She was headed for Seagull Rock. She flipped her radio on. "Shots fired in area of Seagull Rock. Repeat, eight shots fired. I am proceeding there."

"Exercise extreme caution," Cunningham said over the radio. "Are you wearing a vest?"

"Affirmative."

"Hold a position on the bike path. Wait for back up."

"Roger that."

Officer DiMartino was both disappointed and relieved by Cunningham's orders. The exhilaration of her first action gave way to the reality of danger. She realized she had plunged herself into the woods without formulating a plan. Staking out a position and following orders seemed a better course of action. She studied her surroundings and began edging her way back. She heard the soft crunch of someone walking on dead leaves. She crouched behind a tree, drew her weapon, and waited. Whoever was coming was headed right for her. She stood up, moved out from behind the tree, and came face to face with a short, burly man carrying a backpack. She pointed her weapon at him.

"Stop right there, sir."

They were no more than ten yards apart. The burly man dropped his backpack. He had a gun. He dove sideways toward the ground. They fired simultaneously. Her bullet crushed his kneecap, and he bellowed out an ear piercing scream. His struck her in the chest, driving her backward into the bushes where she lay motionless. He was in agony but still had his wits about him. Despite the pain, he was able to open the backpack and dump the contents on the ground. Pieces of a sniper rifle fell out, along with a first aid kit, a small knife, a canteen, and food. He was prepared for this kind of emergency. He cut a slit in his pant leg and tore it apart up past the knee. He took a thick, antiseptic pad, the size of his hand, out of the kit, tore it open and pressed it against the wound. He let out another yell as he cupped his two powerful hands over the pad and pressed down to apply maximum pressure. He secured the pad to his knee with adhesive tape. He looked for rope to set a tourniquet, but was interrupted by the sound of a police siren and someone shouting. He pushed himself up and stood on one leg looking through the trees toward the cemetery. A large man with a gun was running through the graveyard toward the bike path, shouting and waving his arms, trying to stop the police car speeding toward Hannon's house. The burly man sat down and quickly reassembled his rifle. He picked up as much as he could reach and stuffed it into the backpack; then stood up and began to hobble in the direction he had come from, using his rifle as a cane.

Max Gallagher had stopped at his granddaughter's grave on his way to Hannon's house. He wanted to convince his friend to take his Colt .45 for protection. When he heard the first grouping of gunshots, he began moving toward the woods where the sound came from. He was almost there when he heard more gunfire. He pulled his .45 out and ran toward it. He spotted the police car and turn toward it, waving his arms and shouting for it to stop. The car stopped, and Cunningham jumped from the passenger seat with his weapon drawn.

"Over there," Max shouted. "In the woods."

"Where?" Cunningham yelled.

"The woods, near the bike path, I just heard more gunfire."

"Oh. Christ," Cunningham lowered his head, "DiMartino is in there."

"Bobby," he called out to his driver. "Get to the house and stay there. Get an ambulance on the double.

The police car sped away. Cunningham turned to Max.

"Can you wait here for Cruz? He's coming on foot from the dock."

"Sure, what about you?"

"I've got to check those shots."

"Can't you wait for Cruz?"

"No. Rose DiMartino is in there."

Max nodded. "I'll head back to meet him."

Cunningham charged into the woods. He hadn't gone twenty yards when he found Rose. He saw the hole in her shirt. There was no blood. The bullet was lodged in her vest.

"Smart girl, Rosie," he said softly.

Her pulse was strong. He called the ambulance, reported an officer down, and gave the location. Then he noticed the debris from the backpack and a trail of blood leading off toward the ocean. He knew the man was hit and couldn't go far. He started to follow the trail. It occurred to him that he didn't have his vest on. The protective vest had saved Rose's life and he had forgotten his. He pressed on. The person he was pursuing was wounded and would be weak and vulnerable. He reached a clearing in the woods, a picnic area. There were four tables with benches and one brick barbeque pit. It was four feet high with a black iron grate covering it. Alexander Kirilova was behind it, lying in wait. He had seen Cunningham following him and was about to open fire when he realized there was one more important thing to be done. He had to call his sister, Marie. She had to be warned about the brothers. She had to run.

Kirilova looked up and saw Cunningham moving slowly into the clearing, hunched over with his .44 magnum clutched in both hands. He popped up from behind the barbeque pit with his rifle at the ready and fired two rounds. The first hit Cunningham in the gut bending him forward, the second smashed into his left shoulder, knocking him backward to the ground. Kirilova slumped to the ground and reached into the backpack for his cell phone. He had killed a police officer in order to make a phone call. He got an answering machine.

"This is Marie. Leave a message."

"Pick the phone up, Marie, and listen carefully," he said quickly. "This is important."

He got no response. He left a message.

"You're in great danger and must leave the country before the Drazinski brothers find you. Take the money and my documents and tapes and leave. Get in the car now and drive to our friends in Canada. They will protect you. I have killed the man who killed your husband, but I am trapped by police. I will not give myself up. Good-bye."

Orlando Cruz and two other officers had reached Max in the cemetery when the last two shots rang out. All three were carrying M16s.

"What's going on? Where's the chief?" Cruz asked.

"There were shots coming from the woods. He went in." Max said.

"Why didn't he wait?"

"Said he couldn't. DiMartino was in there."

"Where's the car?"

"He sent it on to Hannon's house. He had the driver call for the ambulance."

"OK," Cruz said. "We've got it sealed off. We're here, and Tom Fisk is offshore on the boat. I've got some SWAT guys on the way."

He started pacing and thinking about his next move. "We can't wait," he said. "We may have wounded. Can you wait here for the others, Max?"

"Sure, glad to."

Cruz sent one officer to his right, the other to his left. When they were both about fifty yards away, he waved his right arm forward and they began moving quickly but cautiously toward the woods, taking cover behind tombstones as they reached them, all three trying to move at the same time. When they reached the trees they went into low crouches and disappeared from view. Max waited anxiously. He turned to look for the SWAT team and saw a black van pulling into the cemetery. When it stopped three armed policemen, wearing plastic headgear and large, black vests, jumped out and began moving toward him.

"Over here," he yelled, waving his arms.

He heard a gunshot. It sounded close. It was. He turned to see a stocky man hobbling toward him, using the rifle he had just fired as a crutch. The man stopped, raised the rifle, and fired two more shots, missing badly with both. He stumbled and pushed the rifle into the ground to keep his balance. Max griped his .45 with both hands and pointed it at his attacker's midsection.

"Get on the ground," he yelled.

The man was less than twenty-five yards away and still coming. He raised the rifle to fire again. Max squeezed off three rounds, two of which hit his charging target, driving him backward into the ground."

Max screamed, "Why didn't you stop?"

Trooper Carl Bucci arrived and took the .45 from Max's hand.

"Why didn't he stop?" Max's voice trembled. "Crazy bastard."

"Looks like he wanted to die," Bucci said. "Some guys have to go like that."

Max dropped to one knee. Bucci and the others cautiously approached the fallen man with their M16s pointed at him. Max lowered his head and closed his eyes. When he opened them, Cruz was back and kneeling over the fallen man. It looked like they were speaking. Max hoped they were. Cruz stood up. "He's gone," he said.

***

Later that same day, Dr. Mark MacMaster came home earlier than usual. He wanted to get his boat out of the water before the storm came. He knew nothing of what had happened earlier, even though he'd noticed the hospital, especially the emergency room, had been busy. Charlotte met him at the door. She was upset. "Someone shot up Hannon's boat this morning" she blurted out. "They think he was on board. He's missing."

"So it was him they were after," Mark answered. "I thought it might be me."

"Isn't that why we have Marco on the payroll and the state police at the ready?"

He didn't answer. He knew the question was rhetorical.

"Come on. I need you to help to pull the boat out."

"I'm tired, Mark."

"I'm sure you are, dear. You were out half the night, but I'm sure you slept half the afternoon. Now get ready."

Ten minutes later they were on the small rubber boat used to reach the schooner. Halfway out Charlotte noticed the harbormaster's boat anchored outside the cove.

"They're still searching for him," she said.

"They better find him fast," he said. "These tides are unpredictable. They could carry him anywhere."

"You hate him, don't you?"

"No more than I dislike the others. They drove us apart."

"That's not true and you know it. It was your work and your goddamned obsession with those who weren't up to your standards."

They reached the schooner and boarded. Something was wrong.

"Someone's been on the boat," Charlotte said. "The padlock on the hatch is broken."

"God dammit," he said. "What now?"

She opened the hatch and started down.

"There's someone down here," she screamed. "My God, Mark. It's Hannon."

Mark jumped down into the cabin. Hannon was lying on one of the bunks, covered with blankets. His left leg was exposed, revealing a crudely applied, bloody tourniquet just below the knee. He had used torn bed sheets and a wrench. First aid for beginners. It had worked. The bleeding had stopped.

"Get my bag," Mark ordered. "It's under the other bunk."

"Is he alive?" she asked meekly.

"I don't know, Charlotte. He's lost plenty of blood. Get the bag."

"Save him, Mark," she begged. "You're a doctor. Save him." Her eyes filled with tears.

Mark got the bag himself.

"Get on the radio," he ordered. "Call the police boat. We need them and we need an ambulance, maybe even a med flight."

She did as she was told and then sat down on the cabin steps to wait.

A moment later he said, "I've got a pulse. Now stop the damn whimpering."

CHAPTER TWENTY-EIGHT

Hannon missed the storm. He could feel himself trying to open his eyes, but they seemed stuck together, so he went to a second option and tried wiggling his toes. He could almost feel himself smiling when it worked. The eyes took longer. When he finally got the lids up, his vision was blurred, but he knew he was in a hospital room. He was going through the same process he remembered from ten years ago when his angina was taken care of. Just a different room. This was only his third time in a hospital, assuming he had been born in one. Slowly he began the challenge of bringing his last memory into focus. It didn't come easily. He was going to need help. He pushed his buzzer for a nurse. She must have been sitting outside the door. She was there before he put the buzzer down.

He chuckled. "What kept you?"

She gave him an attractive smile, the kind only attractive women can pass out.

"Glad to see you've still got your sense of humor," she said. "How do you feel?"

"I'm a little fuzzy in the head. I have some questions."

"You're in Mercy Hospital with a gunshot wound in your leg. You were brought in Friday afternoon, and you've been out ever since."

"How long might that be?"

"It's early Sunday morning."

"Wow, almost two days. What else can you tell me?"

"You have a busy day ahead. I've got people to notify you're awake."

"Can you drag your feet a little?"

"Not really, but Dr. Murray has to see you first."

"Take your time calling him."

During the twenty minutes that followed, Hannon was able to reconstruct his conversation with Kiralova, including the name he had been given. His thought process stopped there. Was that what the assassin had really said? More importantly, had he said it to anyone else? Dr. Murray's appearance put those questions on hold. He quickly pronounced Hannon well enough to talk to the police and left. Orlando Cruz arrived only moments later, long before Hannon had time to get his thoughts together.

"You got me before breakfast, Big O," he said as Cruz came in.

"Probably egg whites and bland bread with fake butter," Cruz said.

"Where's Cunningham?" Hannon asked.

Cruz told him. He also told him about Officer DiMartino.

"She's OK. The vest saved her," he said.

"Is Cunningham dead?" Hannon asked.

"Not yet, but it doesn't look good."

"Christ, I've brought bad times to our town."

"Not your fault some psycho wants you dead."

There was a pause while Hannon tried to decide what he should tell Cruz. He decided the truth was easier to remember.

"I know a bit more about that particular psycho than I did before."

Cruz nodded, but didn't say anything. Hannon told him everything he remembered about the attack.

"Did you get the name?" Cruz asked.

"I did. It was Margaret Hopkins."

"What about the name of the person who hired him?"

"Hell no. I went into the water and he started shooting."

"I didn't get it either."

Hannon was surprised. "You caught him?"

"We had him cornered. He made a suicide charge on Max Gallagher. Max shot him."

"Max was involved?"

"He was on his way to your place to give you his gun."

"And you spoke with the guy."

"Yeah, just before he died."

"And you got the same name?"

Cruz nodded. Hannon smiled. "I guess I just passed a test," he said.

"With flying colors."

Hannon wondered if he would have passed if Cunningham had been doing the testing. "So where do we stand now?" he asked.

"Not exactly at square one. We have someone's motive, but we don't know whose and we don't know if they'll send someone else."

"Or come after me themselves."

"That's not likely."

Hannon's breakfast arrived. Cruz had been right. It was egg whites and toast.

"Looks like you won't have to find your teeth to eat that," Cruz joked.

Hannon smiled. "What I chew with is all mine. How'd I end up here?"

"You made it to the MacMaster's boat. The good doctor and his wife found you about six hours later. They were pulling their boat out before the storm hit."

"So they saved my ass."

"Don't sell yourself short, old man. The doc said you fixed yourself up pretty good before you passed out."

Hannon took a sip of his decaf. He didn't like decaf, and it was cool already.

"Charlotte was very upset," Cruz said.

Hannon nodded and smiled. "What about Linda?"

"Remember, I told you she ducked out of town. She's not back yet."

"Where the hell is she?"

"Baltimore, we think."

Hannon shook his head. He didn't say anything. Cruz continued.

"The chief got pretty upset when she left. He thinks you may have tipped her off."

"I didn't."

"He got a warrant and searched her apartment. She'd bought an Amtrak round trip ticket to Baltimore, left late Wednesday, due back Tuesday."

"Did he put out an all-points bulletin?" Hannon said, chuckling.

"No," Cruz answered. "He might have if she hadn't bought a round-trip ticket. He's certain she's involved."

"She can't be," Hannon insisted.

"Maybe not, but I have to follow up on it."

"Yeah, I know. You're the chief now."

"Acting chief, for the moment. I'm glad you told me what you did. I knew you would."

Hannon nodded. The attractive nurse came in to pick up his tray. He hadn't touched it.

"I'll leave that a while longer," she said. "You need to eat some real food."

"When real food arrives, I'll gobble it up," Hannon said.

"Don't be difficult," she said, and she left.

"I'll be back later," Cruz said. He started to leave.

"Hold on, will you? I've got a question."

Cruz sat down.

"What happens now?" Hannon said. "Someone thinks I killed Margaret Hopkins fifty years ago. Well, I didn't, but I have no clue why anyone would think that. Where does it go? I know what the guy said can't be ignored."

"You got that right, but it won't be my call. The state police have a unit that handles old cases."

"Will it be Costello?"

"Maybe. Someone's already working on it. They've got samples of your blood to get DNA."

"So I'm a suspect?"

"A person of interest."

"Do I need a lawyer?"

"Not unless they come up with a lot more than the hearsay they've got. Can I go now?"

"Sure, take your time coming back."

After Cruz left, Hannon ate his egg whites and the attractive nurse took him for a short walk around the corridors. He had to use a cane, and his leg gave him a good deal of pain. The nurse offered him some narcotic relief but he declined. One addiction per lifetime was enough. He had a brief nap, and his lunch was filling and almost good tasting. He took another lap around the corridor and fell asleep again. When an older nurse woke him up for supper, she gave him a message from George McCarty.

"He said to tell you one of your problems is over, and you should call him tomorrow afternoon," she said, handing him a piece of paper with a phone number on it.

After she left, he tried to contact Linda. He dialed her cell phone and was surprised when she answered. She sounded as if he'd woken her up.

"Why haven't you called me?" she said.

He told her what had happened.

"Oh, my God," she said. "You're in the hospital?"

"Yeah, but I'm all right. It's just a flesh wound."

"I tried your to call you several times. Your voice mail wasn't on."

"I lost my phone overboard."

"This is awful. I'll be back Tuesday. Will you still be in the hospital?"

"I don't know. I hope not. Where are you?"

There was a pause. "Baltimore," she said finally.

"Cunningham wanted to interview you again. He thought you skipped town."

"No, that's not right. This is a personal matter. I'll explain Tuesday."

"What's going on there?" he asked.

"It's a long story. I'll fill you in Tuesday." She sounded evasive.

Before he could respond, she hung up.

CHAPTER TWENTY-NINE

It took Hannon a long time to get to sleep after his conversation with Linda. He finally did, but only slept a couple of hours. He woke up at three o'clock with a new thought in his mind. He remembered dropping his phone as he dove off the boat, but what about the .32? He had it in his jacket pocket, Where was it now? He tried to remember what had happened. It took him another hour to go back to sleep. The night nurse woke him up early the next morning. She took his vital signs and told him the doctor was on his way. He was surprised when Mark MacMaster came in.

"How are you feeling?" he asked.

"Just fine. Anxious to go home."

"My wife asked me to look in on you. She's quite concerned."

"She's a concerned person."

"Yes, that's true."

Mark sat down.

"Cruz told me you and Charlotte found me," Hannon said. "You saved me."

"I woke you up. You're very fit for a man your age. You saved yourself."

"I don't remember. I don't know how I got on your boat."

174

"It will come back to you."

"Well, thanks. I know I'm not one of your favorite people."

"Thank my wife. You're one of her favorites."

Hannon thought it might be a good time to change the subject.

"How's Chief Cunningham?"

"Touch and go. One of the bullets came close to his heart."

"Is he conscious?"

"No."

"How much longer will I be here?"

"Stay with us one more night, Mr. Hannon, just to be on the safe side."

After Mark left, Hannon pushed the button that lowers the bed. On the way down, he asked himself a question aloud. "What was that all about?"

He didn't mind staying another night. The hospital was as good a place as any to rest and put his thoughts in order. He wasn't happy about being a murder suspect, and he wondered what affect it would have on his friends, especially his old classmates. They were sure to become involved in any investigation. Would they believe he was innocent? Could they possibly believe he was not? He began to count the number of people who'd been at the beach party so many years ago and were still alive. He came up with at least six, but those were only the ones who still lived locally. Should he let them know what was going on? He'd have to talk to Cruz first. It would be better for him to find out what was really going on before alerting others. What about Linda? What would she tell him when she came back? Suddenly, it didn't seem like George's checking her out was such a bad idea. He found that thought unpleasant, almost hypocritical. He decided to use patience as his main weapon. Let things play out. See what the actions of others were and react. It was defensive but it was his nature. It always had been and it usually worked.

Cruz was his first visitor of the day. He arrived shortly after noon with bad news.

"An up-and-coming assistant DA named Laura Lundregen is having a press conference at eleven tomorrow morning," he began. "She's going to announce the reopening of the Margaret Hopkins murder case."

"Will I be named as the chief suspect based upon the deathbed statement of a professional murderer?"

"No."

"So how will it play out?"

"They'll be an investigation. You and some of your friends will be interviewed."

"You mean interrogated."

"They'll be interviewed. You'll be interrogated. I shouldn't be telling you this."

"I appreciate the heads-up."

"Have you heard from your girlfriend?"

Hannon told him about his contact with Linda.

"Christ, Hannon, something's not right here."

"I trust her. Trust is a big part of our relationship."

"I've got to question her the minute she gets back. You understand that?"

"Yes, of course."

After Cruz left, Hannon's day became uneventful. By the time dinner arrived he'd reach a stage of downright boredom and was wishing he'd lobbied for an early discharge. Fortunately his nurse reminded him of the phone call he'd forgotten to make. He pushed his meal aside and grabbed the phone. George's new wife told him George was already in Rhode Island and would be in to see him during the evening or tomorrow morning. He was happy with that.

By the time ten o'clock rolled around, he'd made two decisions. Cable TV had nothing to offer him, so he was glad he didn't have it in his home, and George wasn't coming. He didn't know how long he'd been asleep when the attractive nurse woke him up.

"A very persistent man who says he's a friend of yours has something to give you." She didn't sound happy, but she looked terrific.

"Is his name George?"

"Yeah," he heard George call out.

"I'm sorry," Hannon said to the nurse. "I think this could really be important."

She gave him one of her best smiles, nodded, and left.

George came in and sat down.

"She's a real looker," he said.

"Yes she is," Hannon agreed. "I think part of it is she gets to wear casual clothes instead of those damned uniforms. What have you got for me?"

"My report," George answered, handing him a larger folder. "It's all in there. You're home free on this one. Read it. I'll be back tomorrow, and we'll talk about it. I need a place to stay tonight."

Hannon gave him the key to his house.

"Think I can get the nurse to join me?" George asked.

Hannon shook his head. "She's here till eight in the morning."

CHAPTER THIRTY

Hannon was anxious to read George's report, but he didn't have his reading glasses. The night nurse solved the problem by lending him hers. It didn't take him long to read the three pages. He was amazed and impressed. He couldn't believe so much information had been gathered in such a short time. George, he thought, was very well connected.

The report was a chronicle of two young Russian hoodlums from Sevastopol, in the Ukraine who took refuge from their enemies by enlisting in the Russian Army in 1980 and serving together in Iraq. Their names were Alex Kirilova and Ivan Balitnacov They became specialists in disarming bombs. During a particular action, one of them saved the others life, but they were separated when the medics took Balitnacov to a field hospital. Several years later Kirilova and his sister, Marie, immigrated to the United States, and he went into business in Upstate New York with two brothers named Dzerzhinsky. They had a legitimate construction company which fronted a host of illegal activities, including assassination. Kirilova experience with explosives was beneficial to the partnership in both aspects of their work. He could handle both construction excavations and murder by explosives. The business prospered in spite of continued surveillance by the FBI. Marie keep house for her brother at their newly-acquired home on Lake Ontario. Years later, Ivan Balitnacov knocked on the door seeking shelter from enemies he had made in the Russian Mafia. During his time in hiding with them, he and Marie fell in love and married. They desperately needed money to seek total safety in Canada under the protection of Ivan's uncle but would not accept it from Alex. When Alex got the contract to kill Hannon, he gave the job and the fee to his old friend without telling the brothers. When Ivan blotched the job, Alexander was in big trouble. No one ever held out on the Dzerzhinsky brothers. He tried to finish the job himself, but that hadn't worked either. He had, however, covered himself over the years by keeping detailed information about the partnership's illegal activities, including tapes of some of their conversations. All this was now in the hands of the FBI, who had detained Marie at the Canadian border Saturday night and placed her in protective custody. All of Alex's information and tapes were in the trunk of her car. One of the brothers was arrested. The other was now a fugitive.

"Wow," Hannon muttered. "George called it. I lucked out."

When he was released from the hospital the next morning, George was there to drive him home.

"I spent some time with Cruz this morning," he said as they drove onto 1A. "I filled him in. It's all set."

"Did he ask you where you got all your information?"

"No, and you shouldn't either."

"What about the fugitive? Will he come after me?"

"Hell no. The FBI found his car in the woods near the Canadian border. They figure he walked over and took deep cover."

"Not that it's really important, but it was Ivan who saved Alex."

"How do you know that?"

Hannon told him about his call from Kirilova.

"Yeah," George said slowly. "Cruz mentioned that. He said they were after you because you killed somebody."

"One of my high school teachers. I didn't, but he said that was the reason they were hired."

"That's a bummer."

"There's going to be an investigation."

"Don't worry. It's just procedure. But it looks like our work isn't done yet."

"I'm glad you said 'our work,' George. I still need your help."

"It's got to be local, Hannon. Nothing to do with Boston."

"Looks that way."

"Get me a list, people who were around back then. What did you say your girlfriend's name was?"

"Linda Rizzo."

"And that's her married name?"

"Yeah, I don't know what it was before."

"Great. Anything else I can do."

"This fugitive brother, can you get me a picture?"

"Sure, I'll bring one along next time."

Hannon felt good when George dropped him off, but it didn't last long. He felt guilty about having jotted down the names of his friends so that George could check on them. He felt like a snitch, but who else was there to investigate?

"What about possible offspring?" he asked himself aloud. He'd have to give that some thought. He got an O'Doul's and noticed he had nothing in the refrigerator to eat. It also occurred to him he had no means of transportation or any way of contacting the outside world, no phone to call Linda or anyone else, and no car. Actually, he couldn't drive his car anyway. No way could he handle a standard shift with his left leg. He limped out to the deck and sat down at the table facing the sea. He took a sip of his beer. He was alone and totally out of touch.

"Welcome home, Hannon," a woman's voice said.

He looked toward the steps. It was Charlotte MacMaster.

"I didn't hear you drive up," he said.

"I walked along the beach. I thought you might need this."

She took his .32 out of her jacket pocket and put it on the table.

"I took it off you on the boat. Before Mark saw it."

"Thanks. You saved me from answering a lot of questions."

"I thought that might be the case. Are you OK?"

"At least no one's trying to kill me. Someone may be trying to put me in jail."

"Yes, I heard about that. Laura Lundregen."

"Yeah. Trying to make a name for herself, I guess—young, ambitious."

"She's been around awhile and wants to be district attorney. You need to watch out for her."

"You know her?"

"She was involved in a couple of Mark's malpractice cases. She's tough—hates to lose."

"That's not good news. I never knew Mark was so involved in medical malpractice."

"He's a crusader. Who'd have thought it?"

"Who indeed." He paused. "Charlotte, you don't happen to have your cell phone with you?"

"You know I never go anywhere without it."

Hannon was more interested in food than information. He used her phone to order a chicken cutlet and spaghetti dinner from Sal's pizza. Information could wait. Charlotte seemed a bit miffed he hadn't ordered dinner for two. After she left, he had his dinner and spent the evening listening to music and thinking about Linda. Was she back in town? Had Cruz questioned her? He went to bed early but couldn't sleep. It was almost midnight when he heard her key turn in the lock.

"Welcome back," he said as she turned the kitchen light on. "You look tired."

"I am tired," she said as she put her overnight bag on the table. "I came right here. I hope you're glad to see me."

"Of course I am. Is everything in Baltimore taken care of?"

"Yes, finally."

"Come to bed. We can talk tomorrow."

"Thanks. Give me a minute."

She disappeared into the bathroom and he heard the shower turn on. He wished he'd done that earlier. He decided to join her.

"Need someone to do your back?" he asked as he slipped into the shower.

"I need someone to do all of me," she said.

They shared a towel on their way back to bed and fell onto it in a locked embrace that lasted until they fell asleep.

CHAPTER THIRTY-ONE

Linda was gone when he woke up. He found a note on the table. She was grocery shopping and wouldn't be long. He had enough coffee to make five cups, so he settled into his recliner with his first one. He had some thinking to do. They would talk when she returned, and he needed to get his thoughts organized. He wouldn't press her about Baltimore. That was her business. He would tell her Cruz was looking for her and perhaps why, if she asked, and he would put any suspicion of her involvement in the attack on him to rest. Kirilova and Balitnacov had been hired to avenge the murder of Margaret Hopkins fifty years ago. She wasn't even alive then. There was no way she was connected. If the killer had been guided alone the hiking trail by someone, it wasn't he. More likely it was one of his classmates, someone local. Perhaps one of them had found out something that made them think the killer was still among them. But why him? Who had fingered him as the guilty one? He heard Linda come in.

"How long have you been gone?" he asked.

"Couple of hours. I had a visit from our new police chief."

Hannon was relieved. He tried not to show it. She put her groceries on the table and sat down on the bed.

"How'd that go?" he asked.

"I didn't get arrested. That's the good news."

"But their treating you as a suspect." Hannon figured he should say it first.

"Yes. How did you know?"

"Cunningham told me at the station."

"Why didn't you tell me?"

"I never got the chance. You jumped in the shower, remember. I was going to tell you this morning."

She smiled. "Yes, the shower. They think I told a little fib about my cell phone so I wouldn't have to get on the boat."

"Because you knew about the bomb," he said.

"Yes. Can you believe that?"

"No, not for a moment."

"Thanks, I don't believe what their saying about you either."

She got up and took the groceries into the kitchen to fix breakfast. He peeled the potatoes for her home fries while he had his second cup of coffee. It was a cold, cloudy day, so they ate indoors.

"They actually think you killed that Hopkins woman," she said when they finished eating.

"I'm the number one suspect."

"Do they have a number two?"

"I don't think so. We'll have to see how things play out."

She took his hands in hers and looked directly at him as she spoke.

"We can't let this come between us. We have to trust each other."

"That's not a problem. We'll get through it."

"I should tell you where I've been."

"You don't need to."

"It's time for us to share our pasts. It can't harm us now." Her voice was soft.

Linda got up from the table and took her dishes to the sink.

"My ex-husband's in prison in Maryland," she began. "He's up for parole. He asked me to testify at the hearing. I felt I owed him that."

"That's all I need to know."

He got up and took his dish to the sink. She kept talking as if she hadn't heard him.

"He killed a man in a fist fight about money. The guy had an irregular pulse, took blood thinning medication. He bled to death—manslaughter."

"And you testified on his behalf at the hearing."

"Someone had to tell the parole board how remorseful he was. He's never been the same."

"Will he get his parole?"

"I don't know. It's over for me now."

Hannon smiled.

Linda called the travel agency and found out she didn't work there any longer. Business was too slow. She seemed relieved.

"I'm going to ride over and clean out my desk," she said. "I'll stop off at the Sail Loft and see if Max can give me some extra hours."

"If you need a recommendation have him call me."

"You don't have a phone."

"True."

"We'll cook spaghetti and meatballs tonight." she said on her way out. "All the stuff is in the bag."

She'd been gone over an hour when Max's Lincoln pulled into the driveway. Hannon met him at the door. "Good to see you," he said. "Want some coffee?"

185

"Nah. Came over to talk."

"How 'bout a drink first? Linda keeps wine here."

Max shook his head. "Just talk."

They sat down at the table. Hannon had an idea what was on Max's mind, but he asked anyway. "What's the problem?"

"Christ, Hannon, I killed the guy. Did they tell you that?"

"Yeah," Hannon answered. "Cruz told me you killed the guy in self-defense, same thing I did."

"I can't get it out of my mind."

"You will," Hannon said. "Time takes care of stuff like that."

"I can't sleep nights." Max's voice was shaking. "I can't stop thinking."

"You don't need to stop thinking," Hannon said. "Just change the thought process. If you didn't shoot him he would have shot you, and we wouldn't be sitting here talking."

"But I took a life. It's a sin."

"It's self-preservation, Max. We all have that instinct. Sometimes it takes a while to catch hold."

"How long did it take you to stop thinking about it?"

"I never thought about it. I was alive and he wasn't. The guy was trash, so was his buddy that you had to shot. Think about it that way."

CHAPTER THIRTY-TWO

By the time Linda got back, Max seemed to be feeling better and was having a glass of her wine.

"I've been looking all over for you," she said. "I need a full-time job."

"You can come to work for me anytime," he answered. "What happened to the travel business?"

Linda sat down, poured herself some wine, and began her explanation. She looked comfortable and he looked interested. Hannon decided he should start the cooking. He had rolled up and seasoned six meatballs when he heard her invite Max to stay for supper. He made more. They were having a pleasant conversation. Linda didn't know she was providing therapy. When she joined Hannon in the kitchen, he got a fire going and played one of his old Broadway show albums. He liked what was happening. The healing process had begun for Max.

"That was wonderful," Max said when they had finished eating.

"It's even better when she helps," Hannon said.

Later in the evening, when Max was leaving, Hannon walked him to his car. He had a question for Max. He wasn't sure it was the right time, but he asked anyway.

"I'm finding out that my neighbor, the good doctor, is a sworn enemy of medical malpractice."

"Most everyone knows that," Max said. "He's been at it for years. My grandchild, Carol, was his first case."

That was what Hannon wanted to talk about. "Was she misdiagnosed?" he asked.

"Maybe. I don't know. It didn't matter. Poor kid never had a chance."

"Were charges brought against the doctor?"

"Yeah, but they didn't stick."

"And Mark MacMaster was involved?"

"Yeah."

"I understand he's made a lot on enemies that way."

"Don't kid yourself, Hannon. Those guys were after you."

"I know that, Max. I was just curious."

"It wasn't the doctor's fault. Everyone knew that, except him. He blamed himself. He was never the same."

"Did he ever practice again?"

"No. He's dead now. Fell off his boat and drowned."

When Hannon got back in the house, Linda was already in bed. "New job starts early tomorrow," she said. "Got to get my sleep."

"That was fast," he said. "No rest for the weary."

She was gone when he woke up the next morning. She had left her cell phone so he would have access to the outside world, but that wasn't much good. The outside world was nothing but voice mail messages. He did get a call from Linda telling him she'd seen his boat at the boat yard. "It looks all shot up," she said. "The police had it towed here."

He hadn't noticed it wasn't on the mooring. It was midafternoon when George called.

"We checked everyone. Doesn't look like your problem's coming from Boston."

"I guess we already knew that."

George ran off the list of names. Lepke and Nunziato were dead, natural cause. Rose Quinlan had been killed in a hit and run auto accident. The driver had never been caught. There were a couple of others Hannon couldn't recall.

"What about Buckley?" Hannon asked.

"He was questioned in Rose's death, but nothing came of it."

"She helped me put him in jail. Where is he now?"

"Lives with his brother in New York. Has dementia."

Hannon didn't bother to ask if it was the city or the state. "So what's next?" he asked.

"Have you heard from the police about the old murder?"

"Not a word."

"OK, I'm still working on the list of locals you gave me. It would help if you got me your girlfriend's maiden name."

"I'll try," Hannon said reluctantly.

'I'll pick it up tomorrow. Get yourself into a thinking position and see what you come up with. You're good at that."

Hannon did exactly what George suggested. He got himself a beer, settled into his recliner, and searched his memory for flashes of the early fifties. He got a clear picture of the beach party but not much else. He had to recreate the times before, during, and after the murder—the people involved, their feelings, and their situations. These people would be his friends, but that didn't matter. Like him, they were there when the murder occurred. They would be his suspects. The police would be looking at him, but he would be looking at them. What possible motive could any one of them have for murder? They all liked her. But someone didn't, and it wasn't him. But should he be looking for the murderer? Not necessary, he thought. He should be hunting for someone who now believes, for whatever reason, that he did it. He needed help. What else was happening in the village in the time before, during, and after the murder? He didn't remember. . His sister, Erin, would know. She kept a diary. He had to contact her. He called Molly Hammond and got her voice mail.

"Damn it," He said aloud. He didn't like the thought that entered his mind. It seemed like the fact that someone was paying money to have him murdered was now sitting on the back burner. With the exception of George, everyone was trying to pin a murder on him. It was up to him to find out who the killer's client was.

A car pulled into the driveway. He went out the front door to see who it was. He saw Molly Hammond coming toward him. There was another woman getting out of the car.

"Hello, Hannon," Molly said. "Look who I found."

He recognized his sister immediately, even though he hadn't seen her for twenty years. He was surprised by her appearance. Her face looked young and radiant and well cared for. Her hair was still light brown. She looked twenty years younger than the age he knew her to be, and she was alive with emotion. There were tears in her eye when she embraced him. They spent their first few moments together hugging and apologizing for not having kept in touch.

Hannon spoke first. "The years have been kind to you."

"And to you as well," she said.

"Are you as happy as you seem?"

"Yes. That is, I was until Molly called me about your problem."

"That's been resolved."

"Has it? Are you sure?"

"There are some loose ends, but I'm safe. We have a lot of catching up to do."

"Yes, we do. More than you know, I suspect."

He wasn't sure what she meant.

"I came to help you," she continued. "Molly told me about Miss Hopkins."

Hannon chuckled. "I've been trying to get in touch for days. You certainly can help."

"She's hard to get hold of," Molly said.

"She just picked me up at the airport," Erin added. "We came right here."

"How long can you stay?" he asked.

"She can stay with me as long as long as she wants," Molly said. "I'm all alone in that big house since Will died."

"That's great," he said. "I need to bone up on the summer of fifty-three."

"We'll start tomorrow," Erin said.

"Got to be tonight."

The two women were tired and reluctant, but they agreed. Linda arrived with ingredients to make fish chowder. After she and Erin were introduced, she did the cooking while Molly went home to get to get an old scrapbook and some high school yearbooks. She returned to enjoy a wonderful dinner with them, after which Linda went home. She wasn't going to be able to help them resurrect their past. Hannon, Erin, and Molly pondered Erin's diary, the yearbooks, the scrapbook, and their memories until well after midnight. At times the two women spoke of their recollections as if Hannon wasn't even there. He couldn't believe how clear their memories were. He listened and learned and, after they left, he felt as if he'd read a book about the time of the murder. He couldn't believe how much he'd forgotten or never even known.

CHAPTER THIRTY-THREE

1953

Erin and Molly grew up across Edger Avenue from each other and were best friends, even though Molly was older. In high school, they both developed crushes on the same young man. Bobby Hinch, Billy Hannon's best friend. The two guys were inseparable, and both joined the National Guard as soon as they were old enough. When their unit was activated during the Korean War, they were in combat together. They returned to Fort Dix, New Jersey, in the summer of 1951. On their first leave home, they were given a hero's welcome. They spent the next two years at Fort Dix and came home for most of their leave time. When they came to Hannon's graduation in 1953, Billy had just reenlisted in the Regular Army but Bobby had taken his discharge to work for his father's construction company. He'd been dating Molly for some time. Billy and Erin were not happy about that. Erin was envious, and Billy was losing his best friend. Needing a companion to go to the Old Howard in Boston's Scolley Square, he finally settled for Hannon. The two brothers had not been close. There was a five-year age difference, and their interests were not the same. Hannon was athletic;

Billy's main interest was music. But Billy had grown up in the army and, in Hannon's eyes, was a hero. He had come to respect and admire him, and he wanted to be like him. On their trip to Boston, they became friends.

Billy had been to Scolley Square many times and was familiar with its ins and outs. On Hannon's first trip, the headline stripper was Georgia Southern, one of Billy's favorites. Midway through her exotic strip, he turned to his younger brother and whispered. "Are you getting a boner, little brother"?

"Nah," Hannon lied. He was embarrassed to have reached a point where partially naked women aroused him. Billy was popular with women. Hannon wanted to be. On the way home, Hannon knew this was the first of many visits he would make to the Square. The neon signs, the bars, the music, and the different types of people had created an awesome hodgepodge of excitement and pleasure for him. So had the almost naked women.

"Do you have a girlfriend, Billy?" he asked.

There was a pause before Billy answered, "Maybe." He said finally, "I'm not sure."

Hannon wasn't sure what that meant.

"Sometimes girlfriends come with problems," Billy added softly. "There's troubles."

They didn't talk the rest of the way home. Billy seemed sad.

The following day Billy got a call ordering him to report back to Fort Dix immediately. Hannon was disappointed but volunteered to drive him to the train station in Westerly. On the way, they stopped at Bobby's work site to say good-bye. Hannon remembered some of their conversion.

"Stay out of trouble," Billy said.

"I'll try, but damn Billy, you know me."

"Yeah, but try to remember I won't be around to bail you out."

"I'll get by. I always do."

At the time, nobody knew Billy and Bobby would never see each other again.

Two days later the Hooper's landing graduates celebrated until four o'clock in the morning at South Beach. It was a wild party, largely due to the presence of Bobby Hinch, who was there with Molly. Hannon had never seen the wild side of Bobby, but it was there. He brought cases of beer and actively encouraged the younger kids to make the most of their graduation by getting "really drunk, which many of them did. He sat for hours by the large bonfire regaling his audience with dirty jokes and crazy stories of life in the Army. Hannon wondered if Billy had ever seen this side of Bobby. He remembered what Billy had said to him at their last parting and concluded he must have. But Hannon had better things to do. He had his father's 1947 Chevrolet coupe, and Bobby had fixed him up with Jane Cummings. She was older and engaged to a soldier stationed in Germany. According to Bobby, she was putting out. Hannon knew what that meant. She did "it"—or at least she knew how to do "it." He was hopeful, but nervous. They got along well as the party progressed. Hannon had his first ever beer. She was on her third when a police car made one of its hourly swings around the parking lot. It wouldn't be back for another hour. Bobby Hinch stood up and got the crowd's attention.

"Time for a come-as-you-wish swim," he shouted. "Everybody in."

Most of the crowd made a wild scramble toward the water. Some kept their clothes on. Others pealed their clothes off to reveal either bathing suits or underwear. A few wished to swim naked. Hannon didn't know what to do.

"Want to join them," he asked Jane timidly.

"My bathing suit is in the car." she answered. "Let's get it."

She ran ahead of him toward his car. He couldn't help noticing how shapely she was. When they reached the car, he opened the door for her. She got in the back seat.

"I'll wait out here," he said. "I got my suit underneath."

"You don't have to," she said quickly. Why don't you climb in with me?"

They never went swimming. They stayed in the car for two, maybe three more passes of the police car. After the first one, he moved his car to a more secluded location so no one would notice the windows steaming up. This was his introduction to a new, exotic, and passionate part of life. She certainly knew how to do "it" and showed an astounding faculty for conveying her talent to others. Hannon fumbled at first, but his energy was relentless, and her patience was never ending.

"Not bad," she said, as they huddled naked while the police car made a pass.

"Very good," was the last rating she gave him while they were getting dressed? They drove to her house in silence. Hannon wanted to see her again but knew he wouldn't.

"I have to write my fiancé a letter before I go to bed," she said when they got there. That cinched it.

The followed day was one of the villages most chaotic. Howling sirens from police cars and ambulances woke him hours before he had intended. He looked out the window and saw a fire engine and two state police cars racing by.

"What's going on?" he called down to his mother.

"There's been a murder. It's on the radio," she said.

He and Erin quickly joined the crown moving up Edgar Avenue toward South Street. It seemed like the whole town was headed that way. South Street was blocked off to traffic and packed with people quick with opinions but short on information. The house where Margaret Hopkins lived was the center of attention.

"She wasn't at the graduation," Erin said.

"No," Hannon said. "She was supposed to give out the diplomas."

Erin went looking for Molly. Hannon spotted Charlie Benson sitting on his front steps, across the street from all the activity. He was hung over and upset. He had been awakened earlier by the horrific and uncontrollable screams of Miss Hopkins's best friend and constant companion, Vera Whitmore, a history teacher who had come over for lunch. After no one answered the door, she'd looked through the living room window. Charlie's father had raced across the street to help her. When he looked through the window and saw the bloody and mutilated body of Margaret Hopkins, he vomited.

"I'll never forget her screams," Charlie told Hannon. "She was on her knees, yelling her lungs out. They took her to the hospital in shock."

"In shock?" Hannon said. "She was always so tough and in charge."

"She wouldn't stop screaming."

Police Chief Melvin Hardy talked to reporters later in the day. The victim had been stabbed several times. No weapon had been found, and there was no evidence of forced entry or theft. The following day Hannon and his classmates were interviewed by police. Other than Charlie Benson, who thought he heard a car start sometime after midnight, no one knew anything. Hannon left for Cape Cod two days later. His father, in an attempt to interest him in landscaping, had arranged for him to work for an old friend who was head groundskeeper at the Cape Coddler Hotel.

During the summer of 1953, Molly continued to date Bobby, and Erin continued to envy her. Hannon's mother kept him up with the police investigation with her weekly letters and newspaper clippings, but he paid little attention to them, largely due to his infatuation with a waitress at the hotel named Edith. Erin, however, maintained a keen interest in the case in her diary. When Hannon returned in September, he painfully informed his father he had no interest in gardening. He had decided to join the army.

"If I get in now, Dad," he said. "I get money for college from the GI Bill."

His father was disappointed but tried not to show it.

"What would you like to do?" he asked.

"Teacher and a football coach," Hannon said.

Three days after he left for basic training, Vera Whitmore was released for the state hospital after being treated for severe emotional trauma and depression. During her confinement, she raved constantly that Bobby Hinch had killed her friend. Chief Hardy visited her on several occasions but found her incoherent. When she returned to her classroom she expressed disappointment to her class that no progress had been made in finding her friend's killer, but she claimed there soon would be. When school got out, she went immediately to Chief Hardy's office, walked past everyone, and barged through his door, interrupting a telephone conversation and placing a large comb on his desk.

"I found this in my jacket pocket," she said sharply. "The one I was wearing the day of the murder. I picked it up on Peg's lawn just before I saw her and put it in my pocket. It belongs to Robert Hinch."

The investigation was invigorated. There was an explosion of renewed interest and differing opinion, and Bobby Hinch became the chief suspect. It was well know that he and Miss Whitmore had not gotten along when he was her student. In the minds of the police, he was the only suspect, though they didn't rule out the slim possibility of a random attack. At the time, Bobby was letting his hair grow longer. This was before it came into style, and to some that made him seem a wild boy in rebellion. That didn't help his case.

"The bitch hates me," he said to Erin and Molly one afternoon.

"Why?" Erin asked.

"Bobby used to do impressions of her," Molly said. "He'd march around the classroom, barking instruction in her squeaky little voice. One day she caught him."

"I apologized," Bobby said. "But it didn't do any good."

"Old Hawk Face tried to get him expelled," Molly said.

They all chuckled. That was what the kids called her behind her back.

"I can't understand why Miss Hopkins is so friendly with her." Erin said.

"Christ," Billy said. "They are inseparable."

Vera Whitmore was relentless in her search for the killer. The pressure she applied to the police put the case back in the news. Bobby insisted he must have dropped the comb when he was leaving from a guitar lesson the day before the murder... The investigation stalled again, but in October, Ray Freeman suddenly remembered seeing Bobby and Molly leaving the party just after midnight. Molly's parents remembered they had heard her come in at about one o'clock, not five, as she had told them. The time of the murder was estimated to be between one and five. Bobby's alibi was gone. Molly overheard her parents telling this to the police and called Bobby at his construction site. He took the call in the onsite trailer. When he hung up, he walked directly to his car and drove away. When the police arrived to take him in for further questions, he was long gone. He never came back.

CHAPTER THIRTY-FOUR

Hannon's late night session with Erin and Molly invigorated him. He woke up the next morning with his mind full of ideas and plans. He knew the direction he should take. He'd get all the information he could about the past and present, especially things he knows now but didn't know then. He now knew why Charles gave the beach house to his father. Would Harry really kill to get the house back? Charles didn't think so. He also knew Charles and Mary had taken in a child as their own. Whose child was it? His father thought it might be Billy's. If so, who was the woman and where was she now. What about his friends. Why had Ray Freeman suddenly remembered Bobby and Molly leaving the party early? Slowly he formed a plan. After he found out everything he could, he'd let his imagination work it over. He wouldn't try to pinpoint what had actually happened. He'd mix and match and come up with all the things that could have happened. Then he'd look for clues, ask questions, and see which scenario made the most sense.

"I can do that," he said aloud. "I've already done it."

And he had. He had figured out the sequence of events and the reasons why the first assassin had attempted two different methods for murder. A bomb wasn't personal enough. He had concluded that the first killer had walked to Hooper's Landing along the hiking trail. The second guy probably got there the same way. And it was he who had figured Patrick car would be at the camp site where the trail began.

He heard a car pulling into the driveway. That would be George. But when he got to the door he saw Erin getting out of a taxi. "Kind of early, isn't it," he called out.

"We need to talk," she said.

"We did that last night."

"There's more," she said as she moved past him into the house.

"More? Like what?"

"I couldn't say anything while Molly was here."

"I didn't think you and Molly had secrets."

"Well, we do."

Hannon made coffee while Erin began the same story he'd heard from Charles MacMaster—his brother's death, the letter, his father's unsuccessful search for a grandchild.

"I've heard this before," he said. "From Charles MacMaster. Dad even hired someone to help him."

"Yes, Florence Bird. God, Hannon, you don't know how awful it was. Mother was such a good Catholic. She didn't want any part of an illegitimate child in the family. But Dad wouldn't quit."

"So she just up and left?" he asked.

"Yes. I think she honestly convinced herself that\ Dad was having an affair with that woman."

"Did she leave a note?"

"Yes, but he wouldn't let me see it."

"How'd you find out where she went?"

"She called and asked me to send her clothes."

"So you went to see her."

"Yes."

"And you didn't come back."

"No, I didn't. I met an old friend and fell in love."

"Anyone I know?"

"Bobby Hinch."

Hannon was taken completely by surprise. Erin couldn't hold back a sly smile. "Don't look at me like that," she said with a chuckle. "I always liked him."

"So did Molly," he said.

"That's why I didn't mention it last night. I never told her. She was crazy about him. They kept in touch."

"And the police never knew?"

"No. I was the only one she told."

"She could have gotten into big trouble for withholding information."

"He never told her where he was and they never put out a warrant for him."

"I guess," Hannon said reluctantly. "All they had was Miss Whitmore's ravings."

Another car pulled into the driveway. This time it was George. Hannon introduced him to Erin and poured him a cup of coffee. They sat at the kitchen table while Hannon and Erin told George everything they'd come up with.

"I think this whole business is local," Hannon said when they were finished. "It's a backyard mystery. It started here years ago and hasn't gone away. It's not about Boston or money. It's about feelings and passions, the actions and reactions of people I've known all my life."

George gave Hannon a thumbs-up. "You might be on to something," he said. "We'll put Boston back on the shelf for now and concentrate on local stuff." He gestured to Erin to continue her story.

And she did. Molly and Bobby corresponded secretly for two years until she became convinced he would never return. He seemed an endless wanderer, constantly on the move, taking odd jobs as he found them, reluctant to reconnect with his old friend, Billy. After four months of not hearing from him, Molly gave up and got married. Erin, who had been privy to Molly's deepest thoughts, called it the best thing she'd ever done.

"She never heard from him again?" Hannon asked.

"Never."

"But you did," George said.

"Oh yes," she answered. "Ten years later he came knocking on our door. My mother opened it and burst into tears. She always liked Bobby."

"And you fell in love with him?" George said.

"On the spot."

Hannon couldn't hide the sudden surge of happiness he felt for his sister.

"Did he stay?" Hannon asked.

"Oh yes. After Mother died, he moved in. We had ten wonderful years together."

"But you never married?"

"No."

"Did you talk about the murder of Miss Hopkins?" George asked the question first.

"Only a couple of times. Enough for me to know he was innocent."

"But he never came back here," George said.

"He couldn't. He knew half the town thought he did it. He had no alibi, and Miss Whitmore wanted him lynched."

"There must have been more going on between those two than we knew," Hannon said.

"I think there was," she said.

"Why?"

"Bobby was ahead of his time in some respects. He thought the two ladies might be more than just friends."

"Lesbians," George said. He didn't waste words.

Erin chuckled. "Was that even a word back then?"

"If it was, we never heard it," Hannon said.

We never thought of stuff like that back then," Erin said. "They were just good friends who did things together."

"You're right," George said. "People didn't talk about it. At least not in public."

"Bobby did." She said.

"As you said, he was ahead of his time. Did they live together?" George asked."

"No. They both owned small homes. They just were always together."

George got up to get himself more coffee. He still had questions. "Were they well liked?"

"Everyone liked Miss Hopkins," Erin answered.

"What about Whitmore?" he asked.

"Not so much."

"She was harsh," Hannon said. "A bitch on wheels in class. She scared people."

There was a knock on the door. Hannon got up to answered it.

"I'm remembering something," Erin said.

"Wait till he gets back," George said.

Hannon was only gone a moment. "Just a reporter," he said when he got back.

"Get used to it," George said.

Erin held up a finger. "Remember, Hannon, when Hopkins and Whitmore went to Italy for the summer together and were late coming back?"

"Yeah, I do. They missed a month of school, passport problem. I was starting my senior year. That was 1952."

"There was lots of talk," she said. "People called it strange."

"That was the 1952 word for *gay*," George said.

"Something else happening then that could be important now," Hannon said.

"How does it fit in?" George asked.

"If they were lovers, it certainly tells us why Whitmore was so relentless about catching the killer."

George didn't seem impressed. "Friendship can be as good a reason to seek revenge as love," he said.

Hannon nodded and turned to his sister. "Do you have any idea what happened to Miss Whitmore?"

"Yes, I do.

CHAPTER THIRTY-FIVE

According to Erin, Vera Whitmore remained as the high school history teacher for six more years. She continued to hound the police about the murder, but as time passed, she became quiet and reclusive. Other than her constant visits to Chief Hardy and her teaching duties, she was hardly ever seen. In her classroom she remained harsh and aloof. In the chief's office she was forceful, full of theories and rumors. Shortly after Erin graduated from college she learned that Miss Whitmore had resigned her position and moved to Maine to live with her recently widowed sister.

"Is that it?" George asked when she appeared to have finished.

"Actually, there's more. And it could be important."

"How 'bout something to eat first," George suggested.

The idea was well received. None of them had had breakfast. There were no leftovers from last night, so Hannon called the sub shop for takeout. When the delivery arrived he went to the door and noticed that the western sky was dark and threatening.

"Got some weather coming," he said to the delivery man.

"Damn right," the man answered. "I just heard thunder."

"Weird for this time of year."

"Yeah."

A driving rain erupted from above. Hannon had moved too far out and was getting soaked, but he didn't mind. The rain felt good on his face. There was a sudden screeching of automobile brakes. He saw an oncoming taxi swerve toward him, barely missing the delivery truck in the midst of a U-turn. A loud blast from the cab's horn followed as the two vehicles sped away in opposite directions. He recognized the cab as the same one that had brought Erin. He knew the driver. The passenger in the back was a bearded man. The taxi raced through the stone pillars and onto the estate. Hannon stood in the rain wondering who the passenger was. Erin's voice startled, "come inside before you drown."

Fortunately, whoever had made the subs was aware of the impending weather and had put them in a plastic bag. They ate at the kitchen table while Erin continued her story.

She had recognized at once that Bobby was different from the person who'd been her brother's best friend. He often spoke of Billy and the times they had together. "I screwed up bad," he once told her. "He would have been disappointed with me."

He had become a wanderer and taken to alcohol and drugs. But, like Hannon, he had straightened his life out and was deeply concerned with making amends with those he'd hurt or embarrassed or offended. And the person he most wanted to apologize too was Vera Whitmore.

"Whoa," Hannon said. "That's some real transition."

"He was dedicated to some step program with AA," she said.

"Yeah, the twelve-step thing. I got into that a little."

"He was fanatical, obsessed."

"Did he ever catch up with Whitmore?" George asked.

"I'm not sure," she said. "I think he must have."

"Why do you say that?" Hannon asked.

Erin had difficulty explaining. Billy was reluctant to share whatever progress he was making in correcting his indiscretions. It was his crusade and she left him to it. He had taken a job in Phoenix that required him to travel to several of the company's other locations, and she knew he sometimes took seemingly circuitous ways to reach his final destinations.

"One time he had to go to Boston, but he flew to Portland, Maine."

"And you think he saw Miss Whitmore?" Hannon asked.

"I think he might have."

Hannon grabbed a dish towel and began rubbing his hair dry. "Any other examples?"

"Yes, but I don't remember specifics."

"Did he keep records?"

Erin had to think about that. "I remember a pocket-size booklet he carried—something from AA."

"Did he write in it?"

"Yes, he did."

"Does he still have it?"

The expression on Erin's face changed. There was quick movement in her head and shoulders, like trembling.

"There's something I haven't told you yet." There was a tremor in her voice.

Hannon knew what was happening. "Bobby's dead, isn't he?"

"Yes."

"Give her a moment," George said.

Erin excused herself and went through the half kitchen to the front door. She opened it and looked out at the driving rain.

"Where's all this going?" George asked.

While Erin was collecting herself, Hannon reminded George of the possibility of Billy having fathered a child back in the fifties. He described his father's search for a grandchild, including what Charles MacMaster had told him about the infant girl who'd been taken in by his wife. He mentioned his brother saying something about a girlfriend on their way back from Scolley Square. George couldn't see the connection. Actually, Hannon wasn't sure there was one. Erin returned to the table.

Hannon continued.

"It's just one of the crazy scenarios that's cluttering up my brain. I'm trying to recreate things that might have happened."

"Just throw everything in the pot and see what kind of stew you get," George said quickly.

"That's about it. I've always done things that way."

"I know," George and Erin said simultaneously.

"You've got to start somewhere," Hannon said. "No matter how farfetched it might be. As long as it's not supernatural or superhuman, it can happen."

"Hannon," Erin said sharply. "Are you making the point that Miss Hopkins may have been the mother of Billy's baby?"

"Something like that."

"That's preposterous."

"I know, but it is possible."

"How old was she?" George asked.

They both looked puzzled. Hannon got up and began to pace.

"Younger than she looked." Back then, teachers tried to look older. It could have happened—stuff like that got hushed up then."

"Let me see if I'm getting all this," George said. "Your brother has a letter telling him his baby's going to be given up for adoption, a baby gets taken in by your rich neighbor, and the teachers are late coming back from Italy. That about it?"

"All in the same time frame," Hannon said.

"And this adds up to a possible angry offspring?"

"Could be, George."

"You come up with crazy ideas." George glanced at his watch. "But I'll do some checking on it, along with the two gay guys, the little girl who didn't die, your girlfriend, and assorted living friends of yours."

Hannon nodded reluctantly. He didn't like the part about Linda.

"Have you heard from the cops?" George asked as he was leaving.

"Not a word."

"Call me when you do."

"Let me know what all this is costing," Hannon said.

"Don't worry about that. Can I give anyone a lift to town?"

"We'll take a cab in. I got some business to do."

"What business is that?" Erin asked after George was gone.

"Got to get some cash to pay George with and see what's going on with the cops."

"Same old Hannon, cash poor as always."

"I was also thinking of taking you to dinner."

"Well, what are we waiting for? I'll call for the cab."

"See if you can get the same driver who brought you here."

"Why?"

"I want to find out who he took to the estate on his next trip."

CHAPTER THIRTY-SIX

Hard rain was bouncing up off the pavement as they drove past Linda's building. The cab driver wasn't the same one and didn't know about the morning trips. Hannon got a quick glimpse of his car still sitting idle in Sam's lot. That didn't surprise him. What did give him a small jolt was the presence of two state police cars parked in the Town Hall lot. Perhaps the investigation was finally underway. When he went in. it appeared it wasn't. Cruz wasn't there either.

"You're not doing so well," Erin said as they approached the Sail Loft.

"Quite possibly not my day."

Max saw them when they got inside and came over. He remembered Erin and gave her a big hug.

"You guys want to eat right away?" he asked.

"Why don't we have a drink in the bar first," Erin said.

"That works. Linda's back at five. I'll put you at one of her tables."

Hannon had hoped that would happen.

"I'll have a Manhattan," Erin said when they were seated at the bar.

"And I know what he wants," Max said. "I'll get 'em."

"I'll need a drink while I tell you about Bobby's death," Erin said after Max left.

"You don't need to do that now."

"Yes, I do."

She seemed determined, so he went no further. Max brought the drinks.

"I'll come get you when Linda arrives," he said before he left.

It took Erin awhile to start. She ordered another drink before she spoke.

"He had so much guilt, and some of it was about Billy."

"How do you know that?"

"I got a peek at his book, and Billy's name was the first one there."

"Did he know Billy had died?"

"I told him. He was very upset."

They hardly noticed when the bartender brought Erin's drink.

"He told me he could never get the guts to face Billy."

"They expected a lot of each other," Hannon said.

"He must have contacted everyone else, but he never felt he'd finished the job."

"What about the book?" he said

"He must have taken it with him the last time he left."

"When was that?"

"Just before the nine-eleven attacks."

"And he never came back."

"No."

Tears began to well in her eyes, but she continued after a sip of her drink. Hannon was surprised and deeply moved by his sister's composure and courage. She spoke softly and in a manner that suggested she was reciting a story she'd rehearsed many times.

Bobby had belonged to a group of AA members who held an annual retreat each September in a secluded campsite on the shores of Lake Erie, just outside of Lake City, Pennsylvania. It lasted only a week, and she became worried when two weeks passed without hearing from him. The horrific news reached her in early October when she had a visit from a member of the group who called herself Alma W. Billy had drowned while on a canoe trip with friends. By his own wish, he had been cremated and his ashes scattered into the lake. Erin was devastated. No personal effects were returned to her, and no account of the accident was given, other than the fact he was not wearing a life jacket. She was told he was given a proper religious service. When she asked about Billy's state of mind before his death, she was told he seemed depressed. The meeting lasted no more than half an hour.

"She told me they knew nothing about his personal life, so it took a long time to find me."

Hannon was surprised they found her at all but didn't say anything.

"I've never really gotten over it," she said softly. "I loved him very much."

Max returned to tell them he had a table ready for them. Erin excused herself to go to the ladies' room. "Everything all right?" Max asked Hannon after she left.

"It will be."

Max sat down and leaned toward him so he could speak softly.

"I'm not supposed to tell you this," he said, "but there's a lot going on at the police station."

"It didn't look busy when I was there."

"It's all downstairs in the integration room. They've talked to a lot of people already."

"Including you?"

"Yeah. I just came from there."

"And the rest of my friends?"

"They've talked to most of them."

"So I'm the number-one suspect."

"Let's just say they have the spotlight on you."

Hannon shrugged his shoulders. "Nobody's called me."

"I think they may be asking them not to," Max said.

"Who might they be?"

"The state cop, Costello, and a woman from the DA's office."

"The heavy hitters, Max."

"Nothing you can't handle. Anything I can do?"

A thought occurred to Hannon. Maybe Max could help. "You know the new owner of the cab company?"

"Sure, I throw a lot of business his way."

"One of his drivers took a fare out to the estate around noon today. Guy with a beard. Can you get me a name?"

Max chuckled. "That's an easy one. It's all over the village. He was one of Mark's brothers."

"Not Harry?" Hannon said.

"Nah, he's already there. It was the other one. I can't think of his name."

"Neither can I, but it looks like something's going on."

Erin came back, and Max showed them to a corner table where Linda was ready to wait on them. After the introduction and pleasantries Erin had lobster; he had shrimp. It was a fine time except for Linda telling him she was staying in her apartment that night. She had to work breakfast early the next morning. It was still raining when they were ready to leave, so Max drove them both home.

"Are you going to watch the game tomorrow?" Max said.

"Who's playing?'

Max turned and gave him a questioning look. "Red Sox and St. Louis, he said. "It's the goddamn World Series."

CHAPTER THIRTY-SEVEN

Hannon got a good night's sleep, largely due to the unexpected and shocking news Max had given him. The Red Sox were in the World Series thanks to a miraculous comeback against the Yankees and him, a long time, suffering, fan, who had never seen them win one, had missed the whole thing He would certainly watch the game tonight—if they were able to play. It was still l raining like hell.

It was a Saturday and he was looking forward to a busy day. He knew George would call, and he fully expected to hear from Cruz. The dinner with Linda as their server had been pleasant, but he couldn't rid his mind of the cops' suspicion of her. He didn't look forward to dealing with that. Suddenly it occurred to him he had no contact with the outside world. His cell phone was somewhere out on the sandbar. And his land line had been a casualty of the strict budget he had imposed upon himself. He owned a fine home on pristine beach property, but other than his eleven-year-old Mustang, which was still at Sam's, he had no assets. He was cash poor, as Erin had said, living from day to day on social security and a small pension. He felt poor and alone, but that didn't last long. Feeling like that never did. He was a strong rebounder. "I got things to do," he muttered. "I'll walk to town."

He attacked his old phonograph console turned storage locker, tearing through it and tossing items onto the floor until he found his father's old rubber poncho. He dressed quickly, threw the hooded poncho over him and headed for the door. He stopped before he got there remembering he hadn't put his shoes on.

"Slow down, old man," he said in a whisper. "You're not at your best when you hurry."

Ten minutes later, he was on the bike path, limping along with his father's old cane and a good deal of pain in his leg. He hadn't eaten, so he'd have breakfast at the Sail Loft. The bank next door was open on Saturdays, and he could also see Cruz. Something ahead in the woods caught his attention. It was a tall person moving quickly in the opposite direction. He or she was wearing some type of camouflage clothing. Hannon concealed himself behind a bush and watched the intruder pass by, heading toward his house. "Dammit," he said softly. "They haven't given up yet."

He followed along in a crouch, keeping the other person always in sight. He was surprised when he or she came to the end of the woods and darted across the street and into the trees near the access road. When the stranger raced past his house and off toward the far side of the peninsula, Hannon knew whoever it was, male or female, wasn't after him. This person was headed for the estate.

Hannon got back on the bike path and began to run toward his house. He had to warn them. He reached the house, charged through the front door, which he'd neglected to lock, and retrieved the .32 from under his bed. He had decided not to carry it to town, but he certainly needed it now. He checked to see that the safety was off as he raced out onto the road and off toward the stone pillars. The rain had become more intense. He was running faster than he had in years, but the pain in his leg was intensifying. He raced through the pillars and started up the road. He heard the loud, almost deafening blast of a gun. The muddy roadway, just a few feet in front of him, seemed to jump up and spatter in all direction as if a small bomb had gone off. He stopped dead in his tracks. He knew a warning shot when he saw one.

"Drop the damned gun and get on the ground," a thunderous voice yelled out.

It was Mark's security guard. Hannon dropped the .32 and raised his hands. The guard approached him in a crouched position with a .44 magnum pointed right at his chest. He recognized Hannon. "What the hell are you doing here?" he yelled.

"I came to warn you," Hannon had trouble getting it out.

"Get on the ground," the guard shouted.

Hannon complied. He was on all fours when a second shot rang out. It wasn't as loud, but it wasn't any warning. He looked up just in time to see the guard tumbling over backward with blood spurting from his face. He reached for his .32.

"You get out of here," a man called out.

Hannon turned to see the camouflaged figure. His face was painted green. He had a hunting rifle pointed right at Hannon.

"This is not your business," the man called out. "This is between me and Mark MacMaster. Get the hell out of here."

"Good idea," Hannon said.

"And don't call the cops."

"I don't have a phone. Finish your business."

The intruder sprinted off toward the house. Hannon sat there considering his options. He decided it was his business. Charlotte was probably at the house, as well as the old man and the guy with the beard. There was no other option. He stood up and reached for the .32. He had one more idea before he started off. He stuck the smaller, illegal weapon into his belt and went to retrieve the security guard's magnum. He saw no reason to check for a pulse. The guard was dead before he hit the ground. He picked up his gun and took off toward the main house. The intense pain in his leg forced him to rely on the cane to hobble slowly toward it. By the time he got there, the camouflaged man was already at the front door. He heard two shots, which he assumed were aimed as the lock. The man was now in the house.

Hannon moved as quickly as he could toward the entrance. He was on the hunt. He glanced through a window and saw his prey starting up the staircase with his weapon at the ready. He reached the entrance and crawled up the three stairs to the open double doors and took cover behind one of them. The man had reached the second floor. Hannon gripped the magnum with both hands and took aim.

"Put the gun down!" he shouted.

The camouflaged man turned and opened fire. He was high and his bullets crashed into the top of the door, sending a storm of shattered wood raining down on Hannon. Quickly Hannon moved to the other door, turning his body toward the staircase and unleashing a barrage of automatic gunfire, shattering the second level banister and its spokes. He lay flat on his stomach behind the door waiting for return fire. None was forthcoming. He heard a door open on the second level. Then he heard Charlotte's voice. "He's not moving, Marco. I think you got him."

"So that's the security guard's name," Hannon whispered to himself. "Get back in the room until the police get here," he called out. He could already hear the sirens.

"Hannon?" Charlotte said. She sounded surprised.

"Yes," he said. "Get back in the room."

The door closed. Hannon dragged himself into the entrance hall and looked for a place to hide the .32.

CHAPTER THIRTY-EIGHT

The next half hour was an eruption of activity in the mansion. It began with the impressive charge of three local cops and two state troopers under the leadership of Orlando Cruz. They raced through the already open door and moved quickly through the hall and up the staircase. Hannon had settled himself into a chair near the door and guessed they didn't see him. Perhaps he was obscured by the umbrella stand, where he had hidden the .32. Actually, he felt as if he were in some type of comatose state, watching a movie, unable to speak or move, having trouble keeping track of the goings on. Finally he was approached by trooper Carl Bucci, who took his statement. Bucci seemed impressed with his story. Suddenly everything else was going on outside. It sounded noisy, cars idling or on the move, tires screeching, the loud clamor of media questions and evasive answers, the chatter of spectators. The same stuff that had made his yard look like a crowded political rally only two weeks ago.

"Mr. Hannon," someone said, interrupting his thoughts.

He looked up to see a tall, slender man with a beard.

"I'm Walter MacMaster, Mark's brother," the man said. "We've never met."

Hannon nodded. The two shook hands.

"You've been away a long time," Hannon said.

"I went back to our roots in Scotland and discovered God."

Hannon noticed the white collar.

"Yes, you're a," he paused. "A Presbyterian minister." He had nearly said priest.

Walter smiled and nodded. "I've come to thank you for what you did."

"I don't think anyone but Mark was in danger," Hannon said.

"Nevertheless, you didn't have to help us."

Hannon shrugged. "Where's Mark?"

"He's tending to our father. He was quite shaken up."

"Are the EMTs with him?"

"Not yet. He called them moments ago."

"And Charlotte?"

"She's with our attorney, Mr. Levine."

"Victor is here?"

"Yes. Family business. That's why I've come home."

"Where's Harry?"

"He was here. He's gone back to Providence with his companion."

"Walter," a voice called out. It was Mark, standing on the third floor landing. "Come up, please."

Walter excused himself and headed toward the stairs. He wasn't going to bother with the elevator. He climbed them briskly. Hannon watched to see if he stepped over anything on the second floor. He didn't. The body had been taken away.

Sergeant Costello enter the hall and spotted Hannon.

"You've been pretty busy since last I saw you," he said.

"I missed you, too," Hannon said.

"Did you give a statement?"

"Yeah. Bucci has it."

"You should have called us."

"I didn't have a phone."

"You didn't have a weapon either, and you must have known he did."

Hannon smiled. He couldn't help it.

"OK," Costello said. "Maybe you did. At least you were smart enough to stash it and use the guard's cannon."

Hannon kept smiling.

"Don't worry," Costello said. "I don't give a shit if you're totting' an AK-47. You should be."

"It's just a .32," Hannon said.

Costello chuckled. "I hoped you weren't crazy enough to go after a camouflaged assassin without a gun."

The EMTs came rushing in, carrying a gurney. They climbed the stairs to the third floor and into Charles' quarters. When they came out, moments later, some-one was strapped onto it. Hannon was surprised. He thought the man he had shot was gone. The two MacMaster brothers emerged from Charles' quarters and stood in back of the banister as if it were a podium. Simultaneously, Hannon spotted Victor ushering the people from outside into the great hall. It took a while. When everyone was in, Walter MacMaster spoke.

"Our lord has seen fit to take our father, Charles, into his care. We hope you will join us in our prayers."

"Christ," Costello whispered. "Three in one day. We won't have room in the morgue."

225

"He died in my arms of an apparent heart attack at eleven sixteen this morning," Mark MacMaster announced.

"May God rest his soul," his brother added.

Hannon looked around the room.

"Christ," he said. "They act like their addressing the United Nations."

"It's a press conference," Costello said.

Hannon didn't answer. The gurney was being carried by.

"On another matter," Costello said, "can you make yourself available Tuesday morning at the station."

"Sure," Hannon answered. "Could you send a car, save me cab fare?"

"I'll run that by Cruz."

Costello left, and Hannon was alone again. He was getting up when he heard Charlotte's voice.

"Are you all right?"

He never got a chance to answer. She was right in front of him before he could react. Victor was behind her.

"You saved us all," she said.

"Mark was the only one in danger," Hannon said sharply.

"But we would have all been witnesses," she argued.

"I was a witness," Hannon said. "He didn't kill me. He was after Mark."

"But he killed Marco."

"Marco would have stopped him if he hadn't. He didn't think I was a threat. Who was he?"

"Roger Rideout," said Victor. "He was a doctor. Mark brought him up on charges of malpractice. During the hearing it came out he was dealing drugs. He did jail time, just got out."

"Didn't take him long to get here," Hannon said.

"The police said he was probably going to kill himself too," Charlotte said.

Hannon nodded. "I'm sure that was his plan."

"Is there anything we can do for you?" Charlotte asked.

"You can retrieve my illegal weapon from the umbrella stand and get me the hell out of here."

Victor obliged Hannon by offering him a ride. He didn't have any trouble walking, so they made their way through the kitchen and out the back door. It was still raining so Charlotte went no further. The two men trudged through the yard, past the hedge maze to the back side of the garages where Victor's car was parked.

"Do you always park so far off the beaten path?" Hannon asked as they approached the car.

"Only when Charles tells me to stay out of sight."

"Is there something big going on?"

"Yes. There'll be an announcement made next week."

Hannon didn't go any further into that. He knew he wouldn't get any more out of Victor, and his attention had been taken over by something else. About a hundred yards to their right was the entrance to the MacMaster's private cemetery which overlooked the cove. There was something there he wanted to look for. He didn't say anything. He would come back later. He would be looking for the gravestone of the little girl Charles had told him he and Mary had adopted in the early fifties. The child whose erratic behavior had driven them to stage a fake death before sending her to an orphanage in Providence, perhaps in the mid-'50s. It was all beginning to fit together in his mind. Billy was back from Korea at that time. He was evasive about having a girlfriend. Hannon was sure he did and almost as sure it was the woman who called herself "Babe" in the letter his father had found.

"Get in the car before you're washed away," Victor called out.

He realized he'd been standing in the rain, deep in thought. He got into the car with thoughts still spinning in his head. Was this little girl still alive, and if so, where was she now? It made sense to Hannon that she could have been the child of his brother and Babe, but it was a long stretch to entertain the thought that Babe was actually Margaret Hopkins. But that was exactly what he was thinking. A school teacher and a younger student, hot media fodder nowadays, but unspeakable then.

"Are you all right?" Victor said.

"Probably," Hannon said.

There was another crowd at the stone pillars and people lining the road all the way to Hannon's house—onlookers, many without umbrellas, and it was pouring. Victor drove slowly past them, his eyes fixed on the road ahead, his mind oblivious to the questions.

They shouted through the closed windows.

"I'm thinking you may not want to be dropped off at your place."

"Correct," Hannon said. "I don't want to be under siege all day."

"Where can I drop you?"

"The Sail Loft. I'm hungry.

"So am I. I'll join you."

"Be my guest."

CHAPTER THIRTY-NINE

They settled into a corner table for lunch. The Sail Loft featured great tuna melts with French fries, which they both promptly ordered along with beers of their choice. Victor spoke first.

"Have you thought about having a lawyer present when the police talk to you?"

Hannon was taken by surprise. "Do I need one?"

"I think its best. The police will expect you to have one."

Hannon had to think about that.

"Last night, Charles asked me to help you out."

"Why?"

"He's always been fond of you."

Hannon drank some beer and shook his head. "I don't know why."

"He may have been envious of the close relationship you and your father had. He didn't have that."

"I didn't think we did either."

"Charles was convinced you did."

The tuna melts arrived. Hannon change the subject.

"I didn't think you were a criminal lawyer."

"I used to be. I was good at it."

"Why does Charles think I need your help?" Hannon asked.

"The woman handling the case is aggressive and ambitious. She wants to be Attorney General."

"So she needs a jump start and I'm it."

Victor nodded.

"You're hired," Hannon said firmly.

They shook hands and finished their meals. Victor took care of the check. When they got outside it was still raining.

"Where can I drop you now?" Victor asked.

Hannon had been disappointed when he hadn't found Linda working. Apparently she'd worked the early shift and was due back to work the evening. He was sure she'd heard of the morning's events and that he was not harmed, but he wasn't sure his sister knew all the details. Besides, he had a question for her. "Can you take me to Edgar Avenue," he asked. "My sister's at Molly Hannon's house."

When they got there, Hannon thanked Victor, got out, and began limping toward the house. Victor rolled his window down and called out.

"I'll be in touch."

Hannon rang the bell, hoping Erin would answer and Molly would be working

He was glad when she opened the door and threw her arms around him. He'd made the right choice.

"God, Hannon, you could have been killed." Her voice was quivering.

"I wasn't," he said.

The television reports had been sketchy, and he had to tell her the whole story before she calmed down.

"It was a crazy thing to do," she said when he finished.

"Yes."

"You killed a man."

"I've killed two men, Erin. The second was easier."

Erin shook her head in disbelief. She couldn't understand her brother's calm, almost icy, demeanor. He was having the same difficulty himself. He changed the subject.

"How did Dad feel about my not becoming a gardener?" he asked.

He was surprised and elated by her answer.

"He was proud of you for making your own choice."

The question and her answer took them into a couple of hours of nostalgic recollections of their childhood—pleasant memories of a close and happy family. Erin was an encyclopedia of those wonderful, but somewhat trying, times, during, and after World War Two. Hannon was enthralled by the things she remembered and spoke about so eloquently. He marveled at the happiness reflected in her voice and began to remember how comfortable and close the family was.

"He loved us all, Hannon," she finally said. "You most of all."

Molly got home from work, invited Hannon to stay for supper, and proceeded to cook a delicious steak dinner. She and Molly had drinks and gave every impression they would continue to do so after he left.

It had stopped raining when Hannon left with his mind spinning like a Frisbee in full flight. Off to the west, the sun was breaking through the last cluster of clouds and closing fast on the horizon, forming what promised to be a perfect, pinkish sunset. He was feeling good about having learned he'd been wrong about his father's feelings for him. It was time now to move on to the clarification of his relationship with Linda. Could she be part of the plot against him? He was sure she wasn't. They had to talk.

He had reached the town hall when he suddenly realized how tired he was. He took a deep breath, exhaled, and sat down on a sidewalk bench facing directly into the sunset. It was beautiful, sinking into the landscape, far away but right in the middle of Main Street, a perfectly round fireball. He closed his eyes.

"No sleeping on this bench," he heard Cruz's voice behind him. "My guy was about to arrest you for vagrancy, old timer. Lucky I came along."

Hannon noticed it was dark. He had fallen asleep. "I could use a little solitary confinement," he said.

"You've had a hell of a day, old buddy," Cruz said. "Come on. I'll drive you home."

They were in Cruz's police car turning off Main Street onto IA before either of them spoke again. Cruz broke the silence.

"That was one crazy thing you did."

"Yes, I know."

"Did you think the guy was after you?"

"At first."

"Why did you follow him onto the estate?"

"I was thinking about making a citizen's arrest."

Cruz chuckled. He couldn't help it. "Glad to see you haven't lost your sense of humor."

"It's got a big dent in it," Hannon said.

"Can we have a serious moment? I know you don't like to."

"I'll try. I'm getting better at it."

"What the hell got into you?"

Hannon had to think about that. They were coming up on Linda's building.

"Can we stop here?" he asked.

"She's not home. She's not at work either."

Hannon was surprised by that, but he answered Cruz's question.

"It pisses me off—people running around killing people or hiring other people to do it for them. I had to do something."

Cruz was impressed.

"I need to see Linda," Hannon said.

"I've got to speak with her again myself," Cruz said. "Let me do that first. Trust me. I'm on your side."

"I know that, but when will *you* see her?"

"As soon as I can The Attorney General's got me tied up on this Hopkins thing."

They turned off 1A onto the access road.

"Seems nobody's interested in who wants me dead anymore," Hannon said.

"Only as it relates to someone who may have proof you killed Hopkins."

Hannon didn't like that. "Sounds like a witch hunt to me," he said

"It's a hot topic. Don't you watch the news?"

Hannon didn't answer. He was thinking about how lucky he was to have Victor as his lawyer and George as his friend. He needed all the help he could get. He needed Cruz.

"I need to tell you something," he said as they pulled up to his house.

It took only a few minutes for him to tell Cruz about his meeting with Charles MacMaster and his theory that Miss Hopkins may have had a baby.

Cruz took it all in before he spoke.

"I won't even ask you why you didn't tell me all this before."

"Sorry," was all Hannon could say.

"You're thinking that this kid, who may have been your brother's and may have been given to Charles and Mary, is now, fifty years later, seeking revenge against you for killing her mother."

"Mistakenly," Hannon said quickly.

"What's that mean?"

"It means I never killed anyone." Hannon hesitated. "Until two weeks ago."

Cruz shook his head. "This is one monster stretch."

"I know," Hannon said. "But it's something we know now we didn't know then."

"But is it related?"

"There was a baby that could have been hers. It's possible motive."

"Why are you telling me this now?"

"I need your help."

"As a policeman?"

"A policeman and a friend."

"I thought you'd never ask."

They got out of the car and walked down to the beach.

"Got any phony beers in your fridge?" Cruz asked.

Hannon nodded and went to get a couple. When he got back, he had an idea.

"Your grandfather and my father worked on the estate together," he said as they walked along the shore. "They were good friends."

"Yes," Cruz answered. "He took care of the cars. Your dad was the gardener."

"Was he there in the fifties?" Hannon asked.

"Yes, he was."

"I wonder if he kept any records."

"I doubt it. He only wrote down stuff about cars or directions to get somewhere."

Hannon was disappointed. There weren't many people around who could provide information about life on the estate when the little girl was there.

"I just thought of something," Cruz said.

They stopped and drank some beer.

"My grandfather. He had a Brownie."

Hannon chuckled. "Would that be a junior Girl Scout or something you bake?"

"No, numb nut, it's a camera." Cruz laughed. "An old Kodak. He loved to take pictures. He took pictures of everything."

CHAPTER FORTY

annon was happy but exhausted when Cruz left, but he couldn't sleep. He needed to relax. The hour they'd spent mapping out a plan had left him limp. Cruz would look in his attic for his grandfather's pictures. He still lived in the house his mother had raised him in after his father had been killed, and his grandfather lived with them after retiring. He was not surprised when Hannon told him that Charles had asked Victor to represent him.

"He was always fond of you," Cruz had said. "And Victor's a good man to have in your corner. The prosecutor's looking to make a name for herself."

Cruz would also issue Hannon a license to carry a firearm. He knew about the .32 and advised him to get rid of it. He didn't ask where it came from.

Hannon hoped he wasn't pressing his luck when he asked to see Chief Hardy's file on the murder. He wasn't.

He got out his original Broadway cast album of *Guys and Dolls* and settled into his recliner to enjoy the show. He didn't get any further than "Fugue for Tinhorns." It was about five o'clock in the morning when he moved from the recliner to his bed. The next thing he knew, it was two o'clock Sunday afternoon, and there was nothing for him to do. He realized it was time to set his mode to patience. He couldn't even try to contact Linda. Everything was on hold, and it stayed that way all day. No phone, no car, no boat, and only Cheerios to eat. He was pleasantly surprised around five o'clock when a car pull into the driveway. It was Molly and Erin.

"We thought you might be lonely." Erin said as they came in.

"What I am is hungry," he said.

"We thought that too," she said with a smile. "We brought groceries."

They cooked supper and stayed for the evening. Hannon didn't have cable television, so they left at eight to get home to watch something on HBO. The only information they could give him was that the police were conducting interviews, and some of his friends weren't happy.

"Everyone's very confused," Molly said as they were leaving. "They don't know what to believe."

"Are you coming into town tomorrow?" Erin asked.

"Maybe. Tuesday for sure if I get a ride."

She left him her phone to call a taxi.

Cruz was on his doorstep at nine the next morning. "I found some pictures," he said when Hannon let him in. "They're grainy black-and-whites. Some of them look like they were taken on the estate."

"When were they taken?" Hannon asked.

"When he first got there—early fifties."

"How can you tell?"

"They didn't like him taking pictures there, so he stopped."

"They liked to keep things in-house, didn't they?" Hannon said.

Cruz nodded and sat down at the table. Hannon got him some coffee.

"There are some good ones of your dad's gardens," Cruz said. "And lots of cars. Too bad they're not in color."

Hannon picked up a few pictures. Cruz was right. They needed color, but he could see the perfect symmetrical layout of his father's floral masterpieces on them. There was one shot of almost twenty children of all ages standing with their teachers in front of the building that housed the schoolroom. Hannon knew the teachers were all family members who lived on the estate. He put the pictures down.

"We're looking for people we know," he said.

Finally he found one of Charles and Mary posing with their four kids. It wasn't hard to tell who was who. Mark was short, Walter was tall, and you could tell Harry had red hair. The little girl had dark hair.

"No one in that picture looks happy," Hannon said.

"I noticed that."

Hannon looked at a second picture. It was the little girl alone in front of the hedge maze. She looked very sad. He thought she might have been crying.

"That one has a note on the back," Cruz said.

Hannon turned the photo over.

"My little wanderer," he read aloud, "who wandered into the maze on her way to heaven."

"But Charles told your father she didn't die, right?" Cruz said.

"He admitted they faked the burial."

"So no one would think they had insanity in the family."

"That's what he said."

"Sounds like something they'd do. I can check that out." Cruz sounded excited.

"George is already working on it."

"I will too, Hannon. I need to do something that gets me out from under the ambitious workaholic in charge of your case."

Hannon was glad to hear that. He started looking at more pictures. "It's like these people lived in their own little world," he said.

"It's all over now."

"Do you know something I don't?"

"Rumor has it they're talking to potential buyers."

Hannon wasn't surprised. He remembered what Victor had said.

"Yeah. Victor mentioned something about an announcement this week."

"That must be it. They're moving pretty fast."

"I'm kind of surprised."

"You got your head in the sand, old timer," Cruz said. "Look at the place. It's had its day. Mark doesn't want to live there. It's falling apart. Plus the taxes are eating him alive. He's wanted out for a long time."

He knew what Cruz was saying was true, but he still had questions. He got up from the table and started to pace.

"I didn't think they had money problems."

"They don't. They just don't like taxes."

"I thought they wanted to give the land to the state as some kind of a recreational sanctuary."

"That's what Charles wanted, but Mark wasn't on the same page. He didn't want to give it away."

"I'm surprised Charles doesn't cut him out of the will."

"Nobody's sure Charles knew much about it."

"He seemed to be in control when I saw him."

"He's very sick. Mark's a doctor, for Christ's sake. He knows that. He can afford to wait."

"He doesn't have to now."

"Yeah, I know."

Hannon had a thought. He considered keeping it to himself. He didn't.

"Is there any chance Mark helped the old man on his way?"

"Hell no," Cruz replied quickly. "He's not stupid. It wasn't necessary to do anything risky."

"They must have argued."

"I understand they hardly spoke to each other."

"Who told you that?"

"Cunningham. He and Charlotte were kind of close."

"Ah." Hannon smiled. "How's he doing?"

"Better. Looks like he might make it."

Cruz had to go to work.

Hannon's day was empty after he left. He did some walking along the beach, relying heavily on his father's cane. It was windy and cold, so he settled inside listening to music. At five o'clock he used Erin's phone to order veal parmesan with spaghetti. In a very short time there was a knock on the door. He was surprised the food had arrived so quickly. It hadn't.

"Good afternoon, Mr. Hannon." It was Harry MacMaster. Jose was with him.

"May we come in?" Harry asked.

"Sure. But the house is still not for sale."

"Nothing like that. We just stopped to say good-bye."

"Going somewhere?"

"Moving to New York City. That's where the action is."

"Too quiet for you here?"

Harry smiled. "I spent many happy hours in this house as a child. Jose and I had thought of it as a summer home. But that's out of the question now."

"How so?" Hannon asked as they moved into the large room.

"Apparently you haven't heard about the sale of the estate," Harry said.

Hannon slipped into his recliner. "Just rumors. I was quite surprised."

"No more than I, Mr. Hannon. Condos, swimming pools, walking trails, horseback riding. Can you imagine? My father's turning over in his grave."

"He's not even there yet, is he?"

Harry sat on the couch. Jose remained standing.

"We buried him at nine o'clock this morning. Family only. Walter presided."

"On the estate?" Hannon said.

"Of course. We have our own cemetery. Everyone's there—generations."

"Of course," Hannon said.

"I was very unhappy living on the estate, being home schooled, so many regimented activities, so many rules. It was like an army base. This house was my only refuge. There was solitude and peace for me here. Thank you for allowing me say good-bye to it."

As they left, Harry and Jose apologized to Hannon for their behavior on the day of the road race. Hannon felt sorry for him. But as he stood watched Harry and Jose speeding up the access road in their Porsche, he realized Harry wasn't unhappy anymore. He was escaping to a new and more exciting life.

CHAPTER FORTY-ONE

The following morning, Officer Rose DiMartino arrived in a police car to take Hannon to the station. "The meeting's been postponed," she said as he got in, "but Chief Cruz wants to see you anyway,"

That was fine with him. "Good to see you back on the job," he said as they sped up the access road.

"Thanks. I'm glad to be back."

"Feeling OK?"

"First rate."

"I'm sorry about the trouble I've caused."

"Don't be. Not your fault. It goes with the job."

Right out of the training manual, Hannon thought, but he was glad to hear it.

"Have you seen Linda?" he asked as they passed her building. She hadn't.

They got to the station in high speed. Hannon couldn't even catch a glimpse of his car at Sam's Garage. When they got there, Cruz did all he had promised to do. Hannon was fingerprinted and photographed, and while the gun license was being made up, he and Cruz did some shooting in the basement firing range. Cruz was impressed.

"You know how to shoot," he said when they were done. "Question is do you know when to shoot?"

"When I fear for my life and I'm backed into a corner with nowhere to run."

"Good. Perhaps a bit cautious, but good."

"I'll keep that in mind."

"OK," Cruz said "Why don't I sell you the .44 mag you're using? It's an extra one."

"How much?"

"You'll get a bill."

"Are you sure you can do all this, Orlando?"

"Damn right, I can. I'm the chief."

Hannon nodded.

He spent the rest of the morning in the evidence room looking over Chief Hardy's file. Cruz was right. There wasn't anything he didn't already know. Margaret Hopkins was a cautious, timid lady who would never have opened her door to a stranger. There had been no forced entry, and nothing was taken. The chief had concluded she knew her killer. The attack had been brutal and bloody, an act of passion and anger, and yet, she had no enemies. Bobby Hinch had been the prime suspect because of his questioning and sometimes lewd interpretation of her relationship with Vera Whitmore. Even after Ray Freeman discredited Bobby's alibi and Bobby ran, there was no real case. And there was no real evidence that the comb produced by the relentless Vera Whitmore belonged to him. When he finished with the file, Hannon invited Cruz to lunch at the Sail Loft.

"Is this some kind of bribe?" Cruz asked.

"Nah," Hannon answered. "Just gratitude for the ride over."

After they were seated the Sail Loft, Hannon spoke first. "I don't understand why they didn't put out a warrant for Bobby," Hannon said

"They questioned him," Cruz said. "But they didn't have enough to go any further. Besides, Bobby's father had a lot of clout."

"They questioned all of us," Hannon said.

"They interrogated him. There's a difference."

"Yeah, I noticed that."

Cruz smiled. "Now you'll be interrogated again."

"They haven't got any more now than they did the first time."

"That's right. That's why they're still looking."

"Any idea when they'll call me in?"

"Couple more days."

Max was there. Hannon asked him about Linda.

"She worked last night," Max answered. "She tried to call you."

"Lost my phone," Hannon said. "I thought I told her that. I've got to buy a new one."

He did exactly that at the Verizon store after he and Cruz finished lunch. He also stopped at the bank and arranged a loan using the beach house as collateral. The loan officer seemed a bit nervous when he asked the reason for the loan.

"Unexpected expenses," Hannon said. "Don't worry, I'm not going to skip town."

He wasn't sure why he said that. The loan officer was surprised and seemed a bit embarrassed. Hannon smiled as he left the bank. Perhaps he was getting his sense of humor back.

His next stop was Molly Hammond's house to return Erin's phone. A smart-looking, younger woman answered the door.

"They went to play tennis," she said. "I rent a room here."

"I'm Erin's brother," Hannon said. "I'm returning her phone."

"Oh, gosh, you're the one who's all over the news."

"I guess so. I don't pay much attention to the news."

"You don't?" She seemed surprised. "Gosh, this is the top story. There are people trying to kill you and you still go out and save your neighbor's life."

Hannon hadn't heard that. "Guess I'll have to watch tonight."

"Yes. You should. I'll give her the phone."

"Can you ask her to call me?" He gave her his new number.

"Sure. Glad to. And good luck."

He was starting to get the message. The whole town knew what was going on, but not everyone would think of him as a hero. No matter how things turned out, some would always wonder if he was a murderer. There wasn't anything he could do about that, but it didn't matter what people thought as long as Linda and his kids were with him.

"What's she thinking?" he asked himself aloud. "What's going on with her?"

He used his new phone to call her but all he got was her voice mail.

He decided to check on his car. He hadn't planned to, but it was only a short walk. He hadn't brought his cane along, so it turned into a painful one.

"You got damn good timing," Sam said when he saw him. "Your car's ready." He was a short, stocky man with no hair and dirty hands.

"I really don't know why I'm glad to hear that, Sam." Hannon chuckled. "I can't drive it yet."

"Never mind. We're ready to close. I'll drive you. My wife can follow in the truck."

They were halfway to the beach house before Hannon thought to ask Sam if the car had been checked for a bomb. Sam gave him a strange look. Hannon felt foolish.

"We haven't blown up yet, Sherlock," Sam said smugly. "Course it's been checked."

"I saw a movie where the bomb didn't go off till the car hit fifty." Hannon tried to cover his blunder.

"We're doing sixty," Sam said.

Sam was younger than Hannon, but his voice sounded older. He was a hard worker and a good mechanic, but he didn't keep himself in good shape, and he was the only person Hannon knew who still smoked. They were good friends.

When they turned onto the access road, Hannon tried again. "What I was asking back there was did they find a bomb and disarm it?"

"Hell no, Hannon. I wouldn't be here if that was the case."

"You started it up?"

"Sure, I had to move it a couple of times."

"Christ, you would've been killed."

"Well, as you can see, I'm still here."

"That's not the point, Sam."

"Sure it is," Sam said forcefully. "Who gives a damn about bad things that didn't happen?"

That hit home with Hannon. He had always felt the same way. He wondered if negative thinking was creeping into his brain. He'd have to watch out for that.

"Thanks much," he said as he got out of the car.

"No problem," Sam said. "I like giving my good customers rides home."

"You gave me a little more than a ride."

Sam didn't understand what he meant.

"You did a little repair job on my thought process," Hannon said.

"I'll add that onto your bill."

Sam got out and walked back to his truck where his wife was waiting. Hannon gave him a wave that was more like a salute as the truck sped off. He had a good feeling as he walked to the house. It had been a good day. He now had a legal weapon, a new cell phone, and a car. It suddenly occurred to him that, at the moment, he wasn't able to drive the car, there was no one to call and, as far as he knew, no one to protect himself from. In short, there was nothing to do and nothing he needed. Actually, there was. He was hungry. He called the sub shop for delivery.

CHAPTER FORTY-TWO

It was warm enough the next morning for Hannon to be having coffee on the deck. He called Linda, got her voice mail, and was leaving a message when he heard her coming in the front door,

"Anybody alive in here?" she called out.

"Out back," he said. "Pour yourself some coffee on the way."

She was already sipping the hot coffee when she came out and sat down next to him facing the cove.

"Careful," he said. "That's hot."

"I've started putting milk in mine," she answered as she slid closer to him'

"I was just calling you on my new cell phone," he said, holding it up for her to see.

"I've been calling you on your old one. I forgot you lost it."

"I got a new number. I thought you were working the morning,

"I switched. I have to go back tonight. I'm a little upset."

He didn't have to ask why. "Sounds like you've heard from Cruz," he said.

"Damn right I have. I'm a suspect in the plot to kill you."

"You're the girlfriend, Linda. That's why. We talked about that."

"There's more, Hannon."

"What?"

"He's still making a big deal about my not getting on the boat with you."

"That's what he gets paid for."

"He insinuated I might have known about the bomb."

"We knew that was coming," he said, taking hold of her arm.

"But I didn't," she said. "You believe me, don't you?"

"Of course I do. Trust me. We need to trust each other, that's all. Everything's going to be all right."

"I hope so."

Linda stayed till early afternoon. She took a shower and fell asleep on his bed while he sat in his recliner thinking of what else he could say that would convince her he was right. He hoped he was doing the right thing. Let the police ask the questions first and then assure her that their suspicions were not his. He had been ordered by Cunningham and asked by Cruz to let it play out that way, and that's what he was doing. On the other hand, he was telling her what she wanted to hear. He wasn't sure everything would turn out alright. He'd had his moments of doubt about her. What the hell kind of trust was that? He was beginning to feel guilty. He didn't like that.

After Linda left for work he called Erin and suggested going out for dinner. She had a better idea. She and Molly would cook. Half an hour later Molly arrived to pick him up. She and Erin had made chicken pie.

"You haven't lost that giant appetite," Erin commented when they had finished eating.

"Just like Mom used to make," Hannon raved.

"It should be. It was her recipe."

They watched *Jeopardy*—one of the few shows Hannon ever watched—while the ladies sipped wine and he drank ice water. He was still pretty good at the game.

"You're a tad slow on the buzzer," Molly noted, "but still pretty sharp."

"Takes longer to get in and out of the vault," he said. "Something to do with age."

Molly gave him a ride home shortly after nine and Erin came with them.

"What's the consensus in town about my guilt or innocence?" he asked as they turned onto Main Street. He could tell by their slow response it wasn't all in his favor.

Erin spoke first. "You know how some people always think the worst."

"Can't win 'em all," he said

"It's just a few," Molly said. "You know Ray Freeman's always been a skeptic, and Charlie Benson's ready to jump onboard any new idea."

"Does that bother you?" Molly asked.

"No," he said. "I know I didn't do it."

"Is that enough for you?"

"Sure. As long as people whose trust matters to me are with me?"

"But that would be a very short list, wouldn't it?" she said.

"Yes, it would."

"You haven't changed," Erin said. "Such a solitary man."

The rest of the trip was short and silent. Hannon had a question for Erin but didn't want to ask it while Molly was there. He would call her in the morning. He would also call the people who were doing his legwork and ask for an update.

CHAPTER FORTY-THREE

Things didn't go well for him the next morning. He couldn't call Erin, because he didn't remember her cell number, and he couldn't expect anyone to call him, because he hadn't given his new number out. Linda was working a double shift and would see him tomorrow. That was her day off. Cruz wasn't available, and George was on voice mail. He left his number with both. He was able to get Victor's office number from the local phone book and talk with his secretary. The meeting with the police was tomorrow. Victor would pick him up at ten o'clock. He was sitting at the picnic table, looking out over the cove, when he heard a car pull into the driveway. A moment later George came around the corner and onto the deck. Hannon felt like a shipwrecked man watching a rescue boat headed for shore.

"You've come in the nick of time," he said. "I was about to walk to town."

George smiled as he sat down across from Hannon and put his briefcase on the table. He took a picture out of it and passed it to him.

"Here's the fugitive brother. You wanted a picture of him."

It was only a head shot of a bald man, but Hannon could tell the body was bulky.

"This is one mean looking man," Hannon said.

"Yeah, he's bad, and he's almost as big as Patrick, but he's long gone."

"You think he's out of the country?" Hannon asked.

"The FBI says he must be. I heard you shot some-body. Another assassin?"

"No." Hannon said. "I got a little crazy, tried to win a Good Samaritan badge."

He told the story about the camouflaged man.

When he was finished, George could only shake his head and smile. After a moment he reached into the briefcase and took out a folder.

"You are something else," he said as he passed it to Hannon. "Take a look at this."

Hannon opened the folder and began reading the first of two pages. It was a report of the investigation of the little girl who'd lived on the estate. George had found that a four-year-old girl had been checked into a state hospital in Warwick in 1956. She had arrived in a chauffeur-driven limousine accompanied by a dis-tinguished gentleman and left there for treatment of fear and agitation. The admission report also indicated she was claustrophobic. She remained in the hospital as a ward of the state for almost four years before being placed in a foster home in Coventry. She was called Lulu and later took the last name of the family she had been placed with. She graduated from high school as Lulu Campanella in 1970.

The report went on to describe an interview George had with Louis Campanella, who still lived in Coventry and worked for the highway department. He'd grown up in the same household, also a ward of the state. They'd been close, well taken care of by the family, but never adopted. He described her as cheerful, well liked, a cheerleader, and active in school activities. She didn't go on to college. There was no money for that. She had a job at the local library for a short time then moved to Providence around 1973. She kept in close touch with Louis for many years. The last he'd heard, she'd married and moved to Atlantic City. He'd given all this information to a woman named Florence Bird sometime in the eighties, but he'd never heard back from her.

"She was working for my dad," Hannon said. "I don't think she got any further."

"I talked to her," George said, "She said your father asked her to stop. I guess your mother was pretty upset about the whole business."

"That's true," Hannon said. "Did she ever get the name of the husband?"

"No, but I think I can."

"What magic do you have that she didn't?"

"It's called the Internet. You know, computers."

"Oh, those things." Hannon bowed his head. He was embarrassed.

George chuckled. "You got anything to drink? I'm thirsty."

"Just fake beer."

"Good enough. I'll help myself."

George got up and started toward the door.

"There's another picture in my case," he said as he moved into the house. "Take a look."

Hannon got the picture out. It was of Linda and was taken a long time ago. She was standing in front of a small house with a man about the same age. They were both smiling and had their arms around each other. They looked very happy.

"So you've been checking on her," he said.

"What?" George called back.

"Where did you get the picture?" He held it up as George got back to the deck.

"Louis gave it to me," George said.

"Who's Louis?"

"The guy who was like a brother to her—Louis Campanella."

It all came together in Hannon's mind. He was stunned.

"It's him and Lulu just before she left Coventry," George continued.

Hannon looked at the picture once more just to be sure. He blinked and looked again. He took a quick breath and exhaled. He was silent, staring at the photograph.

"What's the matter?" George asked.

"Lulu's been changed to Linda," Hannon said. "Her married name is Rizzo. This is a thirty-year-old picture of my girlfriend."

CHAPTER FORTY-FOUR

"What now?" George asked after a short period of silence.

Hannon didn't answer.

"It doesn't mean she's part of the plot to kill you," George continued.

"It's an option," Hannon said.

"We got lots of options."

"But this one fits, George."

"Run it by me again."

"We know my brother and someone called Babe had a baby, and she gave it to a rich lady. Mary MacMaster was a rich lady who had three boys and wanted a girl without going through the whole birth process again. She got a girl. You just gave me a picture of her."

George didn't say anything.

Hannon got up and started to pace.

"Years later, after my brother dies, my father goes looking for her. He doesn't find her, but now, you do. What am I missing?"

"You don't know Babe and the Hopkins woman are the same person," George said.

Hannon knew George was right, but he wasn't done.

"Remember my sister told us about Hopkins and Whitmore going to Italy and coming back late. That's probably when she had the kid."

"They said it was a passport problem," George said.

"Bullshit. They couldn't come back till the child was born."

"That's just speculation, Hannon. How do we prove it?"

Hannon had to think about that. "DNA," he said finally.

"That's a stretch," George said.

"Yeah. What's your take on all this?"

"Well, we don't know Hopkins had a baby, and it's pure conjecture to say she did and it was his."

"I'd rather call it a hunch."

"Call it whatever you want. It's still no more than a possible coincidence that makes your girlfriend your niece."

That hadn't occurred to Hannon. "Oh, Christ," he muttered.

"Let's not tackle that yet," George said. "It may not be all that bad at your time of life."

Hannon shook his head. "Yeah," he said softly. "No kids. It's not like we knew."

"Maybe we should look for this Whitmore lady," George said. "Maybe she's still alive."

"If she is," Hannon said, "she's pushing ninety."

"I'll get someone up to Maine. If she's alive, we'll find her, and maybe she'll still have some of her faculties left."

Hannon nodded in agreement. He stopped pacing and sat down on the bed. He was still thinking about Linda being his niece.

"Are you really concerned Linda may have a motive to kill you?" George asked.

"No, but the police are."

"We don't have to tell them about this."

"I've already told Cruz about Billy's baby."

"Was that wise?"

"I think so. He's on my side, and he's already helped."

"How so?"

Hannon got the photographs Cruz had given him and showed him the four kids together.

"His grandfather worked on the estate. He took them."

"The girl looks sad," George said.

"I noticed that."

"But she certainly looks like the girl who grew up to be this girl." He held up his picture of Linda and Louis. "Are you going to show this to Cruz?"

"No, not till I figure things out."

"That's good," George agreed. "So what's your next move?"

"I'll talk to Linda tomorrow."

"Be careful how you handle that. You could screw things up."

"Don't I know it? But I've got to get it cleared up. That's what's most important to me now."

George smiled. "Yeah." He understood how Hannon felt. He wasn't going to weigh in on that. "I'll be on my way now. Call you tomorrow."

They walked to George's car together. George was in the car and halfway out of the driveway when he stopped and put his window down.

"I don't think your girlfriend will remember living on the estate."

"How come?"

"She had a lot of therapy. Her hospital records said she lost all the memories of her time on the estate. Guess that's how she got well."

"So it's like she was born in the hospital," Hannon said. "Already five or six years old."

"Something like that," George said. "When's your meeting with the police?"

"Tomorrow."

"Are you worried?"

"No, not about that."

George smiled, gave him a thumbs up, and drove away leaving him in an uncomfortable state of mind. He had to do some walking and get his thoughts together before he talked to Linda. He wasn't looking forward to that. He'd made her happy after her meeting with Cruz, but that could be undone. He would have to be careful how he went about questioning her. He had to make it seem like an effort to get the two of them on the same page. He had to tell her what he'd found out and, hopefully, she would understand and put his thoughts to rest.

Suddenly he was ashamed of his lack of complete trust and the fact that he would be questioning her.

"What the hell kind of trust is that?" he asked himself the same question he had asked the day before aloud. He still didn't have any answer.

CHAPTER FORTY-FIVE

Surprisingly, he was able to sleep when he finally went to bed but the question was still unanswered. It wasn't from lack of trying. He had walked the beach and paced the floor, burned a dozen logs in the fireplace and listened to countless records, all to no avail. The only thing he hadn't done was eat. He had to talk with Linda. He would be unable to concentrate on anything until he did. The guilt and the fear of failure would be with him till them.

He was having coffee when Officer Fisk called from the police station to inform him that his meeting had been postponed until later in the day. That was good. He'd forgotten about it anyway. He was pouring his second cup of coffee when he heard her key turning in the lock. Showtime.

"I've got something to tell you," he said after she poured herself coffee and sat beside him.

He didn't tell her the whole story. He left out the part about his brother's possible involvement. They would deal with that if his theory proved to be correct. She sat and listened quietly to his carefully chosen words. When he was finished, she knew Margaret Hopkins may have had a baby girl and given it over to Mary MacMaster.

"That's the woman who was murdered?" she asked when he was finished.

"Yes. Over fifty years ago."

"The woman they say you murdered."

"Yes."

"What about the baby's father?"

He shrugged his shoulders and turned his palms up. "Don't know," he lied.

"And you're thinking this child might be me."

"Something like that."

"How much can you back up with facts?"

He showed her the picture of the "little wanderer" standing in front of the hedge maze. She had no noticeable reaction, but she didn't give it back. She continued to stare at it like someone in a trance. Hannon waited until she spoke.

"Where's this little girl now?"

He showed her the picture of Lulu and Louis. Still no reaction. He continued to wait.

"Oh my God," she said finally.

"Sorry to drop it on you like this," he said.

"I don't remember this one," she said, holding up the picture of the little girl. "But this," she said, indicating the second picture. "This I remember quite well. How did you get it?"

"Charles told me about the little girl, and George traced you through the hospital they sent you to. He got the picture from Louis."

"George is your detective friend?" she said.

"Yes. He brought the picture to me yesterday."

"It seems George is very competent."

"It's what he does."

"How is Louis? We've been out of touch for many years."

"George found him still living in Coventry."

"I knew he'd never get out of there," she said. "Got any more pictures." She sounded sarcastic. He couldn't blame her.

"I was just looking for someone. I never thought it would be you."

"It's a small world, Hannon." He sensed anger in her voice. "Turns out it is me. Now what?"

"We deal with it."

"How, Hannon? How? I can't help you here. I have no recollection of my life before Coventry. I don't know who my real mother and father were. We should have talked about stuff like this years ago. Dammit! I knew something like this would happen."

"Nothing's going to happen," he said.

"It's already happening." Her voice was rising.

"That's not right," he said emphatically.

"Oh really," she shouted. "Tell me you and your god-damned detective friend aren't thinking I found out you murdered my mother and I'm out to get you."

"I'm not thinking that," he said without hesitation.

She stood up and leaned forward, placing her hands on the table and looking directly at him. "Then what the hell are you thinking?" she demanded.

He didn't have a quick answer for that. He would never have gotten to speak anyway.

"Do I really have to tell you I'm not part of this?" she said. "Have you forgotten how I feel about you? Have you lost your trust in me?"

"No, no, and no," he said firmly. "I'm simply telling you what's going on. This is an update, not an accusation."

"Why now?"

"Because now is when it's going on. Now is when it needs to be dealt with it."

What he said seemed to calm her down.

"Do you really think I'd want to harm you, Hannon?"

"Of course not."

"Tell me this," she said. "When you first saw the picture, didn't you feel you'd uncovered a motive for murder?"

"I knew that's what the police would think," he said.

"I don't give a damn about the police, Hannon. What was in your mind?"

He didn't speak quickly enough, so she answered her own question.

"You didn't know what to think, so you thought the worst. You had a suspicion, a lack of trust. That shouldn't happen when people trust each other."

"We're not perfect, Linda. Nobody's perfect."

"I guess I thought we might be," she said. "And we're not."

He didn't have an answer for that.

"I need time to think about this," she said.

"I've been thinking about it all night. It doesn't do much good. You just have to keep going."

"Yes, call me tomorrow. I need to leave now."

He didn't argue. They needed thinking time.

"Will you tell the police?" she asked as they walked toward her bicycle.

"Course not," he assured her.

"Will they find out?"

"I don't see how. There not even looking. All the attention is on me."

"I think we've lost something today," she said. "Trust for each other."

"Don't say that, Linda.

"Trust can be hard to hang on to, Hannon. We should have come clean about our past before we got involved."

"We didn't," he said. "We chose not to."

She didn't answer. She got on her bike and rode away, leaving him to ponder if he had done the right thing. He wasn't sure. They'd gone through their share of disagreements, but nothing like this. He remembered talking about making a nuclear weapon out of a cherry bomb. Is that what they had done? He wasn't sure. One thing he was he was sure of was that he was worried. People had tried to kill him, and the police had made him a suspect in a murder case. Yet what he was worrying about was his future with Linda. He didn't give a damn about the rest.

CHAPTER FORTY-SIX

Hannon wasn't sure what to do after Linda left, but he knew he had to do something. He didn't want to wander around thinking about what had happened. He needed to involve himself in something else. He called the police station. Officer Tom Fisk answered.

"Anything new on my meeting?" he asked.

"Nah," Fisk answered. "Nobody's here yet."

"Where's Cruz?"

"He's out on the water."

"What's he doing out there?"

"He's still the acting harbormaster, you know."

"Is something going on?"

"How the hell should I know? They never tell me anything."

Hannon couldn't cover up a chuckle. "OK," he said, and he hung up. What Fisk had said was true. He was usually kept in the dark, and Hannon knew a better source of information. Max Gallagher would know what was happening.

"There's been some kind of boating accident," Max said when he finally got to the phone. "Cruz took off in the harbormaster's boat. He got a call from the Coast Guard."

"Sound's big," Hannon said.

"Looks that way. I heard him tell DiMartino to call some of the other harbormasters for help."

"That's really big. Anything else."

"Nothing yet."

"Can you keep me posted?"

"Sure. How you doing?"

"Alone and hungry, Max. I feel like I fell off the planet."

"I'll send some food out."

Hannon got his binoculars and set up on the deck to scan the water. The sea was calm with nothing in sight all the way to the horizon which was well past the mouth of the cove. He began working his way back along the north side of it. His eyes settled on the MacMaster's mooring. The schooner wasn't there. He set the binoculars on the table and shook his head. He didn't remember if it was there before. Mark and Charlotte were taking it off the water almost two weeks ago when they found him. He knew they hadn't got it out then, but had they done it since? Was it there yesterday or the day before? He hadn't noticed. Were they in trouble on the water now? He didn't know.

"Damn," he muttered.

He went into the house and turned on the TV. All he got were soap operas, game shows, and ads. It wasn't time for the news. He turned on his clock radio and sat down on the bed to listen. Before he got any news, Max called back.

"It was the MacMaster's boat," he said. "Somebody went overboard."

Hannon slumped back onto the bed. He felt a sickly shiver slip into his stomach. He had trouble getting the question past his lips.

"Was it Charlotte?"

"No," Max said quickly. "It was a guy."

Hannon pushed the air out from his lungs. "Walter," he said softly.

"Yeah," Max said. "I think he was Mark's brother. They haven't found him."

"How long have they been looking?"

"Couple hours."

"Did he have a life jacket on?"

"Don't know."

"Probably not," Hannon said.

"I'm going down to the dock, see what else I can find out. I'll call you back."

"Thanks, Max."

Shortly after the call, a young kid showed up at the door with a couple of tuna salad and American cheese sandwiches courtesy of the Sail Loft. The cheese wasn't melted so Hannon spread butter on the bread and grilled them. They didn't taste quite as good as the ones he had at the Loft. He would have to ask Max what the grilling secret was. It was after dark when his phone rang again.

"I guess he didn't have a jacket on," Max said. "The search has been called off till tomorrow."

"He may be washed up on the shore by then," Hannon said.

"Yeah," Max agreed.

"Are they going to search the cove if he doesn't come in?" Hannon asked.

"I doubt it, Hannon. Mark gave them their location when the accident happened. They were out of the cove headed for the boat yard to haul the boat out.

"What was the accident?"

267

"I guess Walter stood up while they were coming about to head in. The boom swung his way, hit him in the head, and knocked him overboard."

"What? He wouldn't stand up if they were coming about."

"That's what Mark told them. He was all shook up. They took him to the hospital."

"He could have been in shock and given them the wrong location," Hannon said.

"Cruz doesn't think so."

"Dammit, Max, they should search the cove. The tide could have pulled him back no matter how far out they were."

Max didn't answer. Hannon realized he was talking to the wrong person.

"I'm sorry Max," he said after a short pause. "I'm uptight today. Is Cruz still around?"

"I think he went home after he talked to the reporters. I don't think it's a good idea to call him tonight."

"You're probably right. I'll try to get him tomorrow. It's not a rescue situation anymore, just a matter of finding the body."

"Get some sleep, Hannon. I'll keep you posted."

"If you see Cruz before I do, Max, tell him I'm thinking about the large conglomeration of jagged rocks and boulders and seaweed surrounding Seagull Ridge. He'll know what I mean."

"OK, I'll tell him."

"And tell him if he doesn't search it, I will."

CHAPTER FORTY-SEVEN

Hannon wasn't kidding. He hoped he hadn't sounded definite or arrogant. He knew from experience the incoming tide was strong and often pull debris into the rocky water around Seagull Ridge. Years ago, he and his brother had regularly snorkeled through the seaweed and jagged rocks searching for lobsters, armed only with a peach basket and a gardening claw. It was illegal but fun, and the family loved lobster dinners. He remembered the many items they'd recovered and made use of that had fallen or been thrown off boats from outside the cove—a compass, oars, deck chairs, even a small refrigerator. Why couldn't a body be picked up, swept back into the cove and jammed into what he and his brother had named the "conglomeration" that led to the massive rocky cliff that rose up to Seagull Ridge.

Early the next morning, he was on the deck, already wearing his hooded wet suit, scanning the cove, eating fistfuls of Cheerios out of the box, and waiting for the phone to ring. His snorkeling mask was strapped onto his forehead. The small inside pockets of the suit were large enough for his phone and his glasses but not the .45. That was OK. He wouldn't need it. He was ready and anxious for the search.

His phone rang. It was Max.

"They won't be searching the cove," he said. "At least not today."

"I'm on my way out there right now," Hannon said.

"Are you sure that's a good idea?"

"No, but I've got hunch he's there."

Max didn't push it. "Is Linda there?"

Hannon hadn't thought about Linda. "No, is she late for work?"

"Nah, I'm trying to get her to come in early. Be careful."

He began to think about Linda as he pulled the row-boat out from under the deck and hauled it toward the water. Where was she? What was she doing? How did she feel? He was on the water and rowing before he realized he could be doing this to keep from thinking about her. He was keeping himself busy until they talked again. Would he find the body? Probably not, but he was active, excited, almost exhilarated, a man on a mission. He was also rowing in the wrong direction. He straightened his course and ten minutes later was tossing his rusty anchor into the water off Seagull Ridge.

It was a perfect tide for snorkeling, but the surroundings didn't look the same. In the past, he and Billy had walked here and arrived at the top of the cliff. Finally he recognized the overgrown path they'd used to climb down to the shelf where they could safely enter the water and swim among the rocks and into the small cave that was under the shelf. That's where they'd found lobsters and other treasures. It was a good place to start.

Hannon pulled his mask down, slipped into the water, and began moving in a back and forth pattern, taking himself closer and closer to the ledge with every turn, using the rocks and seaweed to pull himself along. The water was clear. If anything was there, he couldn't miss it. When he reached the shelf he decided to dive under it into the small cave. A couple of strokes was all it took to bring him under and up into the air space, face-to-face with the dead body he was searching for. His head snapped backward and a rush of air pushed the snorkel from his open mouth along with a resounding yell of surprise and fright. The face was bloated and grotesque, but there was no doubt it was Walter MacMaster. Hannon steadied himself and tried to turn him around, but he couldn't. The body was wedged between two large rocks. He took a deep breath and tried to pull it out. He couldn't do that either. He needed help. He managed to reach into the dead man's pants pocket and dig a wallet out. He wondered if he should be doing police business.

"What the hell," he muttered. "Why not?" He needed proof of his find. He dove down and swam back under the ridge. After he pulled himself up onto the top of it, he pulled his phone out of the wet suit and called the police station. Rose DeMartino answered.

"Guess who found what beneath Seagull Ridge," he said.

"Hannon?"

"The very same."

"You're at Seagull Ridge?"

"Yes, in the water."

"Why?"

"That's where the body is."

He gave her the details and requested she send the police.

"Are you sure it's him?" she asked.

Hannon squelched an urge to ask her who else it might be.

"I've got his wallet, "he said. "It's him."

After she hung up he looked through the wallet. It was all the usual stuff. He focused on a laminated family picture—Walter with his beard, an attractive, slightly overweight woman, and three grown, clean-shaven men.

"Wife and three kids," he muttered. "Damn shame." He continued looking at the picture without knowing why. There wasn't anything special about it. He rested on the shelf a few moments before deciding to climb up to the ridge and meet the police there. They had divers who could pull the body out. He was starting to feel his age.

It didn't get any better as he climbed up the crocked path. He was breathing hard and his legs felt heavy. He heard footsteps as he neared the top. He look up to see who it was. He saw only what looked like a baseball bat swinging down toward his head. He moved his left hand up to ward off the blow, but it did little good. The bat struck him on the side of his forehead, catching part of the mask and cracking the plastic face. He fell backward from the cliff and plunged into the water inches away from the sharp edges of the ledge. Barely conscious, he managed to grab a handful of seaweed and pull himself under it. There was blood coming from his cheek when he ripped his mask off. He covered the wound with one hand and used the other to turn himself to face out. He was underwater and needed to breathe, but he couldn't go that way. There were bullets zipping down through the water and into the sand outside the ledge. Someone was shooting at him. He slid back into the air space to breathe and wait.

No use pulling the cell phone out. He wouldn't get any signal in the cave. He applied pressure to his cheek with his hand and submerged to look out. No one had come into the water so he slid out into the open air. He was pulling his cell phone out when he spotted the harbormaster's boat headed right for him. He sat on the rocky ledge and waited while the boat came in as close as it could and a diver went into the water. He thought it would be Cruz and was surprised to see Officer Tom Fisk pull his mask off.

"How come they let you out of the office?" Hannon asked.

"I swim," Fisk answered. "And I'm bucking for the harbormaster job."

"Good for you," Hannon said. "The body's stuck in the cave. I can't get him loose."

"There's a cave down there?" Fisk sounded surprised.

"Yeah, a small one. You'll need help getting him out."

"How does he's look?"

"Awful."

Fisk didn't look happy with that. "I better take you back first," he said. "He can wait. You need medical attention."

Hannon agreed, and they made their way back to the larger boat. Fisk gave him a thick gauze pad to put pressure on the cut. On the way back they called the station and reported the incident.

CHAPTER FORTY-EIGHT

Cruz was waiting on the dock when they got back. He didn't look happy.

"You crazy son of a bitch," he yelled at Hannon. "What the hell were you thinking?"

"I'm not sure," Hannon said. "I think I was just bored."

"That's bullshit," Cruz shot back.

Hannon knew Cruz was right. He took the gauze pad off his cheek to see if the bleeding had stopped.

"What the hell is that?" Cruz asked when he saw Hannon's eye.

"Son of a bitch clubbed me with a baseball bat. Knocked me off the ridge."

Cruz shook his head as he moved to get a closer look. "Can you see out of that eye?" he asked.

"Not really."

"Get in the car. I'm taking you to the hospital."

"I don't need any hospital."

"Yeah, you do," Cruz said firmly. "You need stitches, your cheek's swelling up over your eye, and you probably have a concussion."

Hannon told Cruz the whole story on the way to the hospital. He had given the wallet to Fisk.

"If the person fired down at you, we should find some spent bullets in the sand, get a fix on the weapon." Cruz said.

"I thought I was done with all this after they broke the Russian gang up," Hannon said.

"I think you are done with them." Cruz said.

"What's that mean?" Hannon asked.

"It means this attack doesn't sound very professional to me."

Hannon thought about that. "Yeah," he said finally. "Who walks around with a gun and a baseball bat?"

"An amateur, I'd say," Cruz said.

Hannon got the point. "You think the person who's been paying the bills has decided to do the job himself."

"It's beginning to look that way."

Hannon took his wet suit off as they drove along. He was mulling the idea over when they arrived at the hospital.

"Anybody know you were going to search the cove today?" Cruz asked.

Hannon didn't like the thought that came into his head. "Yeah," he said. "Max Gallagher. He's the only one I told."

The two men turned and looked at each other. Neither liked the idea. Finally Hannon said, "Someone could have been watching me."

"I have to check it out," Cruz said.

Hannon nodded and started to get out, but Cruz took him by the arm. "Hold on. I got something to say."

Hannon thought he knew what was on Cruz's mind and was surprised when he said, "I'm worried about you, my friend. Something about your state of mind."

Hannon gave him a questioning look.

Cruz continue. "A lot's happened to you over the past three weeks, and you're walking around like you don't remember any of it." Hannon tried to respond, but Cruz kept going. "It's not natural. Four attempts have been made to kill you, and you've killed two men. It's not normal for anyone to experience stuff like that without some sort of emotional reaction."

Hannon interrupted him. "I've always tried to keep my feelings to myself."

"I know that," Cruz shot back. "Just let me finish. What's happened is unbelievable. You've been incredibly lucky. You should be dead, and yet you keep putting yourself in harm's way. You're treating it like a game, and you seem to be enjoying it."

Hannon didn't know what to say. Cruz kept right on going.

"I've seen it all before and it ended badly."

Hannon realized where Cruz was headed. He knew what was coming. He knew the story.

"This is about your father."

"Yes," Cruz said. "I'm beginning to see a lot of him in you."

Hannon was stunned and confused. He tried to think of a response, but all he could come up with was, "I don't understand."

Cruz tried to explain. "You know my father was a detective."

"And a very good one," Hannon said.

"He was the best. He loved his job. He made it fun, like a game. My mother told me he seemed infatuated with danger. He thrived on it. It scared her to death, but whenever she tried to confront him, he always said,

'Don't worry, love. They won't get me today. Someday, maybe, but not today.' It was like he felt invincible, and then one day, he wasn't."

"Killed in a drug bust," Hannon said softly.

"Yeah. He had plenty of close calls before, but that day was his someday."

"I appreciate what you're trying to say, Orlando, but—"

"I just think you should give it some thought."

"I will."

"Ask yourself how you felt when you were chasing the guy who was after Mark MacMaster, or when you went looking for the body today."

Hannon was already doing that. He didn't answer.

"Think about how short a time you've had to deal with real danger. It probably took years for my dad to have as many episodes as you've had in three weeks."

That hit home with Hannon. If the adrenalin rush of danger was addictive, he could be in trouble.

"I'm done," Cruz said. "Get in there and get that cut fixed."

Hannon started out, but Cruz grabbed him again. "Thanks for finding the body."

He spent the rest of the day in the emergency room getting the cut on his face stapled and convincing Dr. Fleming he didn't have a headache. He was released into the care of Erin shortly after six o'clock with the understanding that he would not be alone for the night.

"Stay with us," Molly said as they drove back to Hooper's Landing. "I got lots of bedrooms. You can put on some of my husband's old clothes."

Hannon was glad to have company for the evening. He got a good meal, some pleasant conversation, a

Jeopardy rerun, and peace and quiet. They were careful not to speak of his day's adventures.

When he woke up the next morning, Erin and Molly had gone to church. He went back to sleep. He got up around noon when he heard them coming in. He was still tired. Fortunately the day turned out the way he hoped it would—quiet and peaceful. He spent it with the girls watching football. They spoke only briefly about his adventures and their concern with his welfare. He got himself another good meal and a second good night's sleep. His only problem was Molly's late husband's clothes were too big for him. The following morning he was up early, anxious to see what Cruz had found out about Max. He borrowed a cane that had belonged to the departed husband and hobbled two blocks to the police station hoping Cruz would be there. He wasn't. Assistant District Attorney Laura Lundregen was. She was sitting in the chief's chair when he waked in.

"You must be Mr. Hannon," she said.

"How can you tell?" he asked.

"You look like someone who might have been struck by a baseball bat recently."

Hannon smiled. "That bad, huh?"

"I've seen worse. I'm Laura Lundregen." She stood up and held out her hand to shake his. She was very tall, slender, and quite attractive. "Sit down," she said. "I was just going to call you."

"About our meeting?" he asked.

"About the cancellation of that meeting," she answered.

"It's canceled?" Hannon was surprised.

"Yes. Your DNA didn't match up."

"With what?"

"Hair from the comb Vera Whitmore gave to Chief Hardy."

A look of disbelief came over Hannon's face. "That's over fifty years ago," he said.

"The comb was checked in the eighties," she said. "Part of the early research on DNA. It didn't start with O. J. Simpson, you know."

"I know that, but still, it's been thirty years."

It was still good. That's possible, I'm told. And now we've got a match on the national data base."

"I'm thinking that would be Bobby Hinch, right?"

"No, that's where things get a little complicated."

"Who's the match?"

"Your brother, Billy Hannon."

Hannon was shocked. He leaned heavily on the cane and sat down. "How can that be?" he asked.

"People in the military volunteered for DNA research testing," she explained. "He must have one of them."

"So how the hell did he get on the national data base? That's for crooks."

"I don't know, but it doesn't matter. He's there."

Hannon was getting angry. He didn't want to do that. "So what happens now?"

"I've already discussed that with your lawyer."

"Fill me in, please."

"He's convinced me to postpone making any statement until we investigate further, find out where he was, if possible."

"He was on duty at Fort Dix."

"I'm afraid that's not right, Mr. Hannon. You should be talking to Mr. Levine. He has all the information. I'm sure he's trying to contact you."

Hannon nodded. Slowly he pushed himself out of the chair and steadied himself with the cane.

"Do you have a phone with you?" she asked.

"No. I think it's still in my wet suit."

"Use this one." She pushed the desk phone toward him. "I've got to go downstairs. Victor's number is right here."

He thanked her. She was right. Victor had been trying to contact him.

"Where the hell have you been hiding?" Victor asked.

"Deep cover," Hannon answered. "It's a long story. "What happens now?"

"Not much, as far as she's concerned," Victor said. "Our problem is there's four days missing between the day your brother left town and the time he got back to Fort Dix."

"Was he AWOL?" Hannon asked.

"No, he got back on time according to his military records."

"That would mean he lied to us about when he was due back." Hannon didn't feel comfortable saying that.

"Looks that way," Victor said.

"But where was he? Why would he lie?"

"Two questions we need answers for. Your friend, George, is already working on that."

"How did he find out?"

"Cruz called him."

Hannon felt good when he heard that. His friends were working together on his behalf.

"How much time do we have until this all leaks out?" he asked.

"Not much. Lundregen is cooperating, but she's anxious to get the word out that she's solved a fifty-year-old murder case."

"Has she got enough to prosecute?"

"There's no one to prosecute, Hannon. Your brother's deceased."

"So she turns it over to the court of public opinion."

"Something like that. Laura's a very ambitious woman."

"I don't want that to happen, Victor. My brother wasn't a killer. I'm going to have to prove she's wrong."

"How?"

"I don't know."

Hannon walked back to Molly's house after his conversation with Victor. He wasn't looking forward to telling Erin what he'd just learned, but he didn't want her to hear it from someone else. As he expected, she was defiant and angry.

"That's crazy!" she insisted. "For God sakes, Billy wouldn't swat a fly."

"I know," Hannon said. "But they have DNA, and he lied to us about his return to duty. He must have had something else to do."

"But what?" she asked. "And why not tell us?"

"That's easy. He didn't want us to know."

They sat looking at each other for a moment. Finally they both spoke, almost simultaneously. "A woman."

The rest of the day provided nothing more, but they agreed that Billy had gone somewhere to be with a girlfriend, perhaps the women called 'Babe'.

They'd eaten, and Molly was driving them to Hannon's house when Erin broke a long and thoughtful silence.

"I just thought of something," she said.

"Let's hear it."

"Billy's funeral. A lot of people I didn't know were there."

"Any of them women in his age group?" Hannon asked.

"Maybe."

"Was there a book to sign at the funeral home?"

"Yes, of course."

"Do you still have it?"

"I don't know. I'll call my neighbor and ask her to look in Mother's old room. There's lots of stuff still there."

"We don't have much time, Erin. If you get anything, call George and give it to him. I'll give you his number."

After they dropped him off, Hannon stood and watched the car drive off. He had thinking to do, but that could wait. He hoped he could go right to sleep, but knew he couldn't. He needed music. *South Pacific* would do the trick. He fell asleep halfway through. It took a phone call from Cruz to wake him up the next morning.

CHAPTER FORTY-NINE

"Where the hell have you been?" Cruz asked.

"Holed up at Molly Hammond's house," Hannon said. "I needed a break."

Cruz got right to the point. "Has George had any luck finding the little girl in the picture?"

Hannon wasn't ready for that. He had to think fast. "He's traced her to a foster home in Coventry. She grew up using the family name, Campanella."

"Anything else?" Cruz sounded determined.

Hannon had the feeling Cruz was testing him again. He figured he'd better come clean. He told Cruz the whole story.

"So your girlfriend is someone who may have a motive to murder you," Cruz said.

"Seems that way," Hannon said. "If my theory about Hopkins and Billy is correct."

"Why didn't you tell me?"

"I needed to talk with her first to be sure."

"How'd that work out?"

"Not well. She said I had no trust in her and walked out. I haven't seen her since."

"Neither has anyone else since Saturday night when she didn't show up for work."

Hannon was stunned.

"I think she skipped town," Cruz said. "Cab driver says he drove her and some guy to the train station in Kingston."

"Christ," Hannon said. "What's happening?"

"I hoped you might know."

Hannon thought it might have something to do with Linda's ex-husband. He told Cruz about her trip to Baltimore. "He may be in some kind of trouble. She feels like she owes him."

"I hope so for your sake," Cruz said. "I've got an all-points bulletin out on them. Do you know what he looks like?"

"No, never met him. What else have I missed?"

"Plenty," Cruz said. "Cunningham's out of intensive care. Mark MacMaster is still being treated for shock. The autopsy shows his brother drowned, but there was a nasty bump on his head, similar to yours."

"Something's out of whack there," Hannon said.

"Don't I know it? They'll be a coroner's inquest."

"Is the sale of the estate still going through?" Hannon asked.

"Just as soon as Mark can sign the papers. It's all his now."

"Lucky him."

"At least you're off the hook for the Hopkins murder."

"But my brother's on it now, and he's not around to defend himself."

"It was a long time ago. Not many people remember. It will pass."

"Not good enough, Orlando."

"Not much you can do about it."

"Maybe not, but I have to try. I owe him that. Billy never killed anybody. I need to make sure he won't be the fall guy."

"How will you do that?"

"I'm not sure now. Call me later. I may have something to tell you."

Cruz didn't push it any further, but Hannon knew he would call back. He hoped to hear from Erin before that. He had forgotten to ask Cruz about checking on Max. He could do that when the call came. First things first. He called George and told him to call Erin. He didn't tell him why. He had toast and coffee and got dressed. It was time to start thinking. Why had Linda left town and who was she with? He suspected it was her ex, was she the child of Margaret Hopkins, seeking revenge. He didn't want to believe that. He also didn't want to believe it was Max who knocked him into the water—or anyone else he knew. But it *was* someone he knew. It had to be. He put on a heavy jacket, got his cane, and went for a walk. It was cold and windy, but he needed the air. He was beginning to relax. When he got back to the house he laid on the bed and fell asleep. It took another call from Cruz to wake him up.

"Any news?" Cruz asked.

"Nothing yet. Can you tell me what it is you're doing?"

Hannon told him about Erin's idea.

"Yeah," Cruz said, "you might get something."

"What about Max?"

"Glad you asked. He's clean. He was working in the kitchen all morning."

"That's good news. Was he upset you were checking?"

"Not at all. He understood. He brought his .45 in. I fired it, and it wasn't a match to the bullet Fisk found when they pulled the body out. It wasn't his gun."

"Anyone else I know own a gun?" Hannon asked.

"As it happens, yes. One of the charter members of your murder club."

"Ray Freeman?" Hannon asked. He hoped it was. He never liked Ray.

"Charlie Benson," Cruz said. "I'm on my way to see him now."

Charlie Benson's name put Hannon back in thinking mode. He was the most determined and passionate member of the club, and he was fond of Miss Hopkins. Her murder had caused him great distress. But was he capable of carrying out an act of vengeance against someone accused of the crime? Hannon didn't think so. He needed to sit down. This time he chose the recliner. He stretched it out till he was almost horizontal. It was very comfortable, a fine place for thinking. I didn't take long for a fresh idea to slip into his mind. It started with the picture in Walter's wallet .There had been something about it that bothered him, and suddenly he knew what it was.

"I wonder," he mumbled as he pushed himself from the chair and headed toward the kitchen table where Cruz's pictures were still scattered. He found the one with the little wanderer, Linda, standing in front of the hedge maze.

"Yeah!" he said. "She got lost in the damn thing and it made her crazy. That's why they put her in the hospital. And when she freaked out while I was talking with Charles, she must have remembered."

But that wasn't what he was looking for. He kept going through the pictures until he found the one with Linda and Charles and Mary and their three sons. Then he found an old photo that Cruz's grandfather hadn't taken. It was the four sons of Earl, all in uniform, ready to go to war. It was taken on the day the iron fence came down.

"That's it," he said softly. "I need to go to the estate."

It was getting dark. Mark was still in the hospital so only Charlotte would be there. Still, he felt a need to protect himself, so he got the .44 and put it in his jacket pocket. He would need a flashlight and certainly his reading glasses. He got those. He also got the keys to his car. Easier to drive than walk His leg was sore and weak. He felt a little foolish. He was acting like an Army Ranger preparing for battle. At least he wasn't covering his face with shoe polish. Another idea came to him. "Oh Christ," he said. "Let's not get carried away here."

He was in the car before he asked himself. "What the hell am I doing?" He remembered what Cruz had said about danger and its possible addiction. Is that what was happening to him? Did he feel like he was playing a game? Was he excited and exhilarated, feeling invincible? He hoped not. He started the car and headed slowly toward the estate. Patience and caution, the older man's offsets for lost ability, were gone. He couldn't stop.

CHAPTER FIFTY

harlotte MacMaster was waiting for him at the front door. She'd seen his car coming up the driveway.

"Nice to see you, Hannon." she said. "How's the eye?"

"Sore and blurred," he said.

"I'm hoping you're here because Linda's left town and my husband's in the hospital." She didn't' mince words, but the look on his face told her he wasn't. "So why are you here?"

He came right to the point. "I'm doing some research on your family tree."

"Not my family tree," she said. "You must mean the MacMaster family tree."

"Yes, perhaps you can help me."

"What are you looking for?"

"Charles's missing brother, Harold."

Charlotte gave him a questioning look. "He's the one who was wounded in the war and couldn't have children," she said. "He's not missing. He's in Texas if he's still alive."

"Anything else?"

"I never met him. He was long gone before I got here. I think he and his father, Earl, had a huge argument about how the family was being run. He left and never came back. I think Earl disinherited him."

"Sounds like something the old man might have done," Hannon said. "My father said he was a real prick."

"How nice," she said. "It didn't matter. Charles said Harold made his own fortune in oil."

"Did they keep in touch?"

"Yes, after the father died."

"Any correspondence?"

"I think Charles has a lot of stuff upstairs."

"Can I take a look?"

"Sure, if you don't mind being in his bedroom with me."

"I'll risk it."

They took the elevator up to the third floor. It seemed even slower than the first time he'd used it. In the ballroom he noticed the screens around the stage had been taken down revealing an elaborately furnished Victorian bedroom complete with a huge four-poster bed.

"That's the biggest bed I've ever seen," he said.

"Care to try it out, Hannon? It's very comfortable."

"Not a good idea."

"I thought you'd say that. Too bad."

He spotted a couple of doors on the back wall behind the ramps. "What's back there?"

"Two rooms that used to be bathrooms. One still is."

"And the other?"

"Charles's private study."

"That's what I'm looking for. Is it open?"

"The key's in the desk drawer." She got it and let him in.

It wasn't a large room, but it had everything a good study needs: a couch, bookcases loaded with books, a cluttered desk, and a file cabinet. He pulled the top drawer open and found a. folder crammed full of papers and letters, newspaper clippings, and photographs. It was simply marked "Hal" in pencil. It didn't take Hannon long to piece together the story of the two surviving brothers whose lives took separate directions but who stayed in touch until Harold's death four years ago. A moment later he found a picture of Harold. He smiled.

"There was a family squabble," he said, "a big one," he said.

Charlotte, who had settled comfortably onto the couch, made no response. He wasn't sure she'd heard him. He continued anyway.

"Harold was adamant about wanting to loosen things up around here—less regimentation, modern techniques—but old Earl wouldn't hear of it. They argued, almost came to blows." He still got no recognition. He turned to look at her, but she had left the room. He found her in the ballroom, looking out one of the windows.

"There's a car outside," she said. "I think Mark is home. This should be good for a laugh."

"Tell him I wanted another ride on the elevator," Hannon said.

She couldn't help smiling. They went out of the ballroom to the top of the stairs. The front door opened below them and Mark came in. There was another man with him. Hannon recognized him at once. Charlotte started for the stairs. He grabbed her by the arm and pulled her back.

"Let's take the elevator," he said, maneuvering her toward it.

"That will take forever," she said'

"That's the point, Charlotte. That's the goddamned point."

"We'll be right down, darling," she called out.

"I certainly hope so," Mark shouted back.

In the elevator, he stopped her from pushing the down button, turned her around to face him, gripped her shoulders tightly and began speaking softly.

"I'm in deep trouble, Charlotte, and unless you know exactly what your husband's involved in, so are you."

She didn't speak. She looked confused and frightened.

"I know who the man with Mark is." he said. "He a Russian mobster and a fugitive, He's what's left of the gang that's trying to kill me."

"What are you talking about?" She said, "I don't understand." Her voice began to tremble.

"Mark hired two of that man's associates to kill me."

"Why! Why would he do that?"

"He thinks I murdered his mother."

Charlotte looked at him in disbelief. She was bewildered. "Mary? Mary wasn't murdered."

"Mary wasn't his mother." Hannon said firmly.

"Are you coming down?" Mark called out.

"Just a minute," Hannon yelled back. "I think the damn thing's stuck."

The elevator jolted quickly and began to descend. Mark had started it from the bottom.

Hannon showed Charlotte the picture he had taken from the folder. "Look at this," he said. "It's a picture of Harold and his two sons."

"What?" She said in disbelief. "Harold couldn't have children."

"Look at the picture, Charlotte, the family resemblance. They look just like him. I saw the same thing this morning when I found Walter. He had a picture of his boys. Even without beards you could tell they were his kids."

The elevator seemed to be going faster down than it had gone up. Hannon stopped it at the second floor.

"What are you saying?" Charlotte asked. She seemed to have regained her focus.

"I'm saying Charles and Mary's kids don't look at all like Charles and Mary, and they don't look like each other. I saw a picture of them when they were little. There was no resemblance at all. I'm saying it wasn't Harold who got his balls shot off in the war. It was Charles."

The elevator started moving again. Hannon kept going. "His father, Earl was a fanatic about continuing the family blood line. He must have made Charles adopt secretly, probably had Mary stage fake pregnancies. They took other people's illegitimate kids and passed them off as their own. They were all adopted, every one of them. I thought it was just the little girl. I think they got Mark from Peg Hopkins."

The elevator stopped. "Get the hell out of here," he whispered. "Get help." He put his car keys in her pocket. "It's behind the garage."

The elevator door slid open. He wasn't ready.

CHAPTER FIFTY-ONE

He should have had his gun in hand ready to shoot. He hadn't thought about that. He wanted Charlotte to understand what was happening. The Russian moved close to him with his hand in his pocket. Through it, he jammed what must have been a gun into Hannon's stomach. He slipped his other hand into Hannon's pocket and removed the .44. "Let's go into the kitchen," he ordered.

"Make Mr. Hannon comfortable, Urie," Mark said. "I'll be along shortly." He turned to Charlotte, who looked to be in some sort of coma. "Why don't you go to your room and rest," he said. "I'll explain this later."

Hannon didn't hear her response. He was being pushed toward the kitchen by the mean looking, bald man with the gun. "Turn around," the man said as they reached the door.

He turned in time to see a huge fist headed toward his jaw. There was nothing he could do. The blow landed exactly where it was supposed to, knocking him back through the open doorway and flat onto his back. He lay there, only half conscience, waiting to be kicked or punched again. The man grabbed his shoulders, pulled him over to the breakfast counter, and sat him up on a high stool. His head slumped, face down, onto the counter.

"That was for Ivan," the man said. "I'll have more after the doctor is done with you."

Hannon was dazed, but he knew what that meant. He was going to be killed, and he couldn't even raise a hand. He was going to have to talk himself out of this. He shook his head, trying to clear his brain He tried to speak but couldn't. He felt his jaw to see if it was broken. It was starting to swell. He tried to speak again.

"You're a forgiving person," he managed to utter. He got no response.

"They screwed you out of the fee for killing me. Ivan kept the money so he could run away from you."

"Our business, Mr. Hannon, not yours. You shouldn't have killed him."

Hannon's mind was clearing. He decided a good lie might be in order. "I didn't kill him," he said. "He tripped and fell on his own knife."

Before he got any response, Mark returned to the room.

"Is he able to speak?" he asked.

"Sure," the Russian said. "He's tough for an old man. I nailed him with a baseball bat the other day and he's back for more."

Hannon shook his head. He was disappointed. He had hoped that was Ray Freeman.

"He looks old and decrepit to me," Mark said. "How about it, Hannon. Feeling like the old man you are."

"I can still cut my own toenails," Hannon muttered as he raised his head up from the counter.

"Urie, can you keep an eye on my wife?" Mark said. "We have business."

Urie nodded and started to leave.

"Oh, Urie," Mark said. "Better leave Mr. Hannon's weapon with me. Make sure it's ready to fire."

What Mark said jarred Hannon's mind into a recollection. He had changed his mind about bringing a second weapon and, at the last moment, had taped the .32 to his left leg. He felt relief but it didn't last long. He would still have to pull the tape off the gun. He quickly diagnosed his situation. He was on the wrong side of the counter. Slowly he slipped down from his stool. He was unsteady from the punch, but his vision was clearing. The counter had stools on both sides and drawers under it. He put both hands on the counter top to steady himself and moved slowly to the other side where he could face Mark.

"Cramps," he said in a voice filled with agony.

"I can relieve you of your pain in an instant, Mr. Hannon."

"I don't believe you want to do that until we complete our business."

"Our business is simply me shooting you."

"You shouldn't do that until I tell you what I know and who I've told."

"And what might that be?"

Hannon pulled himself onto a stool and got his right foot planted on the foot bar. He leaned forward and, reached down toward the tape. He had bought some time with his remark but was beginning to feel the shivers of fear creeping into his body

"It was Charles, not Harold, who couldn't have children because of his war wounds," he said. "You and the others were adopted in black-market fashion, and they passed you all off as their own to keep the blood line going. I think you know this. I also think you could be the child of Margaret Hopkins and, perhaps, my brother. Miss Hopkins was murdered fifty years ago. I think you've been told recently it was me who killed her. I didn't."

"This is preposterous," Mark stopped him.

"No," Hannon said firmly. "I can prove most of it. You're not Charles and Mary's child, and you know it."

Mark didn't answer right away. While he considered his response, Hannon lifted up the pant leg on his leg. "I recognized the man you came in with," he continued. "He's a Russian mobster on the run. I can't think of his name, probably couldn't pronounce it anyway. But he's a member of the group you hired to kill me."

Hannon could see Mark was surprised. He began moving his fingernails over the tape, searching for the beginning. He could feel sweat forming on his forehead. "I also believe you've used the Russians before," he continued, "perhaps to punish one of your malpractice target's you couldn't get to any other way." He was thinking of Max's granddaughter whose doctor drowned after having not lost his license because of a mistaken diagnosis. Mark was speechless. His shoulders slumped. He took a step backward and leaned on the door frame. His arm dropped down so that the gun was aimed at the floor. On the other side of the counter, Hannon's index finger found the break in the tape and began to peel it off. "I don't hear you calling all this preposterous," he said. Still no response from Mark.

Hannon took a verbal shot in the dark. "Did you murder your father and brother?"

Finally Mark responded. "Why would I do that?"

"Money!" Hannon said quickly.

"Oh, that old thing," Mark said weakly. "Well, as you've pointed out, they weren't kin. Charles was about to kill the deal for the property, so I deprived him of his oxygen."

"And Walter caught you in the act," Hannon said.

"Hell no," Mark's voice was growing stronger. "That moron wanted to give his share to his damn church. I couldn't have that."

Hannon freed the .32, from the tape, slipped the safety off, and moved it up to his lap. "How did you find out you were adopted?"

"So, at least we have one piece of the puzzle you haven't come up with." Mark seemed pleased.

"Enlighten me," Hannon said. He was getting his confidence back.

"I suppose I should. You've got this far. A sweet old lady came to my medical school graduation. Charles and Mary seemed to know her."

"Vera Whitmore," Hannon said.

"That's correct," Mark said. "I'd appreciate it if I could tell my story without your egotistical interventions."

"Sorry."

"She was pleasant. She came for dinner that night. I didn't see her again for two years. She came to visit me at the hospital where I was doing my internship. We had coffee. She told me everything. At first I didn't believe her, but she had plenty of proof."

The Russian hurried into the room. He looked perplexed.

"I can't find her," he said.

"She's not in her room?" Mark said.

"No."

"Find her, God dammit. We need her here. Is her car out there?"

Urie shook his head. He didn't know. He went to find out.

"What proof?" Hannon asked quickly. He had to get Mark going again.

"Birth certificate from a hospital in Rome, signed agreement between my mother and Mary MacMaster that I would be brought up as their child, pictures of my mother, this Hopkins woman. I looked just like her."

"Yes," Hannon said. "Family resemblance is a sure-fire clue."

"She was totally obsessed with finding my mother's killer. I'm sure they had been lovers. She wanted my help in finding and punishing the man who came between them. She was sure it was Bobby Hinch. She was relentless. She wanted him dead." Mark raised his arm and pointed the gun at Hannon. "I should kill you now," he said.

"Why the hell would you kill me, anyway?" Hannon shouted back. "I never killed anyone."

"Of course you didn't. I knew that."

Hannon was surprised. "Then why?" he demanded.

Mark MacMaster smiled and began to laugh. Hannon sat up straight and brought the .32 up to the edge of the counter.

Mark pushed himself off the door fame. "You fool," he said, still chuckling. "You don't have a clue, do you?"

Hannon was confused, but not for long. Suddenly, it all came together. "Charlotte," he said. "This is all about her."

"Bulls-eye. My wife that you took away from me. Good for you."

Hannon, had to say something. He wasn't happy with what came out. "It was an affair, for Christ's sake. It happened years ago and it's over. There were others. You know that."

"None before you, Mr. Hannon. You were first, and she fell deeply in love with you."

Now it was Hannon's turn to be speechless. He hadn't seen that coming.

"She still loves you," Mark ranted on. "The others were just fill-ins until she could get you back. She lost all feelings for me."

"But why now? Five years later?"

"I hoped she'd get over you, but she never did. When I decided to sell the estate and told her we were moving to Newport, she refused to go. She wouldn't leave as long as you were here."

"So you called on your Russian friends."

"Yes, just as you surmised, I've done business with them before."

"Did they kill Bobby Hinch?" Hannon took another verbal shot in the dark.

"They killed him for Miss Whitmore, not me. The damn fool visited her asking forgiveness for the troubled he caused. He told her about his yearly retreat on Lake Erie. She and I had kept in touch and she passed the information on to me. I had it done for her."

Hannon had one more question. "Why did you tell the Russians I killed your mother after you told them Bobby did?"

"I said Miss Whitmore had made a mistake. I wasn't going to tell them a man like you took my wife away from me. I have pride."

"You also told them to make it very personal, to be sure I knew why I was dying."

Mark smiled. "I didn't tell them that," he said. "It was their idea, some kind of silly code about killing men who've taken other men's wives. I just wanted you dead"

"Now what, doctor?" Hannon asked.

They heard the Russian running toward the kitchen.

"Nothing's changed," Mark said. "You still need to be dead."

"I can't find her," Urie barked as he entered the room. "Her car's still out back."

"Does she have your car?" Mark demanded of Hannon.

"I doubt it," Hannon said. "Unless she knows how to hot-wire a car."

"Did you give her your keys?"

"Of course not, maybe she picked my pocket."

"What did you tell her?"

"Pretty much everything I just told you."

"You told her to get the police."

That got Urie's attention. "What the hell's going on here?" he demanded.

"We have a situation," Mark said. "I've got to think."

"You said I'd be safe here until I could get out of the country." Urie voice was rising.

"Shut up, I'm thinking," Mark yelled. "Mr. Hannon has sent my wife for the police."

Urie's face filled with rage. "How could this happen?" he shouted.

Mark didn't answer. He stood limp, looking as if he might collapse. Urie moved quickly toward him and put his massive hands on Mark's shoulders. "Say something, you little shit," he shouted.

The gun in Mark's hand exploded. Urie bolted backward, stunned. Mark turned his head to the side and fired again. Urie staggered back but still didn't fall. Mark fired again still looking away from his target. This one tore into Urie's left arm, turning him around so that he fell face down on the floor

"Plan B," Mark screamed. "Plan B is a go!" He didn't see that Hannon had the .32 pointed right at him. He started moving toward Urie.

"What do you think of this?" he called back to Hannon. "I shot him with your gun. Now I shoot you with his gun. His gun in his hand, your gun in your hand, and I'm back in the hospital, asleep in my office. Plan B. Perfect."

Hannon didn't want to argue the point with a madman. He pulled the .32 up from his lap and fired. The bullet hit mark in the right forearm. The gun flew out of Mark's hand as he fell sideways, screaming in pain. Hannon slipped off his stool and moved around the counter, steadying himself on it.

"Help me," Mark pleaded.

Hannon didn't answer. He wanted to make sure Urie was dead. He knelt down and turned him over. He wasn't. He threw his fist up at Hannon, striking him in the cheek. It wasn't much of a punch. Throwing a meaningful punch from the prone position isn't easy. Hannon switched the .32 to his left hand and punched the Russian in the face with his right. That wasn't effective either so he pushed the .32 into Urie's face between the nose and upper lip. "Give it up, or I'll blow your face in half," he said. The Russian heaved a huge sigh and his entire body went limp. He was done.

Hannon pulled himself up using the counter and went to check Mark. He didn't look good. The bullet had gone through the arm and into his side just above the hip. Hannon knelt down and tried to get a pulse.

"You need to stop the bleeding with pressure," Mark said weakly.

"The police are coming," Hannon said.

"That's good," Mark said. "They won't believe your story. It's my word against yours."

"I don't think so," Hannon said. "The Russian's very much alive. He's wearing a protective vest, and he's mad as hell at you."

Hannon could see the hope draining from Mark's face. He was calling 911 when he heard the front door being forcefully opened and footsteps rushing around the large entrance hall.

"In here," he yelled. He hoped it would be Cruz, but it wasn't. He put his weapon down before two state troopers burst in. They were all business. They entered the room crouching, one at a time, weapons drawn, ready to fire. Hannon put his hands up.

"On the floor, face down," one of them shouted.

He wasn't going to argue with that. In short order, he and the Russian were face down on the floor, handcuffed. Hannon ended up on the other side of the counter from Urie and Mark. He heard an ambulance siren. He hoped Mark was still alive. Several other people arrived, but he couldn't tell who. There was a great deal of commotion. He began to think they had forgotten he was there. It was Sergeant Costello who finally took the handcuffs off.

Hannon sat up and looked at him.

"What kept you?" he asked.

"We need someone to tell us what happened." Costello said.

"I'm your man."

CHAPTER FIFTY-TWO

Hannon's interrogation lasted until midnight. Everyone was there—Cruz, Costello, Laura Lundregen, and even Victor. They all had questions, comments, and opinions but, when it was over, they were convinced that Hannon's explanation was correct. Mark was in the intensive care unit at the hospital, clinging to life. Urie was also in the hospital, under arrest and waiting for the FBI to take him. His vest had stopped Mark's bullets from doing any serious harm and he was being cooperative in corroborating everything Hannon had told them. A coroner's inquest would be held to determine the cause of death for both Charles and Walter. The trooper who had handcuffed Hannon and left him out of sight apologized. Before he could say he was "just doing his job," Hannon said it for him. They shook hands and parted.

"Good job, Hannon," Costello said. "I knew you had a little cop in you."

"I was wrong most of the way," Hannon said. "A fifty-year-old murder was just a jealous husband."

"Mark was a fanatic and a murderer," Costello said. "He would have killed again."

Hannon nodded and slid off the stool he'd been sitting on. He was tired. "I need to speak with my lawyer," he said.

Victor was sitting on a sofa with Laura Lundregen in the big hall.

"So what happens now?" Hannon asked as he sat down.

"Cruz is meeting with the media now," Victor said. "You'll be something of a hero tomorrow."

"What about my brother?"

'There's been a development. Can we give you a ride home? I'll explain on the way."

"Sure," Hannon said. "My car's missing."

"It's out on the access road," Victor said. "Charlotte was stopped for speeding by the trooper who keeps an eye on the estate. He called it in and they came here."

"Ah, yes," Hannon said with a smile. "Good girl."

When they got into Victor's car, Laura Lundregen gave Hannon some good news. "Your sister called your detective friend early this morning and gave him information about strangers who attended your brother's funeral."

Hannon nodded. "I knew about that."

"George never had much luck getting information from the army," Victor said. "So he called me. I knew Laura had spoken with someone about the date Billy got back from his furlough in 1953, so I asked her to call them."

"They were very cooperative," Lundregen said. "The first thing your brother did when he got back to Fort Dix was request family housing for his new bride and infant daughter."

A comical look spread over Hannon's face. "Wow," he said before breaking into laughter. "Billy got married. I bet his wife's name was Babe."

"Barbara," Laura said. "Barbara Worth"

"What was the little girl's name?" Hannon asked.

"Rachel."

"And they were at his funeral?"

"They both signed the book," Victor said. "They were living in Port Washington, on Long Island. That's where the wedding was. In a synagogue."

"She was Jewish," Hannon said, surprised. "How 'bout that? Are they still alive?"

"Oh yes," Lundregen said. "And still living it Port Washington."

Victor nodded. "I spoke with Barbara just before we came here. She and your brother were staying at the Plaza on the night of the murder."

"You guys work fast," Hannon said as they reached his house. "That puts Billy in the clear, right?"

"That's correct," Victor said.

"Have you told my sister?"

"Not yet."

"I'd like to tell her myself," Hannon said. "Can you take me to Edgar Avenue?"

"Certainly," Lundregen said.

They were on 1A before Hannon spoke again. "So the old murder's back to square one?"

"Most everyone's settled on Bobby Hinch," Lundregen said.

"That is square one, Laura," Victor said.

"Yes, of course," she said.

Hannon thanked them both as he got out of the car at Molly Hammond's house. There were no lights on, but his knocks were quickly answered. Erin and Molly had been sitting in the dark waiting to hear from him.

"Max called and filled us in," Erin said. "We were hoping you'd come here."

"I have news," he said. He told them everything that had happened and what he'd learned. When he seemed to be feeling his way through the part about Erin and Bobby, Erin interrupted him.

"I've told Molly about Bobby and me," she said. That made it easier and a lot quicker. When he finished, there was a period of silence before either of them spoke.

"I knew there was more to his death than I was told," Erin said.

"My God, he was murdered," Molly said. "And for nothing. He never killed Miss Hopkins. There was no violence in him. He hated going to war."

"And Miss Whitmore had him killed," Erin sobbed.

"She badgered Mark to avenge the murder," Hannon said. He began to think about what he just said. What Mark's exact words were. He didn't remember but something hadn't sounded right.

"And what a shocker Billy getting married was," Molly said, jogging Hannon's mind back to the conversation.

"I'm stunned," Erin said. "All those years and we never had a clue."

"I had a feeling there was someone he cared about," Hannon said.

"God, Hannon, it's unbelievable," Erin said. "You weren't around. Actually, we didn't see much of Billy either."

"Now you know why," Hannon said.

"But why wouldn't he tell you?" Molly asked.

"Molly, you knew what a devout catholic my mother was. A baby being born before the wedding? Are you kidding? And with a Jewish girl? She would have had a fit. You know how things were then."

"They're different now," Molly said. "Will you contact them?"

"Of course. I have a sister-in-law and a niece. I want to meet them. Will you get me a phone number, Hannon?"

"Sure."

"Will you go with me?"

"Yes, if you go, I'll go with you." He wasn't sure he ever would. His first priority was Linda.

It was three o'clock when they got to bed. Hannon got the same room he'd had before but had trouble going to sleep. He kept thinking about Linda. He would go to the Sail Loft tomorrow and see if Max had any news. In the next room, he could hear Erin crying. She was thinking about Bobby.

CHAPTER FIFTY-THREE

Hannon got a hero's welcome when he and Erin got to the Sail Loft the next afternoon. The lunch crowd gave him a round of applause while he was being seated, and several stopped at their table to offer congratulations while they ate their tuna melts. After they finished, Hannon looked for Max and found him in the kitchen. Danny spotted him first.

"Man of the hour on deck," he called out. "Attention." Danny was a navy man.

Max grabbed his hand and shook it. "You crazy, old son of a bitch," he thundered. "You did it."

Hannon got high fives from most of the kitchen help, and a female server kissed him before he could get Max aside and ask him about Linda.

"I don't know," Max said, shaking his head. "I haven't heard from her since she left."

"Did she say anything to you?"

"Just she was sorry, but she had no choice."

"How was she last time you saw her?"

"She seemed upset. You guys having a problem?"

"Yeah. Kind of a trust thing."

"She'll be back, Hannon. She belongs here. You'll talk and patch it up."

Hannon smiled. "I hope so. I miss her."

"We all do," Max said.

When Hannon got back to the table, Erin was ready to leave. "They won't take our money," she said. "It's on the house."

"We'll leave a good tip," he said.

On their way out they noticed Max waving them over to the front desk.

"Guess he's changed his mind about the bill," Hannon joked.

That wasn't it. He had just heard that Mark MacMaster had died. Hannon shrugged his shoulders. The news didn't bother him. Max had one more question.

"Did he have the doctor who misdiagnosed my granddaughter killed?"

"I'm sure he did," Hannon said. "He'd been using the Russians to handle that stuff for years."

"Was it hard to kill him?"

"No, Max, it gets easier."

Helen and Tom Cogsworth were coming in as he and Erin were leaving. Helen gave him a big hug as Tom shook his hand fiercely.

"It's finally over," Helen said. "You did it."

Hannon didn't say anything, so she kept on going. "We've got to celebrate. I'll arrange everything with Max sometime next week. You'll be our speaker and tell us how you solved the murder. You will be sure to come, won't you?"

"Sure," Hannon said. "But I'm not sure it's solved yet."

"Of course it is, Hannon. Everyone's locked in on Bobby Hinch."

Hannon knew how that must have sounded to Erin. He was surprised she didn't say something. He spoke for her. "That's not a lock yet, Helen. I'll explain at the party."

They had walked to the Sail Loft earlier and were halfway up Main Street on the way back before either spoke.

"I don't like the way this is ending up," Erin said. "Bobby did it. Case closed."

"Me neither," Hannon said.

"What is it you're going to explain at the party?"

"I really don't know."

"So you said that to give me a little hope."

"More than that. I can't explain yet."

"Something bothering you?"

"Yeah. Something Mark said didn't sound right."

"What?"

"Trying to remember. When I do, you'll be the first to know."

They stopped at the police station. Erin sat on a bench while Hannon went to see if Cruz was there. He was sitting at his desk.

"I'm glad to see you took my advice," he said.

Hannon smiled and sat down. "I was possessed."

"Same thing used to happen to my dad," Cruz said.

"It won't happen to me again."

"Feeling your age, are you?"

"Yeah."

"Then you should act it."

They both got a chuckle out of that. Cruz opened one of his desk drawers and took a plastic bag out. Hannon's two guns were in it. He'd forgotten about them.

"How'd you get them away from the state cops?" Hannon asked.

"Costello. He thinks you may want to go to work for George."

"He's wrong."

"Glad to hear it. Are you done with all this now?"

Hannon didn't answer right away. "I guess so," he said finally. "It officially over, isn't it?"

"Yes, but are you onboard with that?"

"I don't think Bobby Hinch killed Hopkins, but I'm not going to start any damn crusade."

"Glad to hear that too," Cruz said. "Can I get a ride home?"

"What took you so long to ask?"

"You know," Cruz said as they were leaving. "We would have had a tough time proving Mark murdered Charles and Walter."

"I know," Hannon said.

"Does that make you feel better about killing him?"

"I never felt bad about that."

CHAPTER FIFTY-FOUR

Cruz drove Erin to Molly's house and took Hannon home. There wasn't much talking on the ride. Cruz could see that Hannon and Erin were uneasy.

"This thing will pass," he said as Hannon got out of the car.

"It already has for me," Hannon answered. "It's my sister I'm worried about. She and Bobby were closer than anyone knew."

Later in the evening, after he'd eaten all the leftovers in his refrigerator and was relaxing in his recliner watching the flames dancing in his fireplace, he remembered what it was Mark had said that bothered him. It was something, he thought, that should be checked out. He needed to call George in the morning. He didn't have to. George was knocking on his door before he was out of bed.

"I was just going to call you," Hannon said when he finally got to the door.

"I talked to your sister last night," George said. "She's upset."

Hannon wasn't surprised.

"I'm meeting her here at ten." George said. "I have information."

Hannon waved him forward. "Come in. I hope you've eaten. I have nothing but coffee."

Hannon put the coffee on and they sat at the kitchen table to wait for Erin. He got the .32 and gave it to George. "You can give this back to Patrick," he said.

George smiled. "I understand you're packing heavier ordnance these days."

"Can't be too cautious," Hannon said.

When Erin arrived, George pulled an envelope out of his pocket and gave it to Hannon.

"The fruits of my labor on your behalf," he said.

Everything they wanted to know was in his report. Vera Whitmore was still alive, a long-time patient at an exclusive psychiatric rest home in Augusta, Maine. She had congestive heart failure and considerable mental issues.

"She's won't be much help," George said. "She's in and out of reality."

"I still would like to speak with her," Erin said.

"Augusta's not that far away," George said. "Maybe you'll catch her on a good day. Want me to set something up?"

"We can do that, George," Hannon said.

"Her doctor's name is Worthman. I'll give you a number."

"Send me a bill," Hannon said. "None of this would have come out right without your help."

"You'll get a bill. My wife takes care of that. Will you join me for lunch at the Sail Loft?"

Hannon and Erin both declined. They wanted things to cool down before they went to the village again. Hannon walked to George's car with him.

"Did you ever speak to Linda about what I found out," George asked as they reached his car.

"Yes. It didn't go well."

"You thought it was a heart-to-heart talk, and she took it as an interrogation."

"Something like that."

"You should have let Cruz do it."

"I wasn't ready to let him in on it."

"This is pure hindsight, Hannon, but just the fact that you didn't want him involved can mean you had doubts of your own."

Hannon hadn't thought about that. George was right. He did have doubts. He was trying to protect her.

"I really screwed up," he said.

"It's kind of like a no-win situation. Where's it at now?"

"I don't know. She's left town."

"How long ago?"

"Last Saturday."

"Is Cruz looking for her?"

"Not anymore."

"Want me to find her?"

"Not yet. She may come back. Actually, I'd want to find her myself."

"Do you have a key to her apartment?"

"Yes."

"That's a good place to start."

Hannon went back to the house as George drove away. He and Erin had a decision to make. It didn't take long. Erin's mind was already made up.

"If I can talk with her, maybe I'll remind her of something," she said.

He was skeptical but didn't debate the point. He knew she had to go and he would take her.

"Soon as I can drive more than a half mile, we'll take a ride up there," he said. She was happy with that.

After she left he decided to walk over to Linda's apartment and look around. Rain and sore leg changed his mind and he was half asleep in the recliner when he heard a knock on the door. It was Charlotte.

"Come on in," he said.

"I can't stay," she said, stepping in from the rain. "I've got a cab waiting."

"Where are you off to?" he asked.

"Away from here. Away from you. I just wanted to say good-bye."

"I'm glad you did."

"I'm going to become a very rich woman. Newport sounds like the place for me."

"I wish you all the best, Charlotte."

"You can cash in on the big windfall yourself, you know."

"You mean the group buying the estate wants this place too."

"Desperately."

"I hope they won't try and kill me for it."

They both laughed at that. She gave him a quick kiss and started back to the cab.

Halfway there she turned back to him. "How about those Red Sox?" she said.

"What about them."

She was surprised. "My God," she said, "you haven't heard. They won the World Series, a four game sweep."

Hannon smiled and shook his head. "And I missed it," he said, "The first time in my lifetime and I missed it. Well, you can't have everything."

"We did. Didn't we?" she said. "If only for a short time."

He smiled and nodded and she was gone.

CHAPTER FIFTY-FIVE

On the day after Halloween, Hannon and Erin headed off to Maine in his black Mustang to visit with Vera Whitmore. His leg had been pronounced strong enough to work the clutch, so he had called the hospital in Maine and arranged a meeting with Dr. Worthman. Erin was elated.

"How long to Augusta?" she asked as they reached Route I 95.

"Four hours," he said. "We'll have time for lunch."

They made good time but didn't get lunch until three o'clock. Hannon had his mind set on Boley's Famous Franks, just outside of Augusta.

"Sean told me about this place," he said as they went in. "Great dogs, homemade French fries."

"Sean was right," she said as they were leaving.

They entered Augusta, drove past the state capital building, and made a couple of lefts into a wooded area. Another hundred yards took them the gate house of the Good Hope Psychiatric Hospital.

"She's been here for over ten years," Hannon said.

"God, that's awful," his sister said sadly.

A high iron fence spread out from the house in both directions. They saw only trees behind it.

"I'll bet it circles the entire property," Hannon said.

The duty guard made a call to verify their appointment and sent them through. It was only a short distance to a huge, immaculately kept lawn that reminded Hannon of the MacMaster Estate in its glory days. But there were no gardens, just massive rolling hills of green grass. The only building, a huge, gray structure, sat majestically at the top of a hill, looming over the lawn, looking very much out of place. A paved road curled its way up the hillside to the main entrance.

"Who are we seeing?" Erin asked.

"Her psychiatrist."

"I need to see her."

"I'm sure you will, but you shouldn't expect much."

"How can she afford a place like this?"

"I'm sure Mark has her paid in full for life."

A tall, thin man wearing glasses was waiting for them in front of the building.

"I'm Dr. Worthman," he said. "Thank you for coming."

"It's good of you to see us," Hannon said. "This is my sister, Erin."

"Are you family?" the doctor asked.

"No, we're former students of Miss Whitmore," Hannon said.

"Good. Why don't we go to my office?"

The office they went to was as impressive and as well-furnished as any Hannon had ever seen. It was business-like but cozy. Though geared for hard work, it featured calming, soft, soothing colors, mostly dark rustic red. There was a semicircle of overstuffed chairs and a sofa carefully placed in front of a large desk. Hannon and the doctor took chairs. Erin remained standing.

"I hope you can help me," Dr. Worthman began.

"Actually, we were seeking help," Hannon said

"Then perhaps we can help each other," the doctor said cordially. "You were students of hers."

"High school history," Erin answered quickly.

"Have you any information about possible traumas she may have experienced?"

"A great deal," Hannon said.

"Perhaps you can share that with me. Her sister told us nothing about the cause of her condition when she brought her here.

"What is her condition, Doctor?"

"Delusional, terrible nightmares that she can't remember long enough to tell. Unresponsive most of the time."

"How is she today?" Erin asked.

"Better than most."

"Is it possible for me to visit with her while you speak with my brother?"

Dr. Worthman paused briefly before he answered.

"I don't see why not. There's no harm, but don't expect a lot."

"My brother already told me that."

"Go back to the main desk and ask for Gregory. He'll take you to her."

Erin thanked him and left.

"Were they close," the doctor asked when she was gone.

"They had a mutual friend. She's seeking information about him."

"And what are you seeking?"

"Information about the event that caused Miss Whitmore's trauma."

"Tell me about that."

***

Erin found the good-looking, muscular black man named Gregory at the main desk, and they took the elevator to the third floor. He was dressed in hospital greens and had introduced himself as Dr. Worth man's orderly.

"She must be on the promenade," he said when they didn't find her in her room.

That was actually a balcony that spread out about fifty feet from the building and ran the entire length of half the structure from the center to the southwest corner. Half of it was glass enclosed, but the large corner section was not. There was plenty of outdoor furniture but not many people. Most of those who were there were inside.

"She's usually outside," Gregory said. "Yes, that's her at the corner table."

"She's alone," Erin said.

"She keeps to herself," he said.

***

Hannon finished telling his story without interruption. He told Dr. Worthman everything he knew about the two mysteries he had dealt with in the past month.

"That's it, Doctor. Any questions?"

"I've taken a few notes. I'm guessing you've come here with some sort of resolve that your brother's best friend and your sister's lover was not a killer."

"We don't see him as being capable of killing. He wasn't an angry person. There was no hatred in him."

"What about his composure?"

"Easygoing, cool. He didn't take things seriously. He just wanted to have fun."

"You must have more than that."

"I do."

"Tell me."

"It was something Mark MacMaster said before I shot him. He said Bobby went to see Miss Whitmore to apologize for the trouble he caused."

"Wasn't that part of his twelve-step AA program?"

"Yes, but he used the word *trouble.* He didn't say he killed Miss Hopkins. He was apologizing for getting her "in trouble." In those days, that meant *pregnant.*

Doctor Worthman had to think about that.

"I see what you mean," he said finally.

"Even on a twelve-step program, you don't go around admitting murder to people who dislike you," Hannon said.

"Not likely," Dr. Worthman agreed.

***

On the promenade, Erin was seated at the corner table with Vera Whitmore, hoping she was only asleep and not dead. In the few minutes she had been there, she had not seen any indication of breathing. Gregory had suggested she let her wake up on her own and assured her it wouldn't take long. The wicker chair was comfortable and high enough for her to see over the wall and the flower boxes on top of it. The view was exceptional, acres of green grass and forest with the sun hovering over it in the blue, western sky. She was nervous when she arrived, but the peaceful setting had relaxed her.

She might have nodded off herself if Miss Whitmore had not stirred in her wheelchair. It was then she noticed how pale and frail and helpless the old woman was. She couldn't have weighted more than eighty pounds, and the blanket that covered her from the waist down showed no signs of legs beneath it. But suddenly there was movement under the blanket and the slow raising of slender arms. Miss Whitmore yawned and opened her eyes.

"I hope I haven't disturbed you," Erin said. She got no response.

"I was one of your students when you taught history in Rhode Island. Do you remember?"

Again, no response.

"Perhaps if I tell you my name. I'm Erin Hannon. I knew your friend, Miss Hopkins."

Erin thought she saw Miss Whitmore's eyelids open a bit.

She pressed on.

"Perhaps you'll remember a good friend of mine."

The old woman shook her head and lowered it. Erin continued.

"His name was Bobby Hinch. I don't think you liked him."

Miss Whitmore raised her head quickly. Erin thought she saw a look of recognition on her face.

***

Back in the doctor's office, Hannon wasn't making any progress.

"I don't think you'll get any information here," Dr. Worthman said. "Miss Whitmore can hardly speak and has no memory."

"I understand she has very little time to live," Hannon said.

"That's true. She's very ill. I told that to the detective who was here."

"So you can't help her now?"

"No. I wish I'd known what you've told me when she first came here."

"I'm sorry I took up your time, doctor. I should go now."

"Not just yet. Maybe we can still help each other."

"How can I help you?"

"I failed your teacher. It'd like to find out why. Give me a moment."

"Sure. I'm in no hurry."

***

Miss Whitmore was trying to speak, and her thin lips were trembling.

"I'm sorry if I've upset you," Erin said.

The old lady reached for the glasses that were on the small table between them. Finally she got the words out.

"Bobby Hinch," she uttered slowly.

"Yes," Erin said. "Do you remember?"

Vera Whitmore repeated the name. She put her hands on her forehead and began rolling her head in a small circle. Erin stood up to give her the glasses. She felt as if she was witnessing someone in a moment of recollection. She was elated. She turned to face the sunshine and raised her head as if she were asking God for a miracle.

"Yes," she heard Vera Whitmore say. "Bobby Hinch."

***

Hannon waited patiently while Dr. Worthman thumbed through a large medical book.

"How many times was Miss Hopkins stabbed?" He asked.

"Ten or eleven," Hannon said. "It was a horrific killing."

"Brought on by uncontrolled rage, I suspect."

Hannon nodded.

"And you don't believe Bobby was capable of such intense rage."

"No."

"I agree, but that doesn't help you."

"It makes me feel better."

"I don't suppose you know the term 'psychomotor epilepsy.'"

"No, of course not."

"Why don't we find your sister?"

"She won't know either."

***

"I don't like the Hinch boy," Vera Whitmore said.

"I know," Erin said. "But he changed. He was very sorry for some of the things he did."

"He makes fun of me."

"He's apologized to you for that."

"Who told you that?" Vera's voice was gathering strength.

Erin couldn't answer. No one had ever actually told her Bobby had gone to see her. She was still standing, looking toward the woods. If she had turned around she would have seen the old lady rise slowly up from her wheelchair.

"Bobby didn't mean all the things he said," Erin continued. "He was so young and foolish then."

Miss Whitmore sidestepped toward one of the flower boxes, took something out of it and began moving toward Erin in short, sliding steps. She was having trouble keeping her balance.

***

"Psychomotor epilepsy is the term for total memory loss due to a fit of rage, Dr. Worthman explained to Hannon as they walked toward the main desk.

"You mean people can block horrible things they've seen out of their minds and not remember?"

"It's not uncommon, Mr. Hannon."

"Did that happen to Whitmore when she found her murdered friend?"

"Something like that."

"What does that mean?"

They had reached the main desk. Gregory was there. Dr. Worthman motioned for him to join them.

"Where are they?" he asked.

"On the promenade."

"Sometimes," Dr. Worthman said to Hannon as they moved toward the elevator, "this condition occurs not when a person sees something horrific, but when they do something horrific."

***

When Erin turned to face Miss Whitmore, they were no more than two feet apart. She was stunned. She was seeing a different person. The woman before her looked larger and not frail. She wore the thick glasses Erin had given her and they magnified her eyes, making them look like holes in the pale, sinister face of a skeleton. Erin screamed."

Where were you at the graduation?" Miss Whitmore demanded.

"I don't understand," Erin said. Her voice was quivering.

"I was worried. I came to see if you were all right. His car was here."

"Whose car? What are you saying?"

"You've taken him back, haven't you?"

"What do you mean?"

"You said you'd never see him again. You promised, and I stood by you. Now he's back. Did you make love with him? Will you be pregnant again?

"Miss Whitmore," Erin screamed. "I don't know what—"

"Bitch," the old lady cried out. "Liar! Whore!"

She raised her arms over her head. The trowel she'd taken from the flower box was clutched in both her hands. Erin raised her hands in defense. The first blow struck her in the shoulder. She blocked a second thrust with her arm but stumbled backward and fell. Gregory stepped between them and took hold of Whitmore's wrists. There was no need to restrain her any further. She was done. The sudden burst of energy and strength that her anger had given had evaporated. The trowel slipped from her hands. Gregory caught her before she fell and put her back in the wheelchair. She was no longer conscious.

Hannon bent down to help Erin up.

"She's bleeding," he said.

326

"She'll be OK," Gregory assured him. "The trowel has a rounded edge. It's not sharp."

"She thought she had a knife in her hand," Dr. Worthman said.

Hannon knew what he meant. Erin didn't.

"What the hell just happened?" she asked.

CHAPTER FIFTY-SIX

Erin didn't get her question answered until they got to a first aid room. Gregory was right. The two wounds were just scrapes, no penetration.

"Even with the adrenalin rush," he said, "she couldn't strike a hard blow."

"It seemed hard enough to me," Erin said.

"She took you by surprise. You didn't realize what was happening." Dr. Worthman said. He had just entered the room with Hannon.

"I knew she was attacking me. I didn't know why."

Dr. Worthman sat down. Hannon remained standing. Gregory finished bandaging Erin's shoulder and arm.

"I've never seen anything quite like it," the doctor began. "Let's see if I can explain it."

Erin didn't know any more about "psychomotor epilepsy" than Hannon did.

"You must have said something to jar her memory back to the crime." Dr. Worthman said.

"After fifty years?" Erin asked.

"It's possible. Do you remember what you said?"

It took her a moment to answer. "Maybe the names, mine and Bobby's."

"That might have done it. Did she speak at all?"

Erin spoke slowly. "She said, 'I don't like the Hinch boy. He makes fun of me.'"

"Present tense," Hannon said.

"Yes," Worthman said. "Her mind was back at the scene of the murder, and you, he gestured toward Erin, "were the Hopkins woman."

Erin gasped in disbelief.

"I don't look like her. She was young. I'm old. She put her glasses on to see me better."

"Those were her reading glasses. They would have blurred her vision. She saw what she wanted to see—a woman she loved who had cheated on her with a man."

"And was doing it again," Hannon added.

Erin sat back in her chair. She was beginning to understand.

"Remember when they were late coming back from Italy in fifty-two?" Hannon said. "They had gone there for Miss Hopkins to have Bobby's baby. They turned the boy, Mark, over to the MacMaster family. Miss Whitmore forgave her."

Erin nodded. "Yes, she said 'you promised, and I took you back.'"

"We heard her yelling that as we ran toward you."

"Did you hear about the car? What was that about?"

"It was Bobby's car she saw," said Hannon. "He'd taken Molly home early from the party and gone to see Miss Hopkins."

Erin lowered her head. She smiled and chuckled.

"Men. If they can't get it in one store, they move on to another."

"We don't know it was for sex, Erin."

"Please, Hannon. We both know what Bobby was like then."

"I think we should move on," Dr. Worthman said. "What's important now is that Miss Whitmore showed up."

"She said she was worried," Erin said.

"She might also have been suspicious," Hannon added.

"Whichever it was," Dr. Worthman said, "she saw Bobby's car and lost control."

"So she confronted them?" Erin asked.

"I don't think there was any confrontation," Walkman said. "She was filling up with rage and jealousy. After Bobby left, she went to the door and rang the bell. Miss Hopkins let her in and she walked right past her to the kitchen. She was in a trance, moving like a sleepwalker, looking for a knife. When she found one, she returned to the living room and began the attack."

"And Miss Hopkins never did anything?" Erin asked.

"She was stunned, just as you were today."

"And there was no talk."

"Miss Whitmore may have said the same words she shouted at you today."

"And she knew nothing of what she'd done?" Hannon asked.

"Not at first. She was aware enough to get rid of the knife, clean the blood off herself and get rid of the clothes she was wearing. She got herself home, but when she woke up the next morning it was all gone."

"Until today," Erin said. "My God."

Gregory got a call on his cell phone. It was brief.

"The police are downstairs," he said as he closed his phone.

After giving their statements to the police, Hannon and Erin were invited to stay the night in the staff residence wing. They readily accepted. After a surprisingly fine turkey dinner with Dr. Worthman and Gregory in the hospital cafeteria, they retired to separate bedrooms for the night. No one seemed interested in talking about the day's events. They left after breakfast the next morning and were halfway out of Maine before Erin brought the subject up.

"I appreciate your bringing me here. I needed to know about Bobby."

"Especially that he didn't do it," Hannon said.

"I was sure of that," she said firmly. "I needed everyone to know."

"Now they will, those still around and interested."

"How do you think it will play out at in Hooper's Landing?" she asked.

"A lover's quarrel, I'm afraid, but far less scandalous than it would have been if it had come out back then."

"Yes, that's right, isn't it? Things have changed."

"What will you do now, go back to Arizona?"

"Not right away. I want to spend time with Molly and there's one other thing I'd like to do."

"That would be go to long Island and meet your sister-in-law and niece."

"Yes, will you go with me?"

"Sure."

They were in New Hampshire when she asked another question.

"Will you look for Linda?"

"Probably."

"With George's help?"

"I'd like to do it myself."

"Where would you start?"

"Her apartment."

Erin gave him a questioning look. "How will you get in?"

"Like you said, things have changed. I have my own key."

Made in the USA
Middletown, DE
14 November 2014